# KIDNAPPED BY A SEX MANIAC

## The Erotic Fiction of Christopher Pierce

Herndon, VA

ISBN 10: 1-934187-65-8
ISBN 13: 978-1-934187-65-4



Published in the United States by STARbooks Press
PO Box 711612, Herndon, VA 20171.

Printed in the United States

Herndon, VA

# Christopher Pierce Titles from STARbooks Press

*As Author*

ROGUE: SLAVE
The First Book of Rogue

ROGUE: HUNTED
The Second Book of Rogue

*As Editor*

MEN ON THE EDGE:
Dangerous Erotica

TAKEN BY FORCE:
Erotic Stories of Abduction and Captivity

SEXTIME:
Erotic Stories of Time Travel

**ACKNOWLEDGMENTS**

Special Thanks to Mickey Erlach and John Nail

**DEDICATION**

For all the readers who have enjoyed my stories, past, present and future

For Bob and Daniel

and

For Master Matt, as is everything

# AUTHOR'S NOTES

These stories are works of fantasy. In real life, please use caution, discretion and protection.

The use of the words "boy" and "kid" in these stories do not indicate minors. All characters in these stories are at least eighteen years of age.

# CONTENTS

# FOREWORD
# By Christopher Pierce

Welcome to the first collection of *my* erotic stories.

There is a lot to choose from here, with works ranging from my very first attempt at erotica, “Headlights,” written in 1993, to “Roped by a Wrangler,” which was written in 2008.

Although most of my stories have contemporary settings, like “The Brute Inside” and “Training Lust,” I hope the reader will enjoy my occasional experiments with genre settings and characters from the supernatural being of “Minion” to the pirates of “Stolen Booty,” the vampire of “Immortal Alone,” and the spaceship captain of “Commander Zann.”

My darker work is well-represented here as well, with the first two stories of my ongoing “Hunters of Men” series included here, “Night of the Hunter” and “Street Hunter,” as well as my tale of vengeance, “Sweaty Revenge.”

No collection of my stories would be complete without a certain tale of abduction, captivity and seduction that has become a fan-favorite, the infamous “Midnight Burglar,” so it closes the show.

I hope new readers of my work will enjoy this collection as much as long-time fans. I appreciate every one of you.

I love hearing from readers.

Please write to me at chris@christopherpierceerotica.com or visit www.christopherpierceerotica.com for news and surprises.

Thank you for reading. Enjoy the stories.

Christopher Pierce

Boynton Beach, Florida

December 2009

# INTRODUCTION
# By Mickey Erlach

Writers who can put themselves into both the minds of the captive and captivator are rare, and most writers only relate what they know through their art. Christopher Pierce knows a lot more than most of us.

The following collection is among his best work, and Christopher shares it with you in the style for which he has garnered thousands of fans.

Mostly written from the first person point of view, these stories display just how talented our scribe is because he jumps from the submissive who resists being captured only to be pleasured beyond belief to the hunter finding his prey only to use his victim for his own pleasure then discarding him like a torn pair of briefs.

Christopher gives versatility a whole new meaning. And, that is what makes this collection so hot, sexy and fun. You expect one thing and get another.

I thoroughly enjoyed these stories and have the sticky underwear to prove it.

Thank you, Christopher, for giving me the pleasure of reading your work.

# I. HEADLIGHTS

The headlights were very bright in my rearview mirror. I glanced up at them, and they almost blinded me. Why was this guy tailgating me so close? He was definitely following me. Whenever I pulled into another lane, he was right there with me, scaring other cars out of the way and always staying right behind me.

To make it worse, it was one of those big shit-kicking four-wheel drive trucks. The cab rode so high on those monster tires that the headlights were right on the same level as my mirror. I was driving back after visiting a friend out of town. After half an hour of this, I got really pissed and just pulled off the road, figuring the jerk would fly past me and that'd be the end of it.

But, he didn't. As if expecting it, the truck pulled off with me. Now I got a little freaked out. I hadn't even signaled, for God's sake. How did he know I was going to do that? I got out of the car and figured I'd find out what the hell was going on.

If I had known what was going to happen, I'm not sure if I would've pulled off the road sooner – or tried harder to lose him.

It was pretty dark, and the truck's headlights were still on, blinding me as I searched for the driver. The cab was already empty, and a figure was walking toward me. I braced myself. Backlit by the headlights, I couldn't make out much except that as he got closer he got bigger, and bigger ... and bigger.

Big guys always turned me on, but this was no time to be getting hot. I didn't know what was going on. He stopped in front of me. God, he must've been 6'4" and weighed 275, all muscle. Just being that near to him made my cock stir and press against my jeans.

His face was mostly hidden by the darkness, but what I could see of it was chiseled and angular, like a statue's. He seemed to be waiting for me to say something, but I didn't know what to say. I was too busy staring at his eyes. They were burning in the dark, seeming to slice right through me.

"Uh ..." I finally started. Instantly, he interrupted me, with a low deep voice.

"You're that model, right? The one in all the magazines?"

God, is that what this was about? My agent had told me to expect this sort of thing, but I had never flattered myself that someone would recognize me ... much less follow me as this thug had apparently done.

"Uh ... yeah, I am." I said, instantly regretting it. Maybe I should have denied it and gotten the hell out of there. He smiled, and his face lit up.

"I've wanted to meet you since the first time I saw you," he said.

God, is this cheesy, I thought, next he's gonna ask for my autograph. He grabbed my hand and shook it firmly, hard.

"It's a pleasure," I said, marveling at the strength in his grip and wondering why he hadn't apologized for freaking me out with his psycho tailgating.

"In fact, it's such a treat to meet you I want you to be at this address tomorrow night at this time." He pressed a slip of paper into my hand and was back in his truck before I could protest.

"Wait!" I called, but the truck was already revved up and tearing down the road. What time was it? I looked at my watch and it said 1:15 am.

Well, that was weird, I thought, as I got back into my car. I considered tossing the slip of paper away but didn't want to litter. I threw it onto the seat next to me and turned the key in the ignition. As I pulled off the road, I tried to convince myself that I was not going to follow the chiseled man's instructions. But I knew I was. I was too intrigued not to. Who in the hell was he to tell me what to do? I wanted to find out.

I didn't think about the incident at all the next day. I was at a shoot most of the time and had to concentrate on looking good for the cameras. I did happen to glance at the address on the slip of paper, and it was in the middle of nowhere! Far out of town along some highway that was hardly ever traveled. I'm not going way the hell out there, I thought.

So, of course, I got into my car at about quarter to one and headed out. The whole time I drove, I was thinking I could always call it quits if I didn't like what happened. Maybe he wouldn't even be there. Maybe it would be someone else. Maybe he was psycho killer or a fag basher. Who knew?

It was another dark night. I found the address and pulled my car off the road. It was an old abandoned barn. I didn't see any other vehicles around. I felt utterly alone and suddenly very foolish. I looked at my watch and it said 1:30. I had only been waiting about five minutes when I decided that this was crazy and that I was getting out of there. That's when suddenly a voice was in my ear.

"You're late," it said huskily. I jumped in surprise, even though I recognized the chiseled man's voice. I turned around, but before I could say anything something grabbed me.

"Hey!" I started, as I felt both of my arms getting forced behind my back. I felt cool metal against them, and then suddenly a click! What the hell was going on? He had cuffed my hands! I started to struggle, but then I found my movement even more restricted – he was looping coils of rope around my arms and torso and tightening them!

"Stop it!" I yelled as I tried to squirm away from him.

"If you didn't want this, you wouldn't have come here," he said as he dropped down and cuffed my ankles together. With more rope, he bound my legs. Within seconds, I couldn't move at all. I was furious and about to piss myself.

"What the hell is going on, man? What the fuck do you think you're doing?" I yelled as loud as I could. He clamped his hand over my mouth.

"We can't have any of that, boy ..." he whispered in my ear. He was sliding something over my head, and my mind screamed in fear when I realized what it was. The leather hood was cool on my skin as it slipped down my forehead. Something was trying to get into my mouth. I shut it tight.

"Open your mouth, boy," he said. I didn't. He hit me roughly on the side of my head. "Open it!"

More surprised than anything else, I opened my mouth, and he shoved the gag in. Then he pulled the rest of the hood down and closed the eyeflaps. As the light disappeared and I felt the straps tightening on the back of my head, I fought against panic. I felt as if my knees were going to give out. I must have stumbled a little because his hands were suddenly holding me up.

I could barely hear him through the hood.

"Don't be afraid, boy," he said, and suddenly my feet had left the ground, and I was sliding into something. I felt a weird sensation sliding up my legs and arms and chest – something like canvas or burlap – and then I realized what he had done.

He had put me inside a big sack. I heard him close the top above my head and tie the drawstrings tight. Thank God there must have been air holes or something because even though I was scared shitless, I could still breathe.

Then suddenly, I was being lifted again, as the chiseled man hoisted the sack over his shoulder. God, was he strong! He was carrying me as effortlessly as if I was an athletic bag he had just tossed over his shoulder on the way home from the gym.

As frightened as I was, I suddenly became aware of another sensation. My cock was throbbing. It was rock hard, and I could feel it rubbing against my kidnapper's shoulder through the canvas. My mind starting tripping out, and I tried to get it under control. Then I was set down onto something soft. There was a loud metallic noise and then muffled footsteps. Where the hell was I? Then I heard a car door open and realized the chiseled man had dumped me into the back of his truck. I started to struggle wildly, then realized how stupid that was.

I thought of what he had said earlier: "Don't be afraid." In some weird way, I began to like the feel of the ropes around me and the hood over my head. I started to feel safe and protected, but fought that feeling down. This was crazy! What was he going to do with me?

I could see the headline: UNDERWEAR MODEL MURDERED BY INSANE ADMIRER. Great. Just what I needed, a celebrity death when I wasn't even a real celebrity. Then I ordered my mind to stop worrying and just relax. I was really tense and starting to get sore from straining against my bonds. I relaxed and tried to think about the feel of the rope on my skin and the texture of the leather on my face. I tried not to think about my raging hard-on.

After what seemed like hours, the truck stopped, and I heard him get out. I was hefted up over his shoulder again and carried somewhere else. He untied the sack and pulled me out of it, throwing me down. Before I could struggle, he had thrown more ropes around me, securing me flat on my back. I couldn't move as I felt his hands all over me. Then I heard his voice through the hood, whispering in my ear again.

"Don't try to get away, boy, or you'll be sorry ..." He was untying my legs. My mind raced with thoughts of escape, but I remembered the pain of his slap and didn't move. He yanked my pants off. Oh my God, I thought, as he pulled down my shorts and my cock sprung up in the air like a periscope, hard as steel.

I was breathing really hard now as he tied my legs back down. I felt the surface I was resting on shift slightly as his enormous weight moved up onto it. I heard the unmistakable sound of plastic and latex that signaled a condom being unwrapped and rolled on.

"Don't be afraid, boy," he said, and then he was splitting my legs apart.

I screamed soundlessly and bit down into the gag as he jammed his dick into the flowering rosebud of my quivering asshole. It must have been huge; it felt as if it was going up past my intestines, into my ribcage.

He moaned in pleasure as he pushed into me. My mind did somersaults, unable to deal with the immense pleasure I felt as he started to move back and forth, in and out. He was pumping me harder than I'd ever been fucked. With every thrust, I thought I could feel the beating of his heart through his throbbing cock as it moved in me, raping, searching, exploring every inch of my soul. I would have been writhing around ecstatically if I wasn't totally immobilized. Then I could feel him start to get close. His breathing quickened as he started to pump faster and faster. My whole body shook as unbelievable sensations flowed through me.

"I'm gonna come, boy, and I want you to come with me. You got one chance – come for me when I tell you to."

I felt lubricant dripping onto my cock and then the exquisite grip of his hand. I struggled against the ropes as he started stroking my dick, fucking me all the while.

Then he started going at breakneck speed, and I knew his countdown had started.

"All right, boy. I'm gonna come. Do it! Shoot for me now!"

In that moment I realized that I belonged to him, that he had claimed me and was marking me. His. Forever. He could do anything with me that he wanted, and what he wanted was for me to share his pleasure. I had no choice.

An apocalyptic flower of pleasure exploded inside me as my back arched and every muscle in my body flexed. With one final thrust the chiseled man plowed into me, and I could feel the milky shower of cum shooting out of my cock like a fountain, splashing all over him. I could feel his dick harden into a titanium rod, and he screamed in ecstasy, shooting like a machine gun as he came.

He collapsed on top of me, and I felt his sweat drip down onto my body. I relaxed as I felt his weight lift off of me. He pulled out carefully, and I heard him yank the condom off and toss it away. Then he was untying the ropes. No thoughts of escape entered my mind. I was utterly helpless, spent, used up.

He gently picked me up in his arms and put me back in the sack and tied the top closed. I fell into unconsciousness as he threw the sack over his shoulder again.

I woke up next to my car with the chiseled man standing over me. The hood was gone. The ropes were gone. And he was taking the cuffs off me.

"I ..." I said, but couldn't finish. I just stared up at him. I missed the ropes and the hood already. My skin felt naked and defenseless without the feel of them all over me.

He looked at me and smiled. Leaning down, he kissed me very gently and whispered in my ear.

"No matter what happens, don't be afraid." He turned to go. My eyes were now adjusted to the dark, and I could see the bard and his truck, parked behind my car.

"Wait!" I said, but there was nothing to say.

"Be good, boy," he said, and was in his truck and gone before I could run over and stop him, beg him to stay, beg him to take me with him. But I just stood there, staring into the night. A few minutes later, I got into my car and drove away.

I never saw him again.

For months after, every time I was driving and some big truck headlights appeared in my mirror, I would get an instant hard-on.

But today, something strange happened. I was at the agency looking at my latest proof sheets, when an assistant came over to me with a message. "It had just arrived," he said. I took it and unfolded it. On it was written an address, and the words 'Don't be afraid.'

As I sit here now, looking at the clock, it's almost time for me to leave. I know what I should do. Throw the message away, go home, do some reading, maybe work out, and go to bed early. I've even got myself convinced that that's what I'm going to do.

But my cock knows better.

# II. MINION

I was cruising through the upper dimensions when I heard the prayer.

Heard actually might not be the best word to describe it. What literally happened was that my corporeal body responded to a prayer of such passion that blood surged into my cock, stiffening it and lengthening it to the size and consistency of a 12-inch steel spike.

Have you ever flown with an erection? Ever felt the wind rushing by it, your dick jutting forward through the air like the prow of a ship slices through water, your wings pumping madly to keep you on course?

No, I suppose you haven't. After all, you probably don't have wings, and I, as you might have guessed, am not human. Oh, I was once, many years ago, but not anymore. Now I'm something else, something beyond human might be a good way to describe it. Who knew you had to die before the real fun starts?

Anyway, I don't usually answer prayers; I leave that to others, but this prayer was special. I couldn't let it go by, wanted it for myself. My eyes searched the dimensions, hunting for the origin of the prayer that was making me so fucking hard, when suddenly I found it! Corporeal Universe … Western Grid … Milky Way Galaxy …Solar System … Planet Earth … North America … United States … Southern California … Los Angeles …

I zeroed in for a closer look.

There he was! In a nondescript apartment building, on the third floor, lived a young man – a very hot young man: mid-twenties, Caucasian, short brown hair, handsome face, in-shape body, bigger than average dick (which happened to be steely-spike hard at that moment from the intensity of his prayer.) I narrowed the scope of my hearing, so I could experience the boy's thoughts.

*Oh God*, he prayed, *no one can give me what I want! My passion is so intense no one can keep up with me. I need a partner with stamina, someone who won't give up! I'll do anything for that, God, anything! Please send me someone who's my equal, anyone who can give me what I want, what I NEED! I'm so horny for someone that loves fucking as much as I do (or more) that it hurts! Please, God, hear my prayer ...*

As he prayed, the young man used his right hand to jack his dick off, and his left to pinch and tweak his nipples. His eyes were shut tight as he silently repeated his prayer, over and over again.

I focused my awareness and, gathering all the facets of my powers, willed myself in sync with the young man's time and space, into a form he could understand.

The walls of his bedroom formed around me, flickering and fading for a few seconds before solidifying. Light from my manifestation filled the room, bathing the young man and his bed in pearly luminescence. The sexy young human stopped jerking off and sat up in bed, staring at me with his mouth open.

I knew what he was seeing.

I was a beautiful naked man with a sculptured, stunning body, gazing at him with eyes that glowed. The huge, white-feathered wings that grew from my back flapped gently, keeping me just high enough above the floor, so my feet weren't touching it. The light that poured from my exquisite body surrounded me like a gigantic halo.

We looked at each other for a few minutes before either of us spoke.

"What the fuck are you?" the boy finally asked.

"I'm the answer to your prayers," I said.

Pointing between my legs, he said, "I didn't know angels got erections."

"Why do you think they're always wearing those robes?" I asked, and then answered my own question: "To hide their cocks."

"Then why aren't you wearing a robe?" the boy wanted to know.

"I have nothing to hide from you," I said. "You know why I'm here. I've come to give you what you want, what you need."

Hope and desire filled the young man's eyes.

"Really?"

"Would I lie to you?" I asked him, smiling.

"No, I guess not," he said. "So … you can do what everyone else can't?"

"I'm not like everyone else," I said, "I can do everything a man can do, and more."

The boy rose from his bed and stepped down onto the floor in front of me. He grabbed his cock in his left hand.

"Let's fuck," he said. "I'm ready. I've been waiting for this my whole fucking life."

"There's one condition," I warned.

"I don't care," the boy said, "I'll do anything for this!"

"You must give yourself to me."

He stopped jerking himself.

"What do you mean?" he asked.

"You must leave your mortal life and become my minion. You will belong to me."

"For how long?"

"Forever."

The boy considered that briefly, then, seeming to come to a conclusion, began jerking off again.

"I've got nothing and no one here worth staying for," he said. "There are worse things to be than an angel's servant ..." He stuck out the hand that wasn't holding his cock. "I'll do it!" he said.

I reached out and took his hand in mine. As my fingers tightened around his, the boy's eyes widened and his mouth opened slightly.

"What's happening?"

"I'm heating your blood," I said. "It'll make your heart pump faster and harder. You'll need that."

"Why?"

I smiled again.

"Because your body is about to receive more stimuli than it ever has before."

I released the boy's hand, and he stared at it. I knew what he was seeing, his veins had changed from blue to orange from my touch. His superheated blood was visible through his skin, flowing madly throughout his entire body.

"On your knees, minion," I commanded. He looked up at me, disbelief registering on his face. I could feel his thought: *What did he just say?*

I gestured suddenly with my hands, willing his knees to bend, and he toppled forward.

"That's more like it," I said. "I am a superior being, and you are an inferior being. You belong to me now and must always show proper respect, or I will force you to show it and punish you for making me do so."

The boy stared up at me from his kneeling position. His face was contorted with confusion, but his cock remained as hard as a shepherd's staff.

"But this," he stammered, "this isn't what I …"

I interrupted him.

"What you want isn't important anymore," I interrupted. "It is what I want that rules your life now, and what I want is to hear less talking from you. I have a better use for your mouth."

I propelled myself forward, and with perfect aim shoved my gargantuan cock into his mouth. He cried out in protest and tried to force the invading organ out, but I held his head firmly with my hands, which, no matter how hard he struggled, kept him frozen in place. He tried to speak, but all that came out were muffled gurgles.

"Suck my cock, human," I said, laughing at him. "Make yourself useful. I am several thousand times stronger than you, so you can give up fighting me. You will never be able to resist me."

The boy obeyed and started blowing me. I'd forgotten how good, how sublime the simple, velvety embrace of a human's mouth on my dick felt. He took in as much of me as he could. It felt spectacular to have him massage and caress my cock with his mouth sliding up and down its rigid length and circumference. And I knew it felt unlike any penis he'd ever sucked: more vibrant, more alive than anything he'd ever experienced. He could feel every beat of my heart through my cock, a beating so strong and fierce that his own, comparatively feeble heart started pumping in time with mine.

But I grew tired of his effort quickly. It was time for me to take what was mine. I shoved my cock even deeper into his mouth. He squealed in surprise, but of course could not fight me. When my penis hit the back of his throat I willed it to curve downward, to maintain its shape and thickness but penetrate further than any cock ever had – literally down the human's throat. He coughed and choked in fear and pain as I forced my dick farther and farther into him. My tube of muscle had completely filled his mouth and throat, and confusion once again joined the other emotions in his desperate eyes.

"Yes, minion," I said, "you are choking. No air is passing into your lungs, and you can't breathe. But don't worry; I won't let you die. You're mine now, and I certainly won't give you up to Death. Let Death find his own minion."

I then started fucking the boy's throat in earnest, shoving my supernatural penis deep inside him and pulling it almost all the way out before pushing it back in again. Eventually he stopped struggling and allowed me screw his mouth without offering resistance. When he got used to it, he resumed jacking his cock, which had not at any point lost its erection.

Soon the pleasure of using this human creature grew far too intense, and I had to let myself come. I let out a snarl and shot my load down my minion's throat – repeated jets of white-hot semen – which he swallowed, but it wasn't over yet. My cock continued to ejaculate, expelling squirt after squirt of cum into him.

After ten shots, I had spent myself and finally released him. He stumbled and toppled onto his back. With my cock out of him, he could breathe normally again, and he coughed and hacked while holding his stomach.

"It's so hot!" he gasped. "It feels like it's burning me from the inside out!"

For the first time since I'd appeared, I let my feet touch the floor and folded my wings behind me.

"Yes, minion," I said, "my seed will burn you. But remember: as before, you will not die, so don't let such trifles as pain trouble you. You'll become quite used to it."

I knew it was impossible, of course, but it amused me to see him trying to grasp that which was clearly beyond his comprehension.

Stepping closer, I looked down on him with my glowing eyes.

"Please ..." he whimpered, backing up.

"I enjoyed being inside you," I said. "I haven't felt that good in several hundred years. I'd like to experience that again …"

"No ..." he cut in, obviously distressed and frightened.

"… but this time through a different orifice," I finished.

He held up his hands as if to ward me off.

"I'm begging you!" he shouted, jumping to his feet and running for the door to his room. He threw it open and was about to run through it but stopped just in time – instead of the hallway outside his apartment there was only space, stretching infinitely in all directions. Distant stars were the only illumination.

"Stay where you are!" I ordered. "Don't presume to think you can run from me; there is nowhere on Earth, heaven or in between that you can hide from me."

"What the fuck's going on?" he said, backing up from the door and turning to face me.

"We are no longer in your room," I said, "haven't been since I arrived. I maintained the room's appearance, so it would remain familiar to you, so nothing would interfere with your decision to give yourself to me."

"I've changed my mind!" the boy shouted, his fear turning to anger. "You can't do this to me!"

I roared like a hundred lions and threw up my hands. The force of my will took the form of a terrible wind that knocked the youth to the floor and tore the room apart. The ceiling cracked, buckled and was hurled away into the void. The windows shattered into a thousand dagger-sharp shards, and the walls crumbled to dust. The boy cried out in fear and grabbed onto the still-standing doorframe to stop himself from being hurled into nothingness.

"Please stop!" he screamed. "Please!"

I let the roar die in my throat, and the wind of my rage slowly subsided with it. All that remained of the room was the floor that I stood on and the doorframe the mortal clung to. Trembling, he looked up at me in terror.

"You belong to me," I reiterated quietly. "Do not tell me what I can and cannot do to or with you." I advanced on him, spreading my wings to their full span. The boy's face was stricken with horror, but I saw him once again drop his hand between his legs to masturbate. My own cock jutted forward as if with a mind of its own. It had tasted human blood and wanted more.

"In the future, you'll learn not to run from me, no matter how frightened you are." When I raised my hands the young man cringed and turned his face away.

"Please ..." he moaned helplessly.

"But for this first time," I continued, "you'll need to be restrained, shown what you truly are."

There was a lightning flash from my eyes, whereupon an invisible force seized and stretched the boy's arms away from his body – slamming them down on the floor, palms up – so that he was unable to defend himself. Several feet above in mid-air, I willed into being two foot-long metal spikes. Before he could beg for mercy, I cast the spikes downward, impaling my minion's hands to the floor. The boy shrieked in agony and terror, unaware of what lay ahead. With a circular motion of my hands, a crown of thorns appeared above his head. It hovered there for a second before jamming itself onto his head, blood springing from where the thorns pierced him.

Willing his legs to rise up and out of the way, his reluctant asshole revealed, I said, "Now you cannot escape me."

My minion screamed in terror as I propelled myself forward and flew into him, impaling him with my cock. His asshole tried to block my entrance, but I forced myself into him, spiking him just as his hands were spiked to the floor. He cried out again as I started fucking, plunging in and out of him.

Doubtless, I was screwing him harder and deeper than anyone ever had. Even as he screamed, I knew I was fulfilling the young man's deepest fantasy. I fucked him for several hours, although to him it probably felt like days. For the first time in his life, he begged a sex partner to stop, rather than the reverse, as the blood from his hands and head collected in blackish pools on the floor beneath us.

All around us, the stars shone, glinting and sparkling, seeming to move as time stretched out – streaking around us, as if we were a sun that held them in orbit. Eventually, however, I could no longer delay the inevitable: I had to allow my climax to peak. Once again gathering all my facets and powers to me, with a cry of conquest and ecstasy, I shot my load into my minion, filling him with liquid fire. As it had before, my cock continued propelling seed into the boy far longer than any human possibly could. Unceasingly, ecstatically, I shot into him, over and over and over. My minion moaned and cried in exquisite pain that mixed, melted and morphed into equally exquisite pleasure. The searing heat of my cum burned inside his body without damaging it, and his skin began to steam as he himself climaxed, with the force of a lightning storm. His seed shot out of his rigid cock and splattered his chest and neck. So hot was his skin that his cum sizzled on it, bubbling and spitting like molten lava. Emitting a primordial scream of bliss and release, my minion's body burst into flames – an inferno that engulfed us both. Likewise, the streaking stars all around us exploded in flames and were destroyed.

Only when the fire had died did I slowly withdraw my cock from my minion. Leaving him spent and exhausted on the floor of what had been his room, I allowed him to rest, despite my desire to seal his fate quickly.

When he regained consciousness, he was surprised and confused to find that the spikes that had impaled his hands and the crown that had encircled his forehead were gone, although he still bore their wounds. His body did not appear burned, although we had both felt the blaze's fury. He stood up and looked around wonderingly at the starless sky, and at me, hovering a few feet above the floor, much as I had been when I'd first appeared, my white-feathered wings flapping slowly.

"What's happened?" he asked me.

"Your fate is sealed," I said. "It is done and cannot be undone."

"My fate?" he asked. "Why would I want it undone?"

"To answer you I must first show you something. We will then depart for your new home."

"Where is that?"

"Home is the place from which I came, the place you will spend eternity … with me," I said.

"Heaven …?" he said with awe. "What are you going to show me?"

"My true form," I said.

"True form? Isn't this your true form?" he asked, gesturing at me in all my glory.

I laughed at him, as a cat would at a mouse if it were able.

"No. This is merely the form I used to ensnare you," I explained.

"I don't understand."

"This is my true form," I said, allowing my disguise to melt away and my actual appearance to re-exert itself as the boy watched with increasing horror, as my round pupils lengthened into vertical slits, like those of a cat. My eyes' serene blue irises changed to reptilian green. Long, curved horns sprouted from my forehead, my rounded ears became pointed, and my face changed from a countenance of benevolence to a visage of appalling cruelty. My lips curled hungrily to reveal the sharp teeth behind them as my pale skin darkened to a deep red – the color of fire and blood. Talon-like claws burst from my fingertips. A forked tail grew from the small of my back and lashed about me like a ravenous serpent. The magnificent feathered wings that sprung from my shoulder revealed their true form – those of a monstrous bat, black and clutching, with leathery membranes stretched between elongated vestigial fingers.

And yes, my cock returned to its natural state as well, still enormous of course, but now studded with spikes and ridges and crowned with horns that would shred whatever they touched.

I grinned at the boy as he screamed in terror and disgust.

"Get away!" he shrieked, his voice breaking. "Don't … come near me!"

"You are mine," I reminded him. "You belong to me."

"No!" he yelled, "I didn't understand!"

"But now it's too late," I reasoned. "You gave yourself to me, and it cannot be reversed."

"You can't do this!" he screamed.

"I can," I confirmed, "and I have."

I moved toward him. He tried to run, but of course there was nowhere to go. My minion crumbled to his knees, shaking his head in blind, desperate denial.

"No! No! No!" he repeatedly screamed, over and over again, until his protest changed to an unending moan of "This can't be happening, this can't be happening ..."

I raised my wings and brought what moments before had been my feet but were now cloven hooves down to the floor. With a hideous shriek, the last remnant of his human world – the floor of his room and its doorframe – cracked and disintegrated into the abyss surrounding us. I flapped my wings to keep myself in place, and grabbed my minion by his wrists to keep him from falling. He burst into tears and moaned piteously.

"Remember when you said there were worse things to be than an angel's servant?" I asked him. "Was a demon's slave one of them?"

I lifted the sobbing mortal and slung him over one shoulder, where he hung, seemingly resigned between my wings.

"Cheer up," I said. "This is the first day of the rest of your life." I slapped his naked ass with one clawed hand, and despite his tears, the boy's cock hardened against my back. Satisfied that my minion was safely in my possession for all time, I began the long downward flight home. You can guess the rest of the story, but if it's a moral you want, it is this: Be careful what you pray for; you never know who may be listening.

# III. THE BRUTE INSIDE

It wasn't until Rick ripped my shirt apart and used it to tie me up and gag me that I realized what was happening. So this is the hidden side, I thought as I fought down panic, this is what he's been hiding from me.

Last night I was lying on the couch with him. It was a chilly night, and I was on top of him under a blanket. That wasn't because I was the dominant one, it was because he is so much bigger than I that I can lie on top of him and he hardly feels it.

We'd been going out a few months, and we really liked each other. I had been completely open and honest with him, but I always had a feeling he was hiding something. It seemed as if he was holding back a side of his personality that he didn't want me to see.

It kind of bothered me but not enough for me to make an issue out of it. In fact I had pretty much forgotten about it until last night. I damn sure remembered then, but it was too late to make a difference. If I had realized what was going on, I might have been able to prevent what happened, but then again maybe not.

Sometimes I think that it was going to happen no matter what because that was the place he was heading all along.

All I wanted to do was lie there, warm under the blanket, with his arms around me. It was getting late, and my mind was starting to swim around in that dreamy place between asleep and awake. We must have been a perfect picture of romantic bliss, an innocent crew-cutted boy of twenty-two lying in the arms of a husky late twenties bodybuilder. I was happy and just wanted to lie there.

That was the problem.

Because I could feel his cock growing underneath me, stretching through the denim of his jeans and pressing against me.

Oh man, I thought dimly. Not now.

But sure enough, he shifted, lifted my face up, and started kissing me. Gently, I pulled away and laid my head back down on his chest. I should have known better. If there's one thing in the world I knew he hated, it was when I pulled away from him. But, usually he got the point and backed off, saving it for another time. I thought he would this time, too.

"Hey," he said, grabbing my face. His strong jaws locked on mine, his tongue forcing itself deep into my mouth. I could never shake the feeling of intrusion when he did that, and I instinctively tried to pull back. His hand clamped onto the back of my head and held me there. His arms locked around my body, holding me tight against him. His cock was getting harder. I twisted my head to one side, breaking the kiss.

"Come on, Rick," I started to say, but suddenly his hand was over my mouth, covering it. What the hell was he doing? He'd never done that before. It irritated me but also made me kind of excited. I had to inhale deeply through my nose to breathe, and his rough masculine smell was intoxicating. I must have whimpered because he shook my face roughly.

"Shut up," he said. "Don't you pull away from me. I've told you a hundred times if you resist it'll make it worse. So don't pull away, boy."

Boy? What was he doing calling me Boy? What was going on here? Apprehension rose in me, and I pulled away for the third time.

"Damn it!" he said loudly. Now I was scared. He'd never used that harsh a tone of voice with me before. He sat up abruptly, and I almost fell off the couch. I tried to stand up and get away from him, but he was too fast. He grabbed my wrist as he stood up and pulled me back.

I work out five times a week and have a tight muscular body, but all my strength was nothing in the face of his sheer brute power. In high school and college football, he had faced down against quarterbacks bigger than he and flung them to the ground, what the hell was I doing struggling against him?

Rick shoved me down on my back and lay on top of me. He was so big, I almost couldn't breathe. He took one of my wrists in each of his hands and held them down. His face was directly over mine now, and my frightened eyes met his. They were the color of the ocean and every bit as deep. Beneath those depths fires were burning.

"Knock it off now," he said. The warning in his voice was unmistakable. "You're my boy, and I've got every right to kiss you whenever I feel like it."

What? I thought. What did I just hear? Now I was getting mad. Since when was I 'his' anything? I didn't belong to him, for God's sake!

He leaned down to kiss me, and I could feel his cock getting bigger and bigger. Now I was wide awake, all thoughts of sleep gone. Now I was ready to fight. When his mouth got close I turned my face to the side, so his lips hit my ear. I jerked my hands upward and his grip tightened so hard I actually cried out in pain. I tried to lift my legs and struggle out from under him, but he pushed down harder, pressing me into the couch.

"Leave me alone!" I yelled at him.

"All right, boy," he said. "That's it." He stood up so suddenly I was too startled to move. The instinct to escape kicked in too late. I tried to get out of the way, but he grabbed my wrists again, pulling me off the couch into a standing position. Without a word, he wrapped one arm around my waist and lifted me completely off the floor. We were moving. He was carrying me under his arm as if I weighed no more than a kid. I tried to struggle but he flexed his arm and it tightened around me painfully.

"Rick!" I said.

"Shut up. Just keep your mouth shut."

He carried me down the hallway into the bedroom. He closed the door behind us and locked it. Then he threw me onto the bed. I wanted to escape, but there was no time – he was on me in a second, pinning me down. The more I tried to get free the tighter his grip got. I could feel panic in the back of my throat as I struggled under his enormous weight. I turned to the last thing left, my voice.

"WHO THE FUCK DO YOU THINK YOU ARE?" I screamed in his face. He recoiled as if I had spit at him. He was still holding me down, but at least he had backed off enough for me breathe. His hand went up in the air. It flashed toward me in a wide arc, then there was a smashing pain on my cheek. The other side of my face slammed into the pillow. He had never hit me before, ever.

No man had ever hit me.

I was so dazed I could hardly understand what he did next.

He grabbed the front of my flimsy T-shirt with his hand and with one pull ripped it down the front. He pulled again, yanking the shirt completely off me. I lay there beneath him as he shredded my shirt to pieces.

He grabbed a bunch of the little pieces of fabric and jammed them into my mouth. I tried to protest, but he yanked me forward and tied one of the longer pieces around my head, securing it in my mouth. He let my head drop back into the pillow, and I looked up at him in disbelief.

He had gagged me in less than five seconds.

Although I wasn't struggling any more, he grabbed my hands and tied them together with another long piece of the shirt. He was livid and flushed, with tiny beads of sweat on his forehead. His face was contorting into a mask of rage and desire that terrified me. I couldn't believe this was happening. I had never seen him this way before.

That's when it hit me. Oh God, I thought, this is what he's been hiding from me? This is the side of him he was holding back?

He got up slowly, as if expecting me to move. I didn't. He pulled my shorts off, and I was amazed to feel my dick spring into the air, totally erect. With the last of my shirt Rick tied my legs together.

"Now I don't have to listen to any more of your crap!" he said, as he stripped off his own clothes. "Now you're going to listen to me."

He yanked his long blond hair back and snapped it into a ponytail. Then he pulled off his tank top and loosened his belt. A second later his jeans fell to the floor. I felt myself get weak, as I always did when I saw him naked. The sight of his perfectly developed and proportioned musculature was so breathtaking he hardly needed to tie me up. With that body, I was his prisoner from day one. His cock was standing straight up, solid as granite. His eyes never left me as he unrolled a condom onto it.

He got back onto the bed and roughly parted my legs with his knees. It hurt with my ankles tied together, but he obviously didn't give a damn. I was lying underneath him totally helpless and vulnerable. Suddenly his hand was on my cock, gripping it hard. I squeezed my eyes shut in pain.

"This is mine, boy, you got that?" he said. "This dick belongs to me." He flipped me over and slapped my ass hard. I squirmed and tried to get away, but he held me tight and spanked me harder. "This ass is mine." He threw me down on my back again and his fingers probed between my legs. "This asshole is mine. Don't ever forget that."

Then he was moving in, coming closer, his legs pushing my own further and further apart until – I threw my head back in pain and ecstasy as he plowed his huge dick into my asshole. I cried out but the gag prevented any sound from escaping. I tried to move my arms, but with one hand Rick grabbed my bound wrists and held them down as he starting fucking me, thrusting in and out.

I shut my eyes. It felt so incredible, it was as if I'd never been fucked before. This was such an amazing feeling – so violent, so primitive, so powerful – it was overwhelming.

"You're my boy," he said. "And I can kiss you or hit you or fuck you whenever I damn well feel like it."

He leaned into me, pushing me up against the wall as he pumped harder and harder, his breathing getting faster and faster ...

"Does my boy want to come?" he said. My eyes flew open. I couldn't believe he was going to let me come when he was so angry. I nodded quickly and closed my eyes again. I heard the slurp of a lube bottle and suddenly his hand was on me again, gripping my cock but this time caressing, stroking, jerking. I could feel every muscle in my body tense as he pumped harder. Any second I was going to explode.

"Just remember this, boy. To everyone else, we're just boyfriends. But don't you ever forget what you really are. You are my property – you belong to me!"

My body convulsed as I came, the spasm rippling through every part of me like a wave. The stream of cum shot over my head and hit the wall behind me. I had never come so hard in my life. Rick pumped me a few more times, then jammed his cock in as far as it would go. As always, he didn't scream when he came, just exhaled loudly into my ear. As I heard the breath empty out of his lungs I knew his cock was shooting serious loads. He pulled out and yanked the condom off. He stood up, looking down at me. I just lay there, staring back at him. I felt amazing. The sensations moving through me were like nothing I'd ever felt before.

I waited for him to take the gag out and untie me.

But he didn't.

After cleaning himself up a little bit, he reached down and took me under his arm again.

"Come on, boy," he said, as he picked me up off the bed.

What's going on? I thought. But my brain was too dizzy to answer. He carried me over to the closet and put me inside, laying me down on the floor. I was naked, covered with lube and sweat.

"Now you're going to stay in there until I come and get you, is that clear? Be a good boy and go to sleep," he said.

What? I thought. Is he crazy? He closed the door, and I was surrounded by darkness. But I wasn't scared. Maybe I'm the one who's crazy, I thought, as I fell right to sleep, enjoying the feeling of my wrists and ankles bound together.

When I woke up I was in bed. Rick was with me, his arms wrapped protectively around me as usual. It was just about time for us to get up.

It was just like any other morning. I was clean and dry, and felt rested and ready for the day. The events of the previous night were already fading in my mind. Did that really happen? Or was it just some bizarre dream brought on by that weird anchovy pizza we ate last night?

I got up, careful not to wake him, and started to walk to the bathroom.

"Hey boy."

His voice startled me so much I almost yelped in surprise. I turned around and he was wide awake, watching me.

I didn't say anything.

"I meant everything I said last night." he said. "To everyone else we can just be boyfriends, but you and I will know the truth – that I own you."

"Okay," I said weakly.

"The proper thing to say is 'Yes, Sir'," he said understandingly. "I'll let it slide this time. But you'll get punished if you forget in the future."

"Yes, Sir." I said.

"Good boy!" Rick said, smiling broadly.

"So from now on, just to make sure you remember what's happened, the first thing you do when you see me is to get down on your knees and suck my cock, no matter where we are. Is that clear?"

"Yes, Sir."

"Good boy. Now go get ready for work so you won't be late."

"I love you," I said.

"I love you, too." Rick said as he wrapped his arms around a pillow and laid his head back down. That was this morning. I haven't been able to think about anything else all day. I can't get it out of my mind. I feel like a new man ... a new boy, who has finally found what he always wanted even though he didn't know he wanted it. Sometimes I wonder about what we're doing, and other times, I wish he had shown me his hidden side earlier.

I could hardly wait to get off work today.

Because Rick said he was coming over tonight.

And I'm ready.

I'm already on my knees at the front door with my shirt off, scribbling in this notebook.

Oops, gotta stop.

I hear his car in the driveway.

# IV. TRAINING LUST

“Come on, man! You can do it! Give it to me, baby, come on, give me all you’ve got!” I glanced up at my personal trainer feeling a mixture of desire and hatred. I desired him totally because he was so fucking hot. And, I hated him for what he was doing to me. The incredible pain I was going through was caused by him. It was all his fault. Of course, I’d asked for it, not realizing what a masochistic thing it was to do.

When I’d asked my friend who looked great how he’d gotten his body in such good shape, he raved about his trainer, who he said had turned everything around for him.

Inquiring further, I got the trainer’s name and phone number. One call on the phone was all it took. The guy was nice, friendly, easy to talk to. He even agreed to train me for free, seeing as I was such a good friend of his favorite client’s.

If only I’d known what I was in for.

“Don’t be a little wimp, dude, come on, I know you can do better than that!”

I’d worked out more or less regularly since high school and considered myself in decent shape, but nothing could have compared me for the torture that Marc would put me through. And, it’s not as if I’m into pain, or anything. I know some guys are, and they’d be happy as a pig in shit if Marc got a hold of them.

But he didn’t.

He had a hold of me.

And I thought I was going to lose my fucking mind.

He was maddening to be around, so good-looking, and such a taskmaster at the same time. From the moment I saw him, I thought, Oh God this can’t be him, I’ll be spending all our time together staring at him and imagining all kinds of wild sexual things. I should’ve known

Marc had encountered that a lot before and knew just how to counteract it. Work 'em and work 'em hard. I'd never worked out harder in my life. Marc totally changed my life, altering the foods I ate, designing exercise program after exercise program for me, taking total and complete charge of my health and fitness.

It was wonderful, I knew – what he was doing for me normally cost guys hundreds and hundreds of dollars, so I kept my mouth shut.

"One more set, come on, I know you can do one more set, it's only fifteen reps, I know you can do it! You don't want all the guys here to think you're a weakling, do you?"

But, he was so hard to be around! So good-looking, so hot, and yet so arrogant and cocky that I wanted to smack him upside the head. Well, why shouldn't he be? He was one of the top trainers in the city, and he knew it.

He had every right to act the way he did.

But, it didn't make him any easier to deal with. The fact that he was so knowledgeable and such a fucking expert at what he did made it all the more infuriating.

Every day we trained, I would take in his image: dark skin from a mix of black and Hispanic blood, short jet-black hair that perfectly framed his beautiful cover-boy face, sparkling white teeth, an absolutely stunning body, every muscle developed and toned to the perfect degree, his skin smooth and hairless as a baby's, round succulent butt-cheeks, each one a mouth-watering handful. And, the way he carried himself, proud, strong, confident, even pompous – a perfect body amid so many merely beautiful bodies.

"Pump it, man, pump it! Give me one more, come on, give it to me, give it to me, give me all you've got!"

Now it wasn't that he made me feel inferior ... or was it? I don't know any more. Ever since what happened the time before is sort of a blur. All I know is that he was hard to be around. I knew that everything he was telling me was absolutely true, and everything he was doing for me and making me do was helping me ... or was it? Sometimes I got the feeling he demanded more from me than he did his other clients, as if he got off on pushing me harder than he knew I could handle. He'd work me until I was a quivering mass of jelly lying on the floor, and then say something like, "Just one more set, man, I know you can do it."

Fuck you, I'd want to say, but didn't, and got up to dutifully follow my trainer's directive. After all, he was the expert, right? He was the one with the degree in health and nutrition and the body that every gay guy in the city lusted after and the hourly rate higher than any other trainer, wasn't he?

Yeah, and it didn't make it any easier to take his prodding and poking, his needling and cajoling, his remarks that rode the border between serious and sarcastic.

I had to do something.

I knew I couldn't let it go on like this.

Something about his training was demeaning me, making me feel less than a man. Somehow this guy whom I had never known before a few months ago was invading my dreams at night, making me feel like a pathetic worm next to him, reducing my confidence and self-esteem to nothing as every day he broke my ego down in front of the mirrors at the gym, stripping away my defenses until all that was left was my pure naked self, just waiting to get abused by him.

No Army drill sergeant could've worked me or pushed me as hard as Marc did. And I was no softy either, that was the killer. No one else could get to me like this trainer did. I knew I was a serious piece of manmeat – 5'11", 175 pounds, pale Norwegian skin, short light brown hair, my facial structure a mixture of my mother's delicate beauty and my father's gruff masculinity.

Anyone's else insults and jibes would just roll down my back. I didn't justify anyone's digs at me because I was hot and I knew it. But Marc? Something about him made it impossible for me to do that. Somehow, I just took everything he had to give, letting him goad me and prod me until I felt like exploding in anger. But he had been nice enough not to ask me to pay him, so I just took it from him, took his bullshit like I had never taken anyone's before. I'd have knocked their block off sooner than take the crap I took from Marc.

But still I took it.

And took it.

And took it – his constant stream of verbal abuse, his killer good looks and the horrifically hard training he was putting me through all combining to drive me absolutely out of my fucking mind.

Day after day, night after night, session after session.

Until something snapped.

It was late at night when it happened. Marc was friends with the guys that owned the gym, so they let him and his clients use the facility after hours sometimes. We were alone in the place, which had closed hours before. Even the janitors had finished their rounds and were gone. It was just him and me, alone in that huge building. Every clank of equipment and every word we said echoed back and forth between the concrete walls.

And I wasn't going to take any more bullshit from Marc.

I had just finished three sets of bench-presses, and I felt like I was made of KY. My arms felt loose and flabby, I didn't know how I could do any more. It was the end of a long day that had been hard enough before coming here and getting reamed out by my asshole trainer.

Marc had been particularly vicious that night, calling me wimp and pussy and weakling when I didn't perform up to his standards. I was just about to blow my top. My temper's fuse was so short I didn't know what I'd do if he pushed me any further.

Whatever I did, it wouldn't be pretty.

"Come on, pussy." Marc said, standing over me with his arms folded. "One more set. You can do it."

I jumped to my feet, seeing red like a bull in a rodeo. With both hands I shoved him away from me, and he fell backwards against the mirrored wall.

"I can do it, all right!" I snarled. "But I'm not gonna do another set, all I'm gonna do is you!"

"What the hell's wrong with you?" he shouted.

"I told you!" I said, fury making my voice sound like a madman's. "I'm sick of your fucking bullshit, and now I'm gonna take it out of your ass!"

"You're out of your fucking mind!" Marc said, but his eyes had widened in fear.

"You got that right," I said as I lunged at him, covering the distance between us in seconds. Grabbing his arm, I pulled him up to his feet and hurled him across the room. He tripped over a pile of weights and crashed to the floor again.

I don't know where my sudden strength came from. Seconds before I'd been totally tired out, but now – the intensity of my rage must have been driving me, finding new reserves of energy to fuel my attack on my tormentor.

"I've taken your crap for three months, Marc!" I yelled at him. "I'm not taking any more! Tonight you're gonna pay for what you've been putting me through!" I lunged for him again.

"You can't do this, Ryan!" he said as he tried to scramble out of my way.

"Oh yeah? Watch me!"

I tackled him, jumping on top of him and holding him down with my heavier weight. He struggled beneath me, my cock hardening as it felt him through the fabric of our gym clothes. Being so close to him for so long, being at such close intimate range with him for all this time without ever touching him, had started a fever in my blood that had reached the boiling point.

"You're a fucking asshole, man!" I screamed down at him as I held him in place. "Who in the hell do you think you are? What makes you think you can treat people this way?" He maneuvered himself so he was on his back, his gorgeous face looking up at me.

"I don't treat people this way, Ryan," he said. "I just treat you this way."

Roaring with rage, I slapped Marc across the face as hard as I could. His head flew to one side from the impact, but when he turned back towards me, he was grinning.

It was a sultry, sexy grin. A grin that made an already attractive face heartbreakingly beautiful, even with a handprint on one cheek. It was a grin that said fuck me.

"Oh, you goddamn cocktease!" I yelled. "You're finally gonna get what you deserve!" I fumbled with the elastic band of my shorts, yanking them down so hard I ripped the fabric. My erect dick popped out, poised and ready for action. Straddling Marc's body with my own, I grabbed the back of his head and slammed my cock into his mouth. He didn't try to resist me, he just lay there and let me do what I wanted to with him.

"Suck my big dick, you fucking asshole!" I commanded him, and obediently his mouth started working me, stroking and massaging my organ with his tongue and the inside of his mouth. My trainer's eyes rolled back in his head and then closed, his whole concentration on my hard dick. I glanced behind me and was amazed to see his shorts being tented by his own erect member. Somehow his fear was alternating with excitement, switching back and forth and mixing together.

"You little fucker," I said, hardly believing my eyes. "You get off on this, don't you? You've probably been pushing me on purpose, pushing me so hard you knew I'd snap and just take you like I'm doing now!"

Marc didn't answer, his mouth stuffed with cock and his eyes clenched shut.

"You've worked me harder than I've ever been worked before, well now I'm gonna fuck you harder than you've ever been fucked, you bastard!"

My balls were churning, the jizz within heating up as my dick got a workout in Marc's mouth. It was so fucking hot, whatever else I could say about him, this man had one talented mouth. He swirled his tongue around the cut ridge of my organ, stimulating every single nerve with delirious pleasure. I could've come right then and there, shooting my load down my trainer's throat, but then it'd be over.

I wasn't going to get distracted by pleasure and expel my spunk too soon. Not when I had an agenda like I did that night. Marc was going to pay for what he'd done to me. I wasn't going to let him off so easily. I wanted to savor this, as I used him and demeaned him and made him the object of my scorn and ridicule just as he'd been doing to me so long.

What he was doing was fucking awesome, probably the best blowjob I'd ever had the pleasure of receiving. But I wasn't going to let him know that. When had he ever praised me? When had he ever told me that I had done good? That he was happy with my progress? Never, that's when! True, I'd seen results in my body; I had made definite strides as my musculature and strength increased under his expert training.

But that almost made it worse.

I knew I was doing good – but my trainer never said it, never praised me. He just kept telling me to do one more set and called me wimp and pussy. Damn him!

Well, now I was getting my revenge, and was it sweet!

Gripping a firm handful of his luxurious hair in my hand, I forced Marc to bear down on my dick even harder.

"Come on, man," I said. "Can't you do any better than that? I know you got more in you than that! Make me feel good, you little cocksucker!"

I fucked his face savagely, forcing him down on me and then off, then down on me and then off, again and again, over and over. But I kept myself from coming.

With Zen-like concentration, I willed myself not to shoot off, not to acknowledge the incredible sensations Marc's mouth was bringing to me.

I wasn't going to give him that pleasure.

At least not yet.

I stood up then, letting go of his head. He started to get up, and I shoved him back down with my foot.

"Get back down there!" I grunted at him. "Stay on the floor, you fucking asshole. It's where you belong."

I started stripping out of my clothes then, letting my shorts fall to the floor. I stepped out of my jockstrap and tore my shirt off over my head. Then I turned around, and shoved my ass in my trainer's face.

"Lick me, you son of a bitch. Lick my ass!"

His tongue was there in a second, burying itself between my cheeks and sending shivers of electricity through my body. It felt so fucking good.

"Goddamn you!" I said. "Can't you do any better? Come on, you wimp, give me everything you got! I wanna feel it! Give it to me!"

Incensed by my taunting, he tried harder, licking and slurping at my asshole with all his might. I wet my hand with my tongue and stroked my hard dick a few times.

Mmmm, was that good.

But not yet.

Denied again, the cum in my ballsack boiled in anticipation – hopefully, anxiously, desperately waiting for the moment it would be released and fly out of my cockhead.

"Come on, trainer boy, you can do it, yeah, come on, don't give up, you little wimp! Work harder! Harder!"

It was heaven to torture him like that, absolute heaven. I loved it. It was the best revenge I could have. Pushing my butt back further and further, I pinned him down with my bigger weight until his head was flat on the floor. Suddenly, I flipped over, so I was facing him. I dropped down on top of him, keeping him down. With both hands I grabbed the front of his tank top and pulled. A loud ripping sound filled the gym as I tore his tank apart.

"Hey …" he started to say, but I slapped him again, hard.

"Shut up!" I yelled in his face. "Shut the fuck up! Just keep your goddamn fucking mouth shut! I've heard enough from you. We're gonna do things my way now, whether you like it or not!"

Tossing aside what was left of his tank, I grabbed the front of his shorts and yanked them down. Marc stopped fighting me then, slipping out of them obediently. Too revved up to care about his shoes, I let him keep those on. But not his jockstrap. No way! One yank of my fist and it was history. But that gave me an idea. I picked up my own discarded jock off the floor and brought it up to my trainer's face.

"Smell it, Marc." I said. "Smell what you do to me, what you've been doing to me for months. Smell it!" He inhaled deeply, sucking in the rank scent of my exertion.

Seeing that made my skin flush with blood. I stuffed my jockstrap in his mouth.

"You better keep that in there, man," I said. "I've heard enough out of you today. That'll keep you shut up."

Now we were both naked, and I couldn't help but pause for a second to admire the incredible beauty of the man I was tormenting. He was every bit as flawless with his clothes off – his gorgeous hairless skin, his wonderful muscles, his full hard cock ... he lay at my feet like a sacrificial victim in a horror movie, lying there waiting to be taken by the monster ...

... to be taken by me.

The time had come.

The time was now.

I reached down and grabbed him under the armpits, yanking him up to his feet. Then I shoved him over to the bench press that he'd been working me on before. I pushed him stomach-down on the bench, so his luscious butt was facing me, his asshole winking up at me like a twinkling star in the sky. The frenzy in my blood was at a fever pitch now. It was time to do what I'd dreamed, wanted and desired since Marc had first started training me and making me the object of his abuse.

"I've waited a long time for this, Marc," I said. "Now, for once, you're going to be my pussyboy!"

And I fell on top of him, pinning him to the bench with my weight. Guiding my rigid cock with one hand, I found the magic spot between his ass-cheeks and slid inside him. My trainer screamed, the jockstrap shoved in his mouth only partially obscuring the sound.

"Go ahead and yell, pussyboy," I said. "There's no one to hear you."

Marc struggled, but I wrapped my arms around him and held him close, like I would a lover. But I didn't love him. I hated him. Didn't I? Or did I? Did it matter?

Anchoring my feet on the floor, I started fucking him, shoving myself in and out of him with a vengeance. It was terrifying and wonderful at the same time. Part of me was shocked, appalled at what I was doing. But this man had pushed me further than anyone deserved to be pushed. He had to be punished for what he'd done. The rest of me was delighted, ecstatic at the savagery of my actions, the pure carnal lust with which I was taking this man, whether he wanted to be taken or not.

Fucking Marc was an awesome experience. My thoughts and imaginations about it were nothing compared to the real thing. The fact that he was moaning and squirming beneath me made it all the more electrifying. The fact that I was raping him on the same bench that he'd used to torture me so many times was fucking mind-blowing!

"Come on, pussyboy," I snarled at him. "Can't you do better than that?! I know this is what you live for. Throwing your legs up in the air like some little whore! Well, you're my whore tonight, and you're not getting away 'til I'm done with you!"

Marc was loving every second of this!

His moans and groans had changed from mixed fear and excitement to total abandon and lust! He was getting off on this just as much as I was. The little fucker.

Leave it to Marc to change getting raped and assaulted into the hottest sex of his life. But I didn't care, because my dick was getting the best ride it had ever had. His whole body was so hot it felt as if it was on fire. I couldn't hold back anymore. It was time to finish this.

"Come on, you motherfucker," I said as I raped his hole. "Give me everything, give me all of it, give it up to me you goddamn cocksucking son of a bitch!"

Marc's head arched back, and his body heaved. As it did I saw him slip his hand under himself. He must have taken ahold of his dick, because his whole body started quivering and shaking. I knew he was jerking himself off, but I didn't care.

I was too far gone.

"From now on you're my pussyboy, Marc, you got that?" I yelled. He nodded his head rapidly to show he understood. "I'm not taking any more shit from you. What I am going to take is you, wherever and whenever I want you. Is that clear?" He nodded again, frantically. We were both seconds away from coming. "From now on, I do three sets, and that's it! I'm never doing four again. You're never going to say 'one more set' to me, got it?"

"Yes, Ryan!" he yelled, the jockstrap muffling his words.

"You're never going to treat me like a piece of shit again! You're going to treat me with the respect and courtesy you should treat everyone with, especially one of your clients, whether he's paying you or not, you snot-nosed punk! Is that clear?"

"Yes, Ryan!" he yelled again.

"Now you're gonna take my cum, and thank me for it!"

The ecstasy overflowed inside me, and I grabbed Marc's hips with both hands as my dick machine-gunned into him. Jizz shot out of me with the force of a hurricane, the long-frustrated cum super-heating like volcanic lava. I roared with passion and primal release. As I did, I felt my trainer's body shudder beneath me, and I knew he was shooting too, oozing his load out onto the bench.

I expelled my seed into him, holding him tightly in place, so he couldn't escape, even if he'd wanted to. Only when we had both drained our ballsacks, and were panting trying to catch our breaths, did I let go of him. Marc slid off the bench, falling onto the floor like the mass of jelly I had felt like before. I leaned over him and yanked my jockstrap out of his mouth, then I put my clothes back on.

The whole time I did this, he just lay there, breathing heavily, not moving. When I got myself together, I went and picked up one of the janitor's mops that was leaning against the wall. I tossed it at Marc, and it clattered to the floor next to him.

"Better clean up that mess, weakling," I said, gesturing at the puddle of cum on the bench. "Don't want to get in trouble with the management."

Figuring I'd had enough of a workout for the night, I headed for the gym's exit. In the open doorway, I glanced back over my shoulder at the man I had just fucked.

"Same time tomorrow," I said.

"Yes, Sir." Marc said weakly.

Now that was more like it!

I walked out into the night, letting the door slam behind me and leaving my trainer lying on the floor of the gym, alone with his thoughts.

# V. NIGHT OF THE HUNTER
## Hunters of Men 1

Harlan adjusted the laser target-finder on his rifle until it was in perfect focus. He was a good enough shot that he didn't really need the targeting system, but if something worked for him he liked to keep using it. When he first learned how to use his rifle, he had depended on the target-finder, so now despite years of practice and accumulated skill, he continued to utilize it. He was the kind of man who liked to do things cleanly, efficiently, crossing all the Ts and dotting all the Is.

He was a consummate hunter, ruthless in his precision. Some called him the best in the business, although he'd never make such a bold statement himself. As far as he was concerned, he was just another working stiff trying to earn a living.

Harlan adjusted his stiff cock in his pants with one hand, keeping a firm grip on the rifle with his other. He got off on hunting, and always had. It was part of what made him so good at it. Unlike other hunters whose sexual excitement distracted them from their purpose, Harlan had found his arousal helped him focus on his goal, his throbbing dick acting like a divining rod searching for water.

Cold from the concrete steps he was perched on seeped through his pants, but he ignored it, as he ignored all discomfort. Discomfort was unimportant, he believed, something to be disregarded. Pain was what really mattered. Pain meant something was wrong. But discomfort? That was just the body complaining, and Harlan detested complaining, of any kind, whether from his clients, his targets, or his own body. He was sitting on the upper steps of a stairwell behind a closed restaurant overlooking an alley. It was dark back here, and quiet to some degree, but caution could not be relaxed. The city's teeming nightlife was bustling on the other side of the building. Restaurants, dance clubs, whorehouses, bars, all within reach, all full of people.

People meant witnesses, and the first rule of Harlan's kind of hunting was no witnesses.

The hunter checked his watch. It was 1:45 am. His target should present himself soon. Observation of target had revealed a pattern: every Saturday night, he went dancing at a certain gay dance club, and after a few hours left the place unaccompanied. Harlan had observed this often enough that it was safe to anticipate the same actions tonight. He couldn't be certain his target would follow this pattern, but anticipate? Yes, he could do that. The only thing predictable about targets was their unpredictability, but the hunter felt confident that soon enough his prey would leave the dance club, and choose this alley as the first leg of his short walk home.

Harlan checked his rifle's magazine again. He knew nothing had changed since the last time he'd checked, but he did it anyway. The magazine contained ten darts, even though all he would need would be one. Other less-skilled hunters might require multiple projectiles in case they missed their marks, but Harlan wouldn't miss.

He hadn't missed in years.

Something was coming! Instinctively the hunter backed deeper into the shadows, disappearing into the darkness that shrouded the stairwell. His body responded so quickly, it took his eyes a second to catch up. A police car had turned off the main drag into the alley, and was cruising slowly down the narrow stretch of pavement between the restaurant and the office building on the other side. The car moved slowly down the alley, the officer within undoubtedly looking back and forth through the car's windows for any sign of disturbance or trouble. The array of lights on top of the vehicle was dark, indicating that this was merely a routine patrol run. Harlan silently watched the car glide past him, its tires grinding noisily on the pavement. Within a few seconds, the police car had completed its run and disappeared at the end of the alley back onto the main road. The hunter relaxed slightly, although he was never fully relaxed while he was working. Hunting required a certain level of tension to be performed properly. A hunter must always be more awake, more alert, more alive than his target. That was what separated them, making one predator and the other prey.

Harlan mentally reviewed his target's appearance, not because he had forgotten it, but merely to confirm one more time before the deed was done. Caucasian, 26 years old, height 5'10", weight 160 pounds, short brown hair, no facial hair, medium build, on the slender side, sexual orientation: gay, first name: Brian. The hunter's client had not shared the target's full name with him, as was customary in this type of transaction. All Harlan needed to know was information pertinent to planning and executing the target's capture. Anything else was irrelevant, and of no interest to the hunter anyway. He didn't care who his target was, only about how much he would get paid by the client for securing him and the logistics of the hunt.

Harlan's keen hearing picked up the sound of approaching footsteps. Someone was entering the alley. Being sure to remain hidden in the shadows, the hunter waited for the walker to become visible.

It was Brian, his target! The hunter's cock flexed in his pants at the sight of his quarry. The young man walked normally, with no signs of intoxication. He didn't look around, evidence of his coming this way many times. The possibility of danger in this alley had long since left his mind. So much the better, Harlan thought. Easy pickings.

The ease of this capture might have bored another hunter as experienced as Harlan. But Harlan took pleasure in every hunt, no matter how uneventful. He would welcome a challenge, certainly, but did not require constant tests of his skill to remain satisfied by his work. A smooth, clean capture was just as fulfilling to him as an arduous hunt for a slippery target.

Brian had almost reached the middle of the alley when the hunter carefully aimed his rifle down through the guard rails of the stairwell he was perched on. Harlan looked through the target-finder and locked his sights on the young man's neck. The targeting system's crosshairs lit up silently, indicating the perfect shot had been lined up.

It was time.

The hunter pulled the trigger of his rifle. The tiny dart that was discharged took less than a second to cover the distance between the hunter and his prey, and imbedded itself into the target's neck. Harlan knew the young man would feel only minimal pain, similar to that caused by an insect bite. The target stopped in his tracks and slapped his hand against his neck with a swatting motion. His eyes widened when his fingers found the dart in his neck, but then drooped as the chemical the projectile had injected into his bloodstream began to take effect. The young man lazily sank to his knees on the pavement. His eyes rolled back in his head, and he slumped to the ground in a heap as unconsciousness claimed him.

Harlan sprang into action. In the space of a few seconds, the hunter disassembled his rifle into its component pieces and stowed them in the pockets of his jacket. Then with the agility of an acrobat, he jumped the fifteen feet from his spot on the stairwell to the pavement below. He knelt next to his fallen target and turned the young man, so his neck was exposed.

The hunter gently removed the dart from his target's neck and covered the hole with a circular bandage he retrieved from his jacket pocket that had been treated with a disinfecting agent. Harlan knew the tiny wound would heal within a few days, leaving no trace that it had ever been there. The second rule of hunting, after all, was don't damage the merchandise. He put the spent dart into a small storage case, so there was no chance of it piercing him when he stored it in a pocket of his pants.

Satisfied, Harlan rose to his feet, grabbing Brian by the arms and pulling him up with him. Then he leaned over and let the unconscious body of his target fall forward over his back. Then the hunter stood erect, hoisting the young man off the ground, up and over his left shoulder like a game hunter would with a deer he'd caught. Harlan hefted his target's body, adjusting it for proper weight distribution. He'd carried prey far heavier than his current catch, so this was hardly a strain at all. He could have carried Brian slung over his shoulder for miles if he had to. But not this time.

This time he just needed to get his target to his truck and out of sight as quickly as possible. There were too many chances to get seen and questioned in this crowded city. After a quick visual search of the ground the hunter determined that there was no evidence of what had occurred. Packing his catch like a sack of laundry, Harlan headed down the alley the opposite way his target had been heading. His truck was waiting for him just on the edge of the alley, in a choice parking spot the hunter had been grateful to secure.

Everything was going well tonight.

"Excuse me!"

The voice, which came from behind him, was loud in the enclosed alleyway. The hunter slowly turned around, trying to not to jostle his burden any more than necessary.

About thirty feet away from him stood a police officer, perhaps even the one who'd driven his car through this same alley a few minutes ago. He must've wanted to do a patrol on foot, so parked nearby and came back this way.

He was tall, probably in his mid-forties, with a mustache and tired eyes. He was pointing a big flashlight at Harlan and looking suspiciously at the unconscious man slung over his shoulder.

"Is there a problem here?" the officer asked.

"No, sir," Harlan answered in a pleasant tone, "my friend here just had a little too much to drink." The hunter patted Brian's leg affectionately. "I'm his designated driver."

"Do you need any help?" the policeman asked.

"No, thank you, officer," the hunter said, "my car's right around the corner. I'll take him home and put him to bed."

"He'll have a hell of a hangover in the morning."

"You said it, sir," Harlan said. "This might keep him out of the bars for a few weeks at least."

"Have a good night," the policeman said.

"Thanks, officer. And thank you for keeping the city safe."

The policeman and the hunter turned away from each other, each heading in opposite directions to where their vehicles awaited them. That was close, Harlan thought, but it turned out okay. He carried his unconscious prey the rest of the way down the alley, then after checking to see if there were any other people nearby, made a sharp right to where his truck was parked.

Harlan's truck was big and black, American-made (of course), with the sizable rear-bed enclosed. Securing Brian over his shoulder with his left arm, the hunter used his right hand to reach into his pocket and find his keys. Pressing a button on a key fob activated the truck's internal systems, and the tailgate of the rear-bed opened quietly.

At the touch of another button the false floor of the bed split and slid aside to reveal three custom-installed compartments, each roughly man-sized. They were well-padded, each with a vent that pumped O2 into them, so the occupants of the compartments could breathe without difficulty.

After another proximity check, the hunter gently slid his target off his shoulder and into the left-hand compartment. Harlan arranged Brian's head and limbs for maximum comfort, then locked the young man's wrists together into a set of handcuffs he pulled from a side pocket and fastening them to a D-ring at the head of the compartment. When his hands had been secured, the hunter did the same with Brian's legs, cuffing his ankles together and locking him to the other D-ring at the foot of the human storage place. Satisfied that his target was secured, Harlan used the buttons on his key fob to restore the bed floor, close the tailgate and lock it.

The hunter got into his truck, started it up, and pulled out of the parking space to join the flow of traffic on the nearby main drag of the city. Even at this late hour, it was still somewhat crowded. Harlan shook his head. It was time for men to be home safe and asleep. When you were out this late, you never knew what could happen. The hunter waved to the driver of the car that was politely gesturing to go in front of him. Harlan pulled out onto the road and headed for home with a feeling of satisfaction.

Another smooth, clean capture completed.

Soon after, the hunter pulled his truck into the driveway of his secluded suburban home. It was almost 3:00 am by now, and the neighborhood was quiet and dark. The touch of a button on the visor, and the garage door opened silently. Harlan pulled his truck into the garage and when the vehicle was all the way in, pushed the button again to close it behind him. Only when the he heard the garage door's locking mechanism click into place did he turn his key in the ignition to turn the truck off. The hunter got out and walked around to the rear of his truck, then opened the tailgate and revealed the compartments under the floor.

His target was still unconscious, sleeping peacefully in his compartment. Harlan examined him briefly and determined that there had been no damage done during the drive to his house. The hunter removed the cuffs from his target's wrists and ankles and gently pulled the sleeping young man from his compartment. Then Harlan maneuvered Brian into a position from which he could hoist him over his right shoulder. Harlan alternated which shoulder he carried his secured targets over.

Of course the hunter was in excellent physical condition anyway, with his regular workouts at his home gym. But since carrying his targets was such a common occurrence in his life, he wanted to make sure his shoulders were prepared. Harlan secured Brian by wrapping his right arm around the young man's legs. He wasn't going anywhere. Then with his left hand he activated the controls that would close up his truck for the night. The hunter hefted his catch and carried him into his house through a door at the back of the garage.

Once inside, Harlan took his target down a flight of stairs to his basement work-room. There he laid Brian down on his back on a padded table with restraints attached to it at each corner. The hunter expertly slid the young man's hands and feet into the restraints and secured them at the wrists and ankles. There was no way he could escape now. For a finishing touch, the hunter tied a black bandana around his target's eyes to function as a blindfold. The third rule of hunting, after all, was never let your prey see you.

Harlan knew that the knock-out drug his dart had injected into his target's system would soon wear off. But since he was securely attached to the table, the young man would be unable to free himself. Not that he couldn't take a slender little punk like this Brian, but Harlan liked things clean, without complications, without mess. Although he'd been working so hard lately he figured he deserved a little indulgence. Maybe later.

He sat down at his desk across the room from the table and unlaced his boots, slipping them off his feet. Then he removed the pieces of his rifle from his jacket and returned them to their holding case, which he left open on the desktop. His jacket came off next, neatly hung up on a hook on the wall next to the desk. A few of the buttons of his shirt were next undone, and he felt much more comfortable.

He felt his hard cock through his pants. His penis was more than good-sized, and he was pleased with it. He picked up the printout of the job detail that was on the desk with his left hand and kept his right on his dick. Harlan started to re-read the specs of the job, not because he'd forgotten, but just to re-acquaint himself with the information.

"Uuuhhh ...?"

It sounded as if the knock-out drug was wearing off. Harlan looked over at the table to see Brian moving slowly, his head turning back and forth.

"Uuuunnnnggggghh...?"

The secured target tried to move his arms and legs and found them to be tightly bound in place.

"Wwwwhhhaaaa...?"

Looks as if the specs would have to wait. Harlan walked over to a small counter that was between the table and the desk. When he reached it he filled a syringe with a longer dose of the KO drug. He left the syringe on the counter and got a dark brown bottle, a small washcloth and a hand towel from a drawer. He brought the last three items to the table and waited for his target to fully wake up. It was time for the indulgence he'd promised himself earlier.

"Wwwhat'sss happening?" Brian asked.

"You awake, boy?" Harlan asked. The bound young man shook his head back and forth, obviously trying to figure out why he couldn't see.

"Yeah, I'm awake, I guess ..." Brian said. "Why can't I see anything?"

"Because I've blindfolded you."

"Who're you?"

"I'm a hunter, boy." Harlan said. "I'm the one who's caught you."

"Caught me?" his target said, confusion in his voice. "What're you talking about? What the hell's going on? Why can't I move my arms and legs?" Beneath the edge of the table, the hunter put his hand into his pants and started stroking his cock.

"You can't move your arms and legs because I've secured them to the table."

"Well, turn me loose, man!" Brian said.

"I can't turn you loose, Brian," the hunter said, and fear replaced confusion in the young man's voice at the use of his first name. "I can't risk you escaping."

"Turn me loose, goddamn it!" the target said as he struggled against his bonds. Harlan could tell he was trying to act tough but was really scared to death.

"No," Harlan said. "You're worth too much to me to release you."

"What the fuck are you talking about?"

The hunter stroked his dick faster.

"I've been offered a sizable sum of money for your capture and delivery," he said.

"I don't know what they're paying you, man, but I'll double it if you let me go," Brian said, his voice quivering with fear.

The hunter laughed.

"You don't have half the money my client's going to pay me, let alone double. Your most valuable asset is yourself, Brian, which is why I've hunted you, caught you, and will deliver you to my client."

With a sudden burst of terror-induced strength, the young man strained against his bondage, trying desperately to free himself. Harlan continued to jerk himself off, hearing fear change to anger in his target's voice.

"You fucking freak!" Brian screamed. "When I get out of this I'm gonna kill you, I swear to God! You goddamn fucking son of a bitch, I'LL KILL YOU!"

Harlan laughed again.

"When you get out of this?" he said, "But you're not going to get out of this, Brian. I'm going to knock you out again and deliver you to my client."

"Help! HELP!! PLEASE!!! SOMEBODY!!!"

"This room is sound-proofed, Brian," the hunter said, "there's no possible way anyone can hear you."

The young man stopped yelling, his head moving desperately back and forth as he racked his mind for any possible way out of the situation he'd found himself in.

"I'm a fag, man, you know that, right?" Brian said desperately. "I'll be your bitch, man, I'm serious, I'm a fucking faggot and I'll be your bitch, you can fuck me, come in me, piss in me, anything, just please don't fucking 'deliver me'!"

Harlan gave his target a big smile that of course he couldn't see.

"That's a flattering offer, Brian," he said, "but again, you're offering me less than what I'm already contracted for. With the money I'm going to get for you, I'll be able to buy myself more bitches than can fit in this whole house."

"Oh God …" the young man whispered, almost to himself, as he realized there was no way out. "Oh God, oh fucking God …" he said, as tears welled up in his eyes and began to run down the sides of his face.

That was all Harlan needed to see.

"OH FUCKIN' YEAH!!!" the hunter said, and came, his spunk splattering onto the edge of the table and onto the floor. "MMmmmmm …" He continued to stroke himself for a few minutes, then put his cock back in his pants and used the hand towel to wipe up the mess he'd made. The young man was whispering to himself as he cried quietly. Harlan noticed with interest that a dark stain was spreading on Brian's pants in the vicinity of his crotch. His target had pissed himself.

"Please …" Brian moaned, "please …"

"Sssshhhh …" the hunter whispered, "it's okay …it's all right …"

He opened the dark brown bottle and splashed some of its liquid onto the clean washcloth. Then he covered his target's nose and mouth with the washcloth. The young man tried to fight him, but it was impossible, and within a minute he had sunk into another deep sleep. Harlan removed the washcloth from the young man's face. After putting the hand towel and the washcloth into a plastic bag to seal in the fumes, he closed the chloroform bottle and returned it to its drawer under the counter. He left the syringe where he had laid it earlier, on the counter ready to go.

Then as his catch slept soundly, the hunter returned to his desk and picked up the job specs printout again. This time, he would read it without interruption.

The hunter read the details of his latest assignment from the client who'd hired him. That client was expecting delivery of the target at 11:00 am the coming morning. Harlan glanced at the clock on his desk. He could still get several hours of sleep before delivering the young man he'd captured to his client.

He considered emptying the syringe full of KO drug into Brian, but decided against it. If the chloroform his catch was currently out from wore off before Harlan woke he could yell all he wanted, no one would hear him.

Yes, some rest would be good. And well-deserved. The capture of the young man, Brian, had not been difficult, or stressful, but pulling off a flawless catch as he'd done tonight took a certain toll on the hunter, no matter how many times he'd done it before. Harlan stood up and took one last look at his prey. Brian was actually pretty good-looking. He hadn't really noticed that before. Well, most men were more handsome when they were asleep anyway, at least to the hunter. He shut off the lights in the room and closed and locked the door behind him, then headed up the stairs to the ground floor of his house. When he reached his bedroom, he stripped down to his briefs, exposing his muscular body to the empty room, and lay down for a nice long nap after setting his alarm.

Several hours later, Harlan awoke to his alarm, took a shower, dressed in clean clothes, and went down to his basement room. Brian was waking up when the hunter retrieved the syringe from the counter and walked over to the table where he was tied.

"What … what are they going to do with me?" the young man asked.

"I don't know," Harlan answered truthfully, "the clients don't tell me, and I don't ask them. I imagine you will be held for ransom, sold to another buyer, sold into slavery, or kept by the client for himself."

"Please …" Brian moaned, "please let me go…"

"Shhh …" the hunter said, gently moving his target's head to one side so his neck was exposed. "it's going to be okay," he said as he inserted the syringe's needle into a vein in Brian's neck and injected the syringe's contents. After the knock-out drug had entered Brian's bloodstream, the young man fell back into unconsciousness. Harlan removed his catch's wrists and ankles from the restraints that were attached to the table, then re-bound his arms and legs with portable hand- and feet-cuffs.

It was time to go.

The hunter took hold of his target's arms and pulled him up into a sitting position on the edge of the table. The he leaned over and hoisted the young man off the table and over his shoulder. He carried him back to the garage and tucked his catch securely into one of the human storage compartments in the rear of his truck, locking his cuffs into the D-rings.

Harlan drove in silence. No music from the truck's stereo or noise from the traffic outside intruded on the hunter's secret thoughts. When he arrived at the designated delivery location, his client was already waiting. The location was the top floor of a downtown parking structure. The floor's security guard has been paid a sizable sum of money to remain in his booth and not make his customary rounds during the hour of the delivery.

Harlan pulled his truck into the deserted corner of the floor, where his client's long black limousine was parked. The hunter stopped his truck and got out, opening the rear area. His client did not get out of the limo, but instead had his driver do so. Without speaking, Harlan opened the compartment containing Brian and unfastened his cuffs from the D-rings. The driver, a burly man about 6'3", gently lifted the sleeping young man out of the storage compartment and deposited him into the back seat of the limo and covered him completely with a black blanket. When the driver closed the trunk, Harlan felt his cell phone vibrate. The hunter checked its tiny screen and smiled. It was an e-mail from his bank informing him that a wire transfer had just deposited $350,000 into his main account.

The driver and the hunter nodded to each other then returned to their respective vehicles. The truck and the limo drove out of the parking structure and then each their own separate ways.

When Harlan returned home, he poured himself a drink and sat down at his computer, where many more e-mails were waiting for him, most from potential clients who wanted to buy his services. He sipped his drink and began to read them slowly, beginning the process, once again, of choosing his next client, and his next target.

# VI. HOT SMOKY NIGHT

The night is hot.

Very, very hot.

The scent of incense fills my nostrils. A light breeze blows in through the window, wafting gently down to where I lie on the floor.

My apartment is small, but big enough for one. I am alone and horny, as usual. The summer evening is making me anxious and sweaty.

It would be simple enough to get another person here. The phone, the computer, the street outside ... sex isn't hard to find around here. Men and boys are everywhere, prowling the bars, the streets, the alleys ... desperately looking for someone to connect with – if only for a night.

But, I don't want anyone else here.

Not tonight.

Tonight, I am enjoying being by myself.

My life is just fine right now without the clutter of other thoughts, other feelings, other lives. I like my solitude. Lying on my back, I am holding a porn mag up in the air with one hand. I hadn't started reading it with the intention of jerking off, but now ...

My cock is warm and hardening, packed tightly in my underwear. Rolling over on my stomach, I start rubbing it against the floor. Mmmm, that feels good. It gets harder, and I rub harder. Yeah ...

No turning back now.

I get to my feet to start my ritual.

First the blinds on the window. I close them against the night, so I can be truly alone. The ringer on the phone and the volume on the answering machine are silenced. A pillow from the bed is tossed onto the floor. Fresh incense is lit. Low chanting tribal music starts on the CD player, low and hypnotic ... I pull off my shirt, enjoying the rough scratch of the fabric on my nipples as I do so.

Catching sight of myself in the mirror leaning up against the wall, I am pleased. The food plan I am on and the new exercise routines my friend recommended are working. After years of working on them, my pecs and abs are finally popping out. They would now join my arms, legs and butt, which are usually mentioned as my best features.

Other than my face, of course. I see sharp dark eyes behind thick full lashes, well-formed cheeks and nose and rows of perfect white teeth behind thick, pouting lips.

I pull a few things out of my closet and put them next to the pillow.

Turning the lights off, I drop down onto the floor. I settle onto my back with my head on the pillow. First I blindfold my eyes with the handkerchief I brought out from the closet. The night becomes even blacker now, as darkness settles over me and into my mind. I feel on the floor and find the pair of dirty underwear I took from my laundry sack. It smells rank and intoxicating as I stuff it in my mouth. An old gym sock is stretched around my mouth and tied behind my head, holding the shorts in my mouth and gagging me tight.

My knees rise to my chest and I loop the torn T-shirt between my ankles and around my feet. Expertly, I cinch the knots and now my feet are tied together.

I force my left arm behind my back and settle onto it with my full weight. It struggles to move but cannot, it is held tight by the sheer mass of my muscular torso. My cock gets harder with each body part that is restricted, the sensations of being tied up awakening deep memories of pleasure from prior lifetimes.

Nostrils flare as I suck in the scent of the incense and feel its mystic moody power enter my brain. I have already begun to leave this place and time without even trying.

I lie on the floor of my home, bound and gagged, and start to imagine.

I need no one else.

No one.

For no one can follow me where I am going.

It is a magical, erotic place.

The deepest recess of my imagination is a place I only go to when I have the courage to face my deepest fantasies.

Now I am truly alone. The music seems to become louder, as if amplified by the darkness surrounding me. My hand finds my crotch, my shorts straining to contain the force of what lies beneath them, coiled and ready to spring. I caress my throbbing cock through the fabric gently.

Then down go the shorts.

My dick is free at last, free to feel the air with the rest of my naked skin.

The summer breeze slips into the room, between the slats of the blinds, to search out my dripping dick and take it gently in its whispering grip. Squeezing the up-turned bottle that I find with my searching fingers, I feel the exquisite coolness of lube settle onto me like dripping candle wax. I match the grasp of the breeze with my own, wrapping my fist around my quivering dick. The cum inside me burns and boils, an organic living presence within my body that is both separate and one with me. It wants out. It too wants to feel the sensual warmth of the night breeze as my skin does.

It demands release from the bondage of my body.

And I have put myself in bondage to give it that release.

My fingers clench around my cock, and I feel the shattering and wondrous feeling of skin on skin. This is the feeling that drives all of humanity – that propels it into madness and beyond. There is nothing we would not do for this feeling, and isolation from it is the deepest damnation one could suffer.

My transportation is complete.

Now there is truly no turning back.

I have entered a state of ecstasy and transformation like a native in a tribal ceremony. I am here to throw myself at the feet of my own body, to worship the forces within me that are both so understood yet totally beyond comprehension.

I imagine the thin wispy smoke of the burning incense filling my vision. It is rising. My hand moves, caressing my cock within its grip. Bliss. Tiny sparks of electricity appear around my hand as it moves. Through the crystalline prism of my mind's eye, I see the incense smoke. But now it is bigger, larger, seeming to form wafts and whorls like the timeless designs of fingerprints, circles within circles within circles.

The circles of smoke are changing now. Or am I just seeing them more clearly? They are not merely circular shapes, but images, pictures in the smoke.

Pictures of men.

Men of beauty, men of power. Men of light and men of darkness. Men of muscle and men of spirit. Men together, doing things to each other. Holding, kissing, touching, fighting, beating, lifting, carrying, hugging, rimming, sucking, fucking and worshipping each other. My vision moves downwards, and I see that the smoke is not coming from any incense. Rather it is from an enormous fire that is burning on a beach at the edge of an ocean.

The fire is enormous, sending fireworks of sparks into the sky and the cascading smoke that I had just been absorbed in. Men surround the fire, chanting and calling to each other. Are they worshipping the spirits within the smoke, or are they calling them forth and controlling them as puppeteers might? Either way, both the men and the spirits are exquisitely beautiful. Naked they are. My eyes drink in every sculpted torso, every full and muscular arm and leg, every inch of skin covered with sensual body paint and brutal exotic piercings, every huge cock flopping and dancing. Their faces are stunning and harsh, not a trace of modern civilization in them. These men are pure as animals, their eyes as steely as those of wolves.

The firelight dances on them and around them, adding its blazing color to their already bright bodies. The men move away from the fire toward something else, something I haven't seen yet. It looks like a platform, made roughly of rocks and tree branches, with torches burning around it. Shadows twist and contort around the platform as the men move to surround it. In the strange light, it is hard to see what has been laid on the platform, or is it an altar? Between the dancing bodies I can make out a shape. It is moving.

It almost looks human – then I recognize it.

It is I.

I am lying on the platform, naked and bound and gagged, writhing in fear – or is it pleasure? And I am there, my consciousness diving forward and down to join my writhing body. The blindfold is gone, I can see freely now. The men chant and howl above me. My hand strokes my dick faster. The fire within me rises higher, almost matching the flashing intensity of the natives' blaze.

What do they mean to do with me? I am their captive, that is clear, their prisoner.

Am I their enemy? Do they mean to kill me in a ritual ceremony as a warning to any others who dare offend their tribe?

Am I to be sacrificed to appease their gods, the man-spirits dancing in the smoke of the fire?

Are they cannibals? Am I to be eaten by these men, cooked alive and devoured like any other wild animal hunted down and caught?

Am I a sacramental trophy, a boy that has agreed to give up his life for the good of the tribe in this ceremony by the ocean?

Or am I one of them? A native boy that has failed his initiation trials – am I a disgrace to them? Was I about to be castrated, my cock and balls sliced off, the jewels of manhood taken from me for now and ever?

I jerk myself faster and faster, my mind reeling in excitement and terror. In my bliss I welcome any of the possibilities, heedless of whether they mean redemption or death. It doesn't matter, for now they are one and the same.

I am a bound and gagged prisoner, a piece of meat to be used however they see fit. My will has been taken and there is no other course for me besides accepting whatever comes. Whatever it is, it will be a further plateau to rise to, as the fire in my cock burns hotter and hotter. My neck strains as I raise my head. What I see sends me further into my ecstasy. All the men's penises are hard as rocks, standing up straight and tall as if in tribute to the night and the man-spirits. Muscles are flexing, flashes of movement filling my sight. The native men are jerking off, standing around me in a gigantic circle. Beyond them, I see more men, and beyond them still more. More than I ever saw before, there are thousands of them, in ever-widening circles.

They are all jerking their huge dicks and staring at me.

Now I realize where I am. This is just another waft or whorl, like the ones within the smoke, a circle within a circle within a circle. These men are forming the largest waft of all. It is as large as an ocean, as full as a galaxy. And I am at the center of it.

I am the focal point for all this energy.

Self-knowledge burns itself in my brain, and I know what I am.

I am one of them ... and I have not failed my initiation rituals. I have passed through my trials by fire unscathed, and now I am about to be marked with the seed of the tribe. I am about to have manhood bestowed upon me!

And the energy that has been building for so long is about to be released ...

... now.

The stars flare as if going nova all at once and the chanting of the natives becomes a crescendo of animal passion. A thousand gallons of hot man-cum shoots at me from all sides, covering me and filling my world. I am swimming in a sea of it.

I am a man.

I raise my head to the sky, where the stars are boiling away into oblivion. The roars of the men become the roar of the ocean I am in. The cum electrifies me, shooting energy and power into every cell of my body. I stroke my dick faster, the slickness of my hand causing more sparks of electricity to shoot out around me.

Now I am truly a man.

The smoke of the torches has entered the ocean of cum with me, permeating it and filling it with its own arcane magic. But a change has happened.

Where am I? I am still bound and gagged as before, tied up and incapable of moving. But where?

I am lost and alone.

And now ...

There is a roof above me.

And the smoke is still there, rising up through my vision as it did before.

But now ...

Inside a building is where I must be.

I force my line of sight down from the wooden planks of the ceiling. The room is quite large, with row after row of bunk-beds going off into the distance as far as the eye can see. Each is covered with a dark green bedspread.

I recognize the color instantly.

Even before I see them I know what will greet my eyes.

Men.

And not just any men.

Soldiers.

Hundreds of them it seems, of all kinds and ranks. All the armed forces are there: Army, Navy, Air Force, Marines ... recruits, lieutenants, grunts, pilots, sergeants, admirals, commanders, captains, privates, corporals ... a mix of men so complex and convoluted my mind stretches trying to wrap itself around it. My wide eyes pick out random details from the crowd: round muscles beneath dark green T-shirts, big full cocks under khaki pants, glittering brass of medals on pectorals, row after row of shiny black boots, piercing eyes, short buzzed hair cuts, heads hidden under caps and berets, guns in holsters, bulging green duffel bags slung over shoulders, dog tags tinkling around necks ...

And the smoke from the natives' fire and torches has become the smoke of these men's cigars, rising to collect at the ceiling of the barracks.

They are all looking at me.

I am naked, bound and gagged, sprawled on my back on a footlocker with my cock standing straight up as if at attention. They are all looking at me, and I feel as if I could die from the heat of their collective gaze.

Why am I here?

Am I a recruit who tried to go AWOL – caught and about to be disciplined by all these men?

Am I an enemy operative, a prisoner of war soon to be tortured and interrogated until valuable information has been squeezed out of me?

Am I a spy who has been working undercover as a grunt, found and exposed at last, now to take my punishment at the hands of the entire U.S. Armed Forces?

My hand pumps my dick faster and faster.

The closest man to me, a hulking drill sergeant with biceps like cantaloupes, walks over to me. He comes around behind me, so I am looking straight up at him with his protruding crotch hanging directly above my face. He looks down at me, his broad face cracking into a smile. It is not a look of malice or anger, not the look of a man about to dole out punishment to another. No, he is looking at me like a child would look at a new toy. His face shows pure unadulterated delight and anticipated pleasure.

Why? What am I? What is happening here?

He sucks deeply on his cigar before setting it down. Then he uses both hands to loosen his belt and unbutton his pants. The dick that springs out from inside those pants is monstrous, surely twelve inches long and five inches wide. It hangs nearly to my face.

What am I supposed to do with this? I wonder.

A second later the man hits me, smacking the side of my head with his hand and grunting gutturally.

Now I know. My mouth stretches open, ready to receive.

The cock falls down, entering my mouth and seeming to fill my whole throat at once. It completely takes up the space inside my mouth, how can I breathe? I inhale deeply through my nostrils, taking in the clouds of tobacco smoke that seem to be filling the room. The drill sergeant, satisfied that his dick is in me as far as it can go, starts fucking my face. There is nothing sensual about this, nothing subtle or romantic. It is pure raw masculine power I am being engulfed by here. He screws my throat in and out, artlessly thrusting as far in as possible before jerking it back out. There is no sense that this is in any way meant to feel good to me.

This is all about him.

And only him. I am a toy to be used and thrown away like a gum wrapper. My life matters only as much as I need to stay alive to keep my mouth open to receive his monster of a penis. My own dick is rock-hard in my hand, seeming to get more and more solid every moment. When his assault grows so forceful I start to slide off the foot locker, the man anchors my shoulders with his hands to keep me still.

Vision is completely filled by the drill sergeant, his massive form covering my sight from side to side. But I can feel the presence of the other men in the room, watching the spectacle of me being used for his pleasure. This knowledge intoxicates me. Suddenly, his cock stiffens like a steel rod, and I feel warm liquid explode in my throat and shoot down my gullet. I swallow and gulp it greedily. With a deep groan of release, the drill sergeant pulls his still-hard dick out of my mouth. When he leaves my field of vision, I can see the rest of the room again. I squint through the clouds of billowing smoke.

What I see staggers my already-overloaded mind.

All the men in the room, all the soldiers and grunts and captains and sailors, have formed a single-file line.

A line that leads to me.

And the wave of self-knowledge that took me on the beach returns to crash down upon me again, and I know what I am.

I am a whore.

I am a captured whore, a hustler boy that has been purchased for the use of all these men. But it is no one's intention to ever let me go, that is why I am tied up.

I am never going anywhere ever again.

All I will ever do, for the rest of my life, is serve these men, serve the line of hard dicks that seems to be getting longer as I watch. The barracks stretches out infinitely in the distance, elongating and lengthening to contain the men who seem to be multiplying before my eyes. But no time for sight-seeing, the next man in line is shoving to get in position above me. He is a young black recruit, with skin smooth as a statue's and his body as hard as cement. He pulls his cock out and sticks it into my waiting mouth.

The men behind him impatiently puff on their cigars, anxious for their own turns. Their smoke fills the entire barracks with a cloud so vast I can see nothing through it.

The recruit's dick plunges further into me, and I can feel the smoke surround me, filling my world as the form of the drill sergeant had minutes before.

Now I can see only the white of the smoke and feel only the rough brutal thrust of the dick in my mouth.

I jerk myself harder.

Something has changed.

My throat is empty.

The dick is no longer there, and I am spinning through space like a leaf in a hurricane. Where am I? What is happening?

There is only the smoke, nothing else.

Am I alone once more?

Yes ...

Alone and empty ...

But now things are getting darker around me, the white of the smoke being invaded by other colors. A surface is solidifying under me.

I am lying on my back, as before.

But I am definitely somewhere else.

What was the sky above the ocean that became the roof of an army barracks has become something else again. What is it now? What fills my vision this time?

It is the ceiling of an apartment.

But not mine.

The huge cloud of smoke is dissipating, dissolving down into a single thin wisp, trailing up into the air like a smoke signal. I glance down and see that the smoke is coming from a single candle that burns near me on the floor.

Am I on the ground?

Yes, bound and gagged, shackled and chained to large metal rings that are imbedded in the floor. A smooth leather collar encircles my neck.

The room is small, with only a few abstract paintings on the walls for decoration. The single doorway opens onto a darkness as vast as that in the barracks.

But now ...

White fills it.

Is it the smoke again? Not this time.

It is a man.

He is tall, nearly 6'5". In his eyes is the blue of the native's ocean. In his massive body is the power of all the men in the barracks combined. He is dressed in white. It is as if the smoke has solidified into fabric that can be worn by a man. A white T-shirt barely contains the expanse of his chest. White jeans grip his butt and legs tight. The cock that shows through them is as large as a hose.

There is no doubt who this man is.

My Master ...

I look at him with eyes that beg, plead, love, adore and worship all at once. All I want to do it serve him, to please him in any way he wants, to do anything for him ...

But I am held down by the chains and cannot move. I strain against them, trying in vain to touch the vision in the doorway.

It is such exquisite torture, I cannot help but jerk myself harder and faster.

There is no doubt what I am.

I am a slave.

An owned piece of property that belongs to this man as surely as his car, his apartment and all his other possessions do.

I live to serve him.

My Master steps into the room, looking down at me with an expression that is unreadable. Surely a creature as basic as I cannot understand the complexity of the mind behind those eyes. But I can long to debase myself for his delight, I can desire to be made to perform every indignity possible for his amusement, I can hope against hope that I will be allowed to bring the god-like presence in from of me pleasure.

My Master drops to one knee between my legs and with a key from his pocket unlocks the shackles holding my feet. Bliss and power flow into me as his strong hands close around my ankles and lift my legs high into the air. The touch makes my heart flutter and skip a beat. The man in white puts both of my ankles in one hand and uses the other to loosen the buttons of his jeans, releasing the cock within. It pops out, the single eye of its piss-slit dripping with excitement. My Master slicks up his hand with the pre-cum and slides his fingers into my asshole.

I catch my breath and moan into my gag. The feel of any part of him inside me is electrifying. The cool stickiness fills my passage, preparing it for the assault to come.

Salivating like a dog, I whimper in desperation. My Master touches his hand to my spit-covered chin and uses it to get his dick wet and shiny. Then it is time. The man in white positions himself and thrusts his cock into me with a single motion. The scream that comes from me is silent but can be heard somewhere by bats and wild dogs.

The pain fills my world as surely as the natives' come and the soldiers' smoke had. But the ecstasy that joins it is inseparable from it, beyond anything I have felt before in dream, fantasy or reality.

What I am feeling within me is cosmic, explosive. I thought my Master god-like, and now I know – he is a god. For what is happening with me as He fucks me is incredible and mind-blowing. I feel as if a world is being created within me, filled with pleasure and pain, fire and water, storm and calm. We have joined together, His cock fusing with my ass and making us one being, a being made of two parts. Symbiosis of the highest and most sacred order – I am a creature who lives only to serve the other. Whatever He needs I will give him, without thought or feeling except gratitude for the chance. With every thrust I am more and more His slave, His possession. The utter mastery with which He uses my body is like that of the almighty power of gravity as it directs and guides all movement of matter in the universe.

He knows exactly how to fuck me.

I belong to Him.

I am His slave to be used for His pleasure in any way He needs or wants.

And then I hear His sweet groan and feel His holy seed shooting within me, igniting every cell with power and glory. My assaulted channel is soothed by its sweet warmth. I am His vessel, the object He uses for His release.

And just as quickly as He entered me, He leaves.

I am barren and empty without Him inside me.

He rises back up to his feet, towering above me and tucking His spent dick back into His pants. I suddenly have the feeling that He is about to leave the room, and me, not to return. Every muscle in me flexes as I twist wildly against my bondage, crying out for Him to please not leave me. I cannot be away from His presence, not now, not ever again. Without a sound my Master reaches down toward me. Fearing being hit for my insolence, I duck my head down. The sound of metal on metal surprises me and I open my eyes to see my Master unlocking all my bonds.

The chains fall to the floor and I am free. I look up at Him with questioning eyes.

The man in white pulls me to my feet and leans forward, slinging me over His shoulder. He walks out of the room down a perfectly white hallway. I am in heaven, hanging over His back and seeing the floor fall away below me. I am not to be abandoned. My Master is taking me with Him. Satisfaction fills me. It hardly matters where we go, as long as I am with Him. My Master brings me to his bedroom. Everything within it is white, and one wall is entirely covered with a mirror. White candles burn on every surface, their smoke gently wafting into the air.

A white bed, white floor, white ceiling ... but in the mirror, I see the opposite white wall – and what hangs on it from a steel hook.

It is a black leather sleepsack, big enough for a man.

Big enough for me.

It hangs entirely off the ground, like a single frozen teardrop from a giant obsidian statue's eye. I am filled with such desire and hope my vision blurs. My mind can hardly grasp the idea before He is carrying me over to it. The exquisite touch of my Master is replaced by the cool kiss of leather as the man in white slides me into the sleepsack. My body fits it perfectly, as if it was made for me.

When all but my head is inside, my Master takes a long last look at me.

Then without warning His hand finds a slit in the leather that gives him access to my forgotten cock and balls. He grabs my dick and starts rubbing it vigorously.

I am a balloon being blown up so quickly I will burst at any second. The gag is the only thing preventing my gasps and cries of pleasure from escaping.

This man is what I have always wanted to find. He has made me into a new being, reborn into my true self: an utter slave with no other thought, no other life. The friction of His hand through the leather is so exciting that I cannot hold back much longer. I am a rocketship that has entered its final countdown before blast off.

There is no turning back now.

Galaxies crash together within me, destroying themselves in order to bring new life into the universe. My final self-realization is at hand, and the absolute knowledge that comes with it burns away all emotion and physicality ... all that remains is pleasure.

My Master is the Alpha and the Omega, the truth and the light, the beginning and the end.

I am a slave.

Slave to this man is my destiny, and I all I shall ever be. I will serve Him, and when I am not serving Him I will be stored in this sack until he wants me again.

That will be the extent of my experience.

And I cannot imagine or more desirable life on heaven or earth.

I come.

The fluid jets out of me, the sparks of electricity becoming lightning bolts that flash as bright as the sun. Splatter all over me it does, covering me from chest to head.

My Master smiles for the first time, and I die and am born again as He gently pushes me down inside the sack and closes the top, cinching it tight.

Darkness surrounds me once again.

But this time I am not alone.

For I know that less than five feet away from me, the man I adore above all others, the man I have given my life to, is getting into bed and settling down for a good night's sleep. I snuggle into the warmth of the leather surrounding me and feel myself begin to doze. The last thing I imagine with my mind's eye is all the white candles ...

... slowly burning down through the night ...

... until nothing is left of them ...

... but thin wisps of smoke, and they go out one by one, until there is only one left ...

Dark.

And sleep.

I stir awake and pull off the blindfold. The first thing I see if a thin wisp of smoke. My incense has burned itself down to the stick.

All that is left is the last threads of smoke.

I pull my arm out from under me and slowly untie my bonds. Dried cum flakes and falls off my torso as I sit up and pull the spit-soaked gag out of my mouth. My jaws and joints are sore. After I have freed myself, I settle back down onto the floor, resting my head on the pillow.

I am still groggy.

Fantasy and reality are still blurry and overlapping.

Or are they?

I wonder if I really do feel the grittiness of sand on my skin as I shift my body on the floor. I wonder if that odor that seems to be all over me really is the smell of cigar smoke. I wonder if the stickiness inside me, that feeling of just having been fucked, is actually there.

I am almost asleep.

I wonder if these things are real or imagined.

I wonder if it matters.

About to descend into dreamless slumber, I wonder if I should put some clothes on. No, I decide at the gate of sleep.

It doesn't matter.

Because ...

The night is hot.

Very, very hot.

# VII. AT THE BACK OF THE BAR

The bar is dark.

There are only a few lights on at all, including the two that have red light bulbs in them. I wonder how the bartender can see what he's doing.

It's late, after midnight. The place is crowded with men. It might be cold outside, but in here it's sweltering – all these horny, hungry men in the small space of the bar generate a lot of heat. Some of them are in leather, others wearing only enough clothing to be street-legal. The odors are dense, concentrated and heady. Sweat, spilled beer, smoke – the smells of men, leathermen to be precise.

From my vantage point at the back of the bar, leaning against the rear wall, I look at a crowd of shadows and silhouettes. My mind fills in the details I can't see – sharp sultry eyes; dark mustaches above parted, wet lips; leather jackets, leather vests, leather chaps revealing pale butt-cheeks, ripe to be swatted and spanked. I put my hands behind my head in a gesture of exaggerated confidence. I hope I look inviting and seductive. Several men look at me, but then turn away, unwilling to maintain eye contact, even in this dim light. Sometimes my looks and attitude intimidate guys, even though I know I'm harmless.

All I want is for some hot man to come along and put me in my place. I'm a cocky, sometimes arrogant young punk, and need another man to take charge of me.

One of the guys looking at me doesn't turn away. I can only see his silhouette in the red, smoky air. It's hard to judge, but I think he's about my height – six feet or so. He's bulkier than I, sort of like a bodybuilder or a football player. From the shape of his head it looks as if he's wearing a leather cap. He makes his way through the crowd, heading my way. I stare at him, even though I cannot yet see his eyes.

He gets close to me, right up in my face. I can see a few more details at this close range. He's wearing a leather jacket with a white T-shirt under it. He has a mustache and goatee, and he's wearing big construction worker boots. I can't tell if he's handsome or ugly, and it doesn't matter. The man exhales in my face, and I smell beer and smoke.

"On your knees," he says, "cocksucker."

Silently I obey, and my denim-covered knees hit the floor of the bar. I know the floor is dirty, but I don't care. The man unzips his pants, and the sound somehow seems very loud despite the noise of the bar. The odors of sweat and musk hit my nose as his crotch is exposed to the air. The man's fat cock flops out, dangling from its root in his forest of pubic hair. It's beginning to get hard with excitement in anticipation of the pleasures my mouth will give it. I part my lips and the un-named man pushes his pelvis forward and his cock enters my mouth. I love the feel of it, the weight of it, this stiffening tube and muscle and flesh resting on my tongue. I receive it hungrily, gladly, gratefully. The dick in my mouth grows to its full length, and I begin to suck it. I worship it with my lips and tongue, caressing it and fondling it for maximum pleasure. I move it in and out from between my lips, creating what I hope is delicious friction. The man groans in pleasure as he penetrates me orally. I glance up at him and see his body quivering slightly, shaking with the sensation of me sucking him off.

It feels so good to serve him this way, to give him pleasure, to take care of him the way a bottom should a top. I don't know if we're being watched, and I don't care. I figure we are, with this many horny men packed in such a small hot space. But all I care about is the cock in my mouth, and the man who owns it standing over me. I need to be dominated this way, to be reduced to a sexual plaything – to be a sextoy for a hot man.

My dick is straining against my jeans, aroused and erect. The music of the bar pounds in my ears. Or is it the flow of my own blood? I realize it must be my heart that is beating throughout my body and resounding in every part of me, filling me with excitement and desire.

"Yeah," the man above me says in a slurred voice, "That's good, cocksucker, that's good …" His voice is low and gravelly, and I love hearing every word. "You're a good little cocksucker, aren't you?" he asks. I answer him, but his dick in my mouth makes it nothing more than a muffled "hhmmff," not that he could hear me over the noise anyway. I hope my performance on his cock is a good enough answer. When I glance up at him, I see his head tilted back in pleasure. He starts speeding up his thrusts into my mouth, and I know he is getting close. He puts his hands on my head, holding it in place. He doesn't want me going anywhere. Neither do I, but he wants to make sure I follow through to his climax. Now his cock is pulsating in my mouth, and I know the time has come. The man comes in my mouth, his penis shooting bursts of salty semen down my throat, and I swallow it gratefully. It feels so good to be used this way, used for his pleasure like a common street hustler. When he's shot his full load and squeezed the last drops out onto my tongue, he lets go of my head and allows his cock to slide out of my mouth.

"On your feet, cocksucker!" the man says sharply. I obey quickly, lifting my sore knees from the hard floor. As soon as I have risen, he pushes me roughly against the wall, my back to him. He presses himself on me, holding me between himself and the wall. It is uncomfortable, but I love it – being pinned this way, in this unknown man's power; it is so sexy and hot. My stiff cock is trapped within my jeans, straining for release. Now the man's hands are on me, reaching around my waist from behind to feel my crotch. He exhales loudly into my ear as his fingers find the shape of my dick through my pants, the sound full of satisfaction and desire. He fondles and caresses me and pushes his groin against my ass. Even through at least two layers of cloth I can feel that his cock is hard again, incredibly, so soon after already shooting once. But, it feels as if he's ready for more, and this time, he needs more than a blowjob.

"Yeah, pussyboy," he growls, "You need my cock in you, don't you?"

"Yes," I say, and he slaps my ass.

"Yes, what?' he asks.

"Yes, Sir?"

"That's better," he says, "Don't forget what you are."

"What am I, Sir?" I ask.

"My pussyboy," he answers. "My cocksucker. The man who'll do anything to get me inside him."

"Yes, Sir," I say. "I'm your pussyboy."

"Yeah, man? You need me inside you?"

"I need you inside me, Sir," I say. Then his hands are at my waist, pulling open my fly. He yanks my underwear down and I feel my cock spring forward, free of its fabric prison. The man pulls down my pants and my bare ass is exposed. The man takes one butt-cheek in each hand and squeezes hard. It hurts but I love it. Then he slaps my ass, sharply, and it stings.

"Thank you, Sir," I say, and the man says "Good boy. You'll take whatever I give you, won't you?"

"Yes, Sir!" is my answer.

"Then take this!" he says and I feel his cock burrow between my cheeks. It's hard and dripping, ready for action again. "You like that?" he asks.

"Yes," I say, "Please put it in me Sir – please fuck me!"

He takes me raw, without lubrication, pushing his cock into my hole. He reams my ass, and I can tell he's going to fuck me long and hard. The man grabs my hips to hold me steady. He pushes into me savagely, then pulls out quickly, then shoves himself back in again. I start grunting with each thrust, a little yelp to match each push in. He does me roughly, with no tenderness or finesse, and I love it. I'm just here to be used.

"Yeah," he growls in my ear. "You're just my little fuck-hole, man, just here to be a warm soft hole for my cock – that's all you are …"

"Yes, Sir," I whisper, "Thank you, Sir …"

He starts fucking me faster, pushing me harder against the wall. He slaps my ass hard. His cock feels so good in my asshole, as if it's meant to be there. I don't care about anything right now – not that I'm getting screwed in a public place, not that men are probably watching, not that I might know some of them. None of it matters. All that matters is that the man who's fucking me is a hot top, and as a bottom, it's my duty to serve him, to give myself to him, to offer my butt as a hole he can fuck. His cock in me is all that matters. I shut my eyes and breathe in deeply, savoring the scents of sweat, beer, smoke and men – this is where I belong, this is where I am meant to be.

The man is growling in my ear as he fucks me hard. My butt starts to hurt, but I love it – this is what it means to be alive, this is what it feels like to be truly wanted, needed, used! It feels good to be taken this way. I love the little grunts he makes as he pile-drives me over and over. I let myself get flattened completely against the wall by the force of his penetration. The wood of the wall is cool and smooth against my palms, and it feels good. But not nearly as good as the slab of manmeat that is pummeling my asshole. Suddenly, the man fucking me wraps his arms around my chest from behind. He yanks me away from the wall and I feel my back hit his chest. I grunt as his cock is shoved deep inside me.

What's he doing? I wonder, but a second later, I know.

The man grabs my dick in one clenched fist, and I gasp as he starts to jerk it. I didn't think there was a better feeling than getting fucked like this, but now I know better. Getting jacked off at the same time is even hotter.

"Come on, pussyboy," he says in my ear. "You gotta come for me; I want you to shoot for me before I finish myself off."

I let my head tilt back in ecstasy to rest on the man's shoulder. His grip is tight, dirty, gritty and feels fan-FUCKING-tastic on my dick. I can't hold out for very long – I have to shoot! I let out a guttural groan as I come, and I feel my cock shudder as it spurts jets of man-juice out onto the wall.

"Yeah, good cocksucker," he says, "Good pussyboy, that's what I need."

I gasp as the orgasm glows inside me, fading slowly. But the pleasure goes into overload – I'm still getting fucked! And the cock inside my ass feels white-hot as it thrusts its way to its climax.

"You want me to come, man?" the man asks me.

"Yeah," I say, "Please come, please come in me, Sir!"

He pushes me forward with his body, slamming me back into the wall again. The breath in my lungs is forced up and out of my nose and mouth as the man crushes me against the wood again and again.

"Aw, fuck man, I'm coming!" he groans in my ear, "I'm fucking coming inside you, pussyboy!"

I push my butt back, wanting to feel his power and his passion as his cock emptied itself in my ass. His frenzied voice in my ear is louder than the noise of the men all around, louder than the music, louder than anything. His groans of exertion and pleasure are formless and wordless. Knowing how good I am making him feel is enough to make my own orgasm seem to go on and on. The man's hands grip my shoulders – tighter, tighter then lets go.

"That was great," the man says as he pulls out of me slowly. My ass feels empty without his dick. I turn around and see him there, the man who just screwed me – hot, sexy, masculine. I think his face is flushed and sweaty, but it's hard to tell in the dim smoky light. A group of men stand around us, watching, then slowly turn away as the action winds down. The man stuffs his cock back in his pants. I pull my jeans back up over my ravaged ass and my exhausted dick. He looks at me intensely for a few seconds, his eyes boring into mine. My whole body feels as if it's glowing, so excited and alive.

Then the man turns and walks away, and is gone into the crowd of men, leaving me alone at the back of the bar.

# VIII. STOLEN BOOTY
## A Pirate's Tale

What was happening?

Where was I?

Someone was shaking my shoulder.

"Wake up!" an urgent whisper said.

Another shake.

"Wake up, lad, or I'll toss you to the sharks!"

I cracked my eyes open.

I was sitting on a chair in some kind of wooden chamber, still wearing the dirty peasant tunic and pants I'd been wearing when I left home. My head hurt and the room was swaying. I tried to move and found my wrists and ankles bound with rope.

"Where …" I started to say, but a sweaty palm was slammed over my mouth.

"Shut up!" the voice said. "Now play it smart, lad, and you'll live to tell the tale. If not, you're gonna be food for the fishes."

The source of the voice walked into view.

He was tall, probably in his mid-thirties, with long dark hair and a week's worth of beard on his chin. His clothes were drab and baggy – I glimpsed a hairy chest through his low-cut tunic. Big boots covered his feet, and sunlight coming through the room's porthole glinted off the wicked-looking dagger that was tucked carefully in his belt.

He looked down at me and narrowed his eyes.

"Now, since I caught you, I figure you're mine by rights. But Captain's orders, all captured booty is to be presented to him for inspection."

I tried to speak, but couldn't through the man's hand.

"Yer gonna keep your voice low and your temper cool, lad?" he asked.

When I nodded, he took his hand off my mouth. "Where are we?" I whispered.

"Why, don't you know?" the man asked. "I mean, haven't ye guessed?" He looked genuinely surprised. "You're on the great vessel Santa Diablo, of course!"

My eyes widened. I realized suddenly, it wasn't I who was swaying; it was the ship I was on! Now that I listened, I could hear the sound of gulls and waves.

"Santa Diablo … the pirate ship?" I asked.

"There be those who call us pirates, aye," the man said, "but we think of ourselves as soldiers of fortune – treasure hunters if ye will."

"What good am I to you?"

"Now, don't be playing dumb with me, lad. I can see the smarts in your eyes, you're no fool. Young buck with your handsome face and strong body's worth a fortune in these waters. Captain Ranjan is lookin' for a new first officer, and we've been needing a new cabin slave. I figure if I give you to the Captain, he'll be so pleased he'll make me his new first officer."

"What happened to the old first officer and the old slave?" I asked.

The man grinned at me unpleasantly.

"They failed to perform to standards," he said, "and they made choice meals for the sharks."

I gulped.

How did I get into this?

I was just a twenty-five-year-old man from a poor village who'd come to the marketplace in the closest port of call.

"Why did you tie me up?"

"Well, I wouldn't want ye to escape, now would I?" the pirate said with a grin.

"We're at sea?" I asked.

"That we are."

"Then where would I escape to?"

He blinked a few times. I could see the wheels turning in his head. Clearly this was not the smartest buccaneer who ever signed onto a pirate ship.

"I guess you're right, lad," he said finally. "I guess you're right."

"So you can untie me, 'cuz there's nowhere I can escape to," I said.

"No funny business now," he said warily. "You're mine; I caught you fair and square!"

"No funny business," I said with what I hoped was a trustworthy smile.

"All right."

The pirate pulled the dagger from his belt and cut me loose from my bonds. With my hands and feet free, I stood up off the chair and stretched. It felt good to be awake and alive. I eyed my sexy captor.

"Now that you have me," I said, "what are you going to do with me?"

"I'd like to enjoy me spoils before I present ye to Captain Ranjan," he said, and I could see a bulge growing in his pants.

"Well," I said softly with a grin, "since you caught me and I'm yours, I'd better oblige you and do exactly what you want …" I dropped down to my knees in front of the pirate and looked up at him with hungry eyes. He licked his lips and stepped forward so his crotch filled my vision. He fumbled with his belt, and his pants fell open, revealing a swollen red cock that was drooling clear nectar from its uncut head. I caught the drop on my tongue before it hit the floor and swallowed it, then took the pirate's cock into my mouth as much as I could. Since he was taller than I and his big dick was upward-pointing I had to struggle a little to suck it, but I did my best. My captor groaned quietly in delight as

I serviced him, with such enthusiasm I wondered how long it had been since he'd been pleasured in this way.

"That's right, lad," he growled above me, "just take my sword right down that throat, take it down as far as she goes, oh yeah …"

My own cock was hard as rock by now, and I rubbed it through the rough fabric of my tunic. The pirate put a hand into the tangle of my hair and forced my head forward. It made me choke on his stiff rod, but it was so fucking hot I didn't mind. His thrusts into my mouth were getting faster – if it had been as long as it seemed since he'd had a good cocksucking, it wouldn't be long indeed before he finished. I wanted to jerk myself off, but sensed that I should concentrate on my captor, at least this time. Soon enough the pirate's groaning turned to guttural grunting, and the moment of truth had arrived. Putting both hands on the back of my head, he speared my throat with his dick and shot five squirts of his booty-juice down my gullet. His grunts became an animal roar that he could barely contain – he seemed to be holding back, and I wondered why. In any case, I swallowed eagerly when he finished and pulled out, strings of cum and spit trailing after his cock as he removed it from my mouth.

There was a loud sound from somewhere else on the ship. It sounded like several men, their voices raised in a drunken toast perhaps.

"Who …" I started to say, but my captor slapped his hand back over my mouth. I was silent but raised my eyebrows questioningly.

"Me mates, lad," he whispered, "they don't know you're here. I've kept you hidden since I caught ye. Don't want them to know about ye 'til the Captain has a look at you."

Someone rapped on the door to the chamber.

"Lojo!" a voice called. "We're gonna drink all the rum and leave none for you if ye don't get yer ass in here!" Lojo (as his name seemed to be) grabbed me by the arm and yanked me to my feet. He gestured to a corner of the room and then shoved me toward it.

"Hide there until I come for you," he told me. "Now, do I need to tie you up again?"

"No, sir," I said, "I'll do exactly what you say."

"See that ye do," he said, and left the room. In the corner where I'd been instructed to hide was a pile of dirty sacks and a few empty rum bottles. I knelt down next to the pile, carefully keeping my balance as the ship rocked around me. There was something familiar about those sacks. I picked one up – it was big, big enough, almost, to fit a man inside. I put the sack to my nose and breathed in. Putrid, it was! Stank of fish and sweat. Then I remembered what had happened to me! A few days before, on my twenty-fifth birthday, I had bid my parents farewell and set out to seek my fortune. I had left the small village I'd lived in all my life and hiked the long road to the great city by the sea. I wandered the streets, staring in wonder at all kinds of amazing sights, sounds and smells I'd never experienced before. It was intoxicating. I suppose that was why I let my guard down enough for a man, Lojo I now realized, to sneak up on me and drag me into an alley. I struggled, but he held a knife to my throat and commanded me to be still. He'd opened a strange vial and held it under my nose. From the vial came sweet fumes that made me sleepy, and soon I was sagging in the man's arms. The last thing I remembered was having one of these sacks slipped over my head, having it fall to the ground and enclose my entire body, and being hoisted up and slung over the man's shoulder as if I was a bushel of fish or a bag of grain.

And now, I was here, aboard the pirate ship Santa Diablo, soon to become the sex slave of a crew of horny cutthroats who'd probably kill me as easily as fuck me. But I knew enough of the world to know that perhaps I could improve my situation. I'd wanted adventure; I'd wanted excitement. And, here it was. The fact that I was brought to it slung unconscious over a pirate's shoulder and not on my own two feet was unimportant. I was here, and the chance was mine to take. I picked up one of the empty bottles and walked back to the door. Through the door, I could hear the rowdy dinner taking place in another chamber close by.

All I had to do now was wait.

After about an hour, the meal sounded as if it was breaking up, with the drunken pirates heading below to what must have been their crew quarters. I stood next to the door, waiting for the footsteps I knew would come. Soon enough, the door opened and Lojo walked through, staggering from liquor, heading for the corner where he'd stashed me without even noticing me. I broke the empty bottle down hard on the pirate's head, and it shattered. Lojo dropped to the floor without a sound. Hurriedly, I closed the door and dragged the unconscious pirate to the corner. I took his dagger, then tied him up and gagged him with the remains of the rope that had bound me. Finally, I piled the stinking sacks on top of him to conceal his body.

Then, quiet as a mouse, I crept out of the room, dagger at the ready. I knew I had to stay off the deck to avoid being seen by the steering crew and the lookout in the crow's nest. I walked through the bowels of the ship until I found what I was looking for – a door under which candlelight was burning. I peeked through the keyhole and what I saw surprised me. Sitting at a desk, inscribing a piece of parchment, was a man only a few years older than I. In one hand was his quill, and in the other he held a long pipe from which he inhaled occasionally. I wondered, could this be the man I was looking for? So young – but how could it not be him? His clothes were far finer than Lojo's had been, and the chamber he occupied was by far the best quarters on the ship.

It had to be.

There was no turning back now.

Within the span of three seconds I had opened the door, stepped into the chamber, and closed it behind me. And yet the young man, who I now saw was quite handsome, was even faster than me. He had leaped at the intrusion and was now holding a pistol to my chest.

"Drop your weapon," he said, and I let Lojo's dagger clatter to the floor.

"Give me one reason I shouldn't kill you right now."

"Captain Ranjan?" I asked breathlessly. The young man moved his pistol from my chest to my throat.

"Knowing who I am is not a reason to spare your life, boy," he said, cocking the pistol.

"Please wait," I said. "I'm worth far more to you alive than dead. I daresay I may even be worth a fortune."

Ranjan grinned, but there was no humor in his expression.

"Perhaps you deserve a few more minutes of life, long enough for you to amuse me with your tale," he said. "Who are you?"

"My name is Teag," I said, "I come from a small village in the eastern province."

"How did you get aboard my ship?"

"I was kidnapped, sir, while the Santa Diablo was in port. I was brought here against my will, but now that I'm here, I believe I can of service to you."

"How?"

"My prowess, for one thing."

"Indeed."

"Will you permit me to show you?"

The pirate Captain pulled his pistol away from my throat, but his expression did not change.

"I will," he said, "but do not think for a moment that I will not kill you if you fail to please me."

"May we move to your bed, Captain?"

"Aye, that we may."

Ranjan backed up, never taking his eyes off me, until he'd reached the foot of his bed. I stripped off my clothes, and although Ranjan tried to appear unimpressed at my handsome body and ample cock, I saw his eyes widen and his hand inch toward his crotch. The young Captain sat back against his ornate headboard and spread his legs. He unbuckled his trousers and released his dick, and I could feel my tongue hanging out at the sight of that mouth-watering member.

Ranjan gestured at me with his pistol.

"Show me!" he commanded me.

A pearl of pre-cum glistened in his piss slit, and I wasted no time in diving for it like it was treasure. After licking it up, I busied myself with tonguing my host's balls, taking them into my mouth and massaging them there, then letting them pop out shiny with my spit. I explored every nook and cranny of Ranjan's crotch, very aware that my performance would dictate his decision – keep me alive or kill me, perhaps by keelhauling me in front of the crew. His groin smelled wonderful, a combination or musk and sweat and salt that was pure aphrodisiac to me.

"Enough with your preparation, lad," he said above me. "Get on with it."

It was funny to be called 'lad' by a man at most two or three years older than I, yet I liked it nonetheless. I opened wide and took the captain's whole cock into my mouth and throat, loving the way it filled me to capacity. This was a cock I could spend many nights at sea sucking. Satisfied at the width and berth of the organ, I proceeded to give it the best service I could.

I caressed every inch of his proud organ with my lips and tongue, covering every bit as if I was swabbing the deck. Low rumbles of pleasure came from my host, and I hoped I was performing well. When he put his hand on the back of my neck I knew I was. Ranjan started adding little pelvic thrusts to our rhythm, causing maximum penetration when I was all the way down on him. Soon, he made a guttural groan, and I was rewarded with a thick wash of pirate cream down my gullet. I swallowed happily and raised my head. Captain Ranjan opened his eyes, but to my dismay it was not his smile but a scowl that greeted me.

"Any cabin boy can suck a good cock," he said, "I need more reason to spare your life than this. Let's see what you can do with that ass of yours!"

Before my eyes, the captain fisted his dick a few times, and it was hard again, as if it hadn't just squirted a load down my throat. Hard it was yet again, hard and stiff as the mast of the Diablo itself.

"Yes, Captain!" I said eagerly, and turned around on my hands and knees so my ass was facing him.

"Sweet booty you have indeed, lad," he said.

I backed up between his legs until I was right above his jutting cock. I noticed with a gulp that the pirate still gripped the pistol in one hand. I better prove my myself or my first sea voyage would be my last. Closing my eyes, I took a deep breath, willing my butt to be as tight yet yielding as possible. I heard Ranjan spit into his hand and slick up his dick a bit. That was good; it wouldn't be as painful that way.

"I'm ready, Captain," I said as I lowered my ass into his crotch.

"Good boy," he growled, and pushed his cock up against my hole and it sniffed at my chute like a pig after truffles. Carefully controlling my speed, I backed down and with a pop the head of the pirate's cock entered me.

It hurt, but I wanted more.

"Mmm, nice ass," he said, and I pushed further back, taking his cock into me an inch at a time. I continued until he was all the way in, and I could feel his bush against my ass cheeks.

"It feels good in there, sir," I said.

"Aye, it does indeed, boy," the captain said. "Now ride me like a dolphin on the waves!"

"Aye, sir." I said. Lucky I had strong leg muscles. Using them I backed off the dick in my ass, then took it back, fisting it with my butt as I would with my hand.

Ranjan started growling again, this time without stopping, a low continuous rumble of passion and lust.

"Faster, boy!" he said urgently, and I obeyed.

I could feel his organ stiffening even further inside me until it felt as if I was being skewered with a steel spike. I knew the moment was right, and I deployed my secret weapon – I flexed my ass muscles, tightening them into what I hoped was the most glorious hole my host had ever fucked. A howl from Ranjan shook the room as the pirate filled me with a second tidal wave of his seed.

"Oh yes!" he groaned, and reached around my hips to grab my cock. I'd been so focused on pleasuring the captain I'd all but forgotten my own dick. It was straining for attention, sticking straight out from my crotch like the prow of a ship. It only took a few strokes of the pirate's fist, and I was splattering his bed with my spunk and roaring my own passion.

When we were done basking in the afterglow, I got up off the bed and cleaned us both with towels.

“Have I served you well, Captain?” I asked.

“Better than well,” Ranjan said with a smile. “I think you’re the perfect boy for the job.” I remembered what Lojo had said about the captain needing a new sex slave for the ship. It wasn’t exactly the fate I’d imagined for myself, but I would do the best I could in my new position.

Later that night, Ranjan called the crew together to make an announcement. I figured he would name me as the new slave and Lojo as his new first officer as reward for finding me. But I was wrong.

Still bound and gagged as I’d left him, Lojo was dragged snarling and cursing onto the deck by his crewmates.

“This is Teag,” Ranjan said, putting a hand on my shoulder proudly, “my new first mate!”

One of the pirates pulled the gag out of Lojo’s mouth.

“But I was the one who brought him here!” Lojo sputtered. “What’s my reward?”

“Indeed, Lojo, you do deserve a reward.” The Captain said, and Lojo puffed out his chest in pride. “You will be our new sex slave. Any member of the crew can take you, any time they wish!”

Lojo’s jaw dropped to the deck, and the rest of the pirates laughed loud and long. Captain Ranjan drew me close, so his mouth was next to my ear.

“Welcome to the Diablo,” he said.

# IX. SATURDAY IS RAUNCH NIGHT

The invitation was printed on a piece of stiff red paper. It said:

SATURDAY IS RAUNCH NIGHT AT SANDER HOUSE!

YOU'VE BEEN CHOSEN TO JOIN THE HOTTEST

MAN2MAN SUCK/FUCK ACTION IN TOWN!

PARTY BEGINS AT 6:00 PM AND WON'T END 'TIL THE LAST DROP OF CUM HAS BEEN SQUEEZED OUT OF THE LAST THROBBING COCK

THIS INVITATION ADMITS ONE

LEAVE YOUR CLOTHES AT THE DOOR

CONDOMS PROVIDED

YOUR HOST:

RUSSELL SANDER

323-555-6969

1267 DENIM WAY #5

I'd never been to a sex party before, so I wasn't sure what to expect. One of my fuck-buddies had sent me this invitation to his latest night of debauchery, and I was ready. If Russell's friends were as hot as he was, it was going to be one fucking amazing event. Some of my other buddies were jealous when they heard about it.

"You got invited to one of Russell Sander's sex parties?" one of them asked in disbelief. "Whose cock are you sucking?"

"Russell Sander's, of course!" I said.

"Tell me how it goes tonight," my friend said.

"I'll call you tomorrow morning," I assured him.

An hour before the party, I got dressed – tight workout shorts to show off my butt, sleeveless T-shirt to show off my arms; tennis shoes, gym socks and no underwear. I'd hadn't had sex or jerked off for three days before the night of the party, I wanted lots of cum churning in my balls to shoot tonight – so I was half-hard and horny just looking at myself in the mirror.

I felt myself through my shorts, pleased with my good-sized dick and my plump, low-hanging ball-sack. I thought I looked pretty damn hot, with my short blond hair, cute face and cleft chin to round out my nice chest, arms, crotch, butt and legs. Hot enough to get invited to one of Russell Sander's notorious sex parties.

I was ready.

Russell didn't live far from me, I knew the way by heart from the times I'd gone to his place for sex. But this time was different – up until now it had only been the two of us – tonight who knew how many horny guys would be there? Who knew what I'd find behind the very ordinary door to Russell's apartment?

I didn't know – but I was dying to find out!

I took a deep breath, adjusted my cock in my shorts, and knocked on the door.

It was opened a few seconds later by a very hot Latino guy with gorgeous thick black hair, sultry eyes and full, pouting lips. He was naked, and I couldn't stop my eyes from roving up and down his sexy body – tasty pecs with big nipples, hard visible abs, a nice length of uncut cock hanging from the bush of pubic hair between his legs, all covered in luscious dark tanned skin.

"You got an invitation?" the Latino said, and I had to force myself to look back up at his face.

"Yes," I said, holding it out to him. He took it, glanced at it, then rubbed the paper between his fingers. While he was doing this I was busy restraining myself from touching him. Luckily for me, I couldn't decide between reaching out and tweaking his nipples or dropping to my knees and sucking his dick, so I didn't embarrass myself in the open doorway. When he was apparently satisfied that my invitation was genuine, the Latino tore it in half and gave me a big smile of bright white teeth.

“I’m Miguel,” he said, “Welcome to Raunch Night.”

“Thanks,” I said, “My name’s Chris.”

“Come on in,” Miguel said as he backed up and opened the door wider for me. I walked into Russell’s apartment and was instantly intoxicated by the aromas – salty sweat, sweet incense, heady poppers and scented candles – thick and heavy in the air. The lights were low, electronic music throbbed in the background, and everywhere I looked were men.

Big ones, small ones, medium-sized ones like me – white, black, Hispanic, Asian – all of them gorgeous, all of them stunning, all of them naked. Russell’s place was big – he was an advertising executive and made lots of money – with hardwood floors, simple but elegant furniture, with framed Bianchi photographs on the walls and Hitchcock bodycast sculptures in the corners.

Miguel closed the door behind me.

“Clothes off,” he said.

“Oh yeah,” I said, realizing I was the only guy in the room not nude. I quickly stripped off my shorts and shirt, peeled off my socks and kicked off my shoes. Miguel took it all from me and stuffed my clothes in a white plastic garbage bag he pulled from a box on the floor. He wrote my name on the bag with a black marker, then put the bag on a shelf in the closet next to the front door, with more bags that I guessed contained the clothing of the party’s other guests.

“You’re ready,” Miguel said with that great smile again. “Have fun.”

“Thanks!” I said, “I hope I see you again tonight …” but he was gone in the crowd of men. I stepped forward from the entryway into the large main room of the apartment. As I said, there were guys everywhere, and the sound of lots of bare feet on the hardwood floor was loud. There were three couches against the walls, all of them occupied. Even with the windows open to the night sky, the air was thick and heady with sex. On the couch closest to me, two guys were sprawled, wrapped in each other’s arms in a passionate embrace, joined at the mouths. I watched them for a minute, loving the sights of their lean muscled bodies entwined. The man on top started grinding his crotch against the guy beneath him, who moaned in response. They continued kissing, never separating as their lips covered and caressed the others'.

My cock stiffened at the sight of this passion, and I took it in my hand, giving it a few strokes – mmm, that felt good! My eyes were drawn to the top guy's butt – two globes of hard flesh, pulsating in the dim light as their owner thrust his hips against his bottom-boy again and again. I wondered what it would be like to feel that ass, to touch it, to taste it, to stick my tongue between those cheeks to find the tender asshole within, to taste his musk and sweat, to push against his tight ring of muscle with my tongue, to get inside.

As if summoned by my imagination, a third man joined the couple. Lean and muscular like them, the third man knelt at the base of the couch and buried his face in the top man's butt. Now it was his turn to moan, and he pushed his ass back, as if to get more of the third man inside him. I jerked myself some more watching this special three-way show. Then I glanced up and saw that someone was watching me from across the room.

He was smaller than I, probably 5'6" or so, slender and tan. A nice-sized cock was standing at attention between his legs. He had light brown hair and was clean-shaven, with a devilish glint in his eye. I looked around to see if it was really me he was looking at. Seeing this, the guy pointed at me and mouthed the word 'you' to me.

He started walking over to me. Other men noticed him, hoping to make eye contact with him, to connect with him …

… but it seemed to be me that he wanted. When he had crossed the distance between us, he stood in front of me, and I looked down into his deep blue eyes.

"You're pretty fucking hot," he said to me.

"Thanks," I said, "Right back at you."

"I haven't seen you at one of these things before," he said. I nodded.

"First time."

"Good," the guy said, dropping to his knees in front of me. "I want to be your first."

"First what?" I asked.

"First one to taste your cock," he said, and engulfed my dick in his mouth down to its root.

"Oh my God …" I said, "it feels so fucking good!"

The cocksucking boy murmured in response as he expertly caressed my dick with his lips and tongue. It was an amazing experience, to be standing there naked in Russell Sander's apartment, with hot men getting it on all around me, myself getting a world-class blowjob from a sexy boy.

"Wow," I couldn't stop myself from saying. "This is unbelievable!" I put my hands on the boy's head and guided him as he took my hot rod in and out of his mouth.

On the couch, the man who had joined the couple changed his position, moving up so his chest was against the back of the man under him. He put one hand between his crotch and the man's butt, and I knew he was getting his cock in position, ready to plunge between those beautiful cheeks.

I was getting close to climax. The cocksucker was worshipping my dick, lavishing his total attention and effort on making me feel good. My balls were boiling with the cum that had been building up for days in anticipation of this very event.

"I'm gonna come!" I said breathlessly.

But instead of pulling off and jerking me the rest of the way to orgasm like most guys do, the cocksucker increased the speed and intensity of his oral stimulation!

"Don't you want to pull off?" I asked, my voice breaking from the shudders of pleasure that were jolting through my body. As best he could with his mouth full of my cock, he shook his head no.

"I'm gonna shoot down your throat if you keep this up!" I said, willing to stop but not wanting to. But the boy made a sound of appreciative affirmation, and I couldn't stop the tidal wave of ecstasy that was breaking inside me.

"Holy fucking shit!" I said as I came, shooting my semen into the young man just as he wanted. The combination of my orgasm and the pleasure of still being inside his mouth was nearly overwhelming, and I leaned forward.

The guy supported me as he sucked up the rest of my load, savoring every drop of it.

"Oh my God …" I whispered, as the young man let my cock slide slowly out of his mouth.

"You're welcome," he said as he stood up.

"But …" I started to say, then trailed off.

"Don't worry about it," the cocksucker said. "Russell screens anyone he wants to invite to the parties. Every guy here is negative."

He put one hand on my chest and pinched my left nipple playfully.

"See you later," he said, "There's lots more to see and do …" and he walked away, flashing those eyes at me one more time over his shoulder. I wanted to pick him up and take him home with me, but I realized that the night had just begun.

As I stepped past the couch where the three-way was going on, I saw that they'd progressed to full-scale fucking, the guy on the bottom's legs high in the air as the guy in the middle plowed his ass with his cock. He himself was getting screwed by the third guy, making what had to be a delicious sandwich of man-meat.

On one side of the room a large TV monitor played porno to a captive audience of five or six guys. They sat on the floor in a half-circle around the TV, staring up at it as enthralled as any congregation rapt at a sermon. On the screen, Ryan Idol was fucking Joey Stefano in the classic scene from *Idol Eyes* as the men watching jerked their cocks in appreciation.

As I walked through the crowd of men, I had my own appreciative audience – random hands reached out and touched me – my butt, my chest, my dick – but I didn't stop, I was exploring. I want to see everything that was happening.

I noticed a few bare butts on their way to the kitchen, and I followed them. I stepped around the guy kneeling on the floor giving a hot blowjob to a guy leaning against the wall, and entered the huge kitchen. There was a small group gathered watching something, and I squirmed in between two of the men, so I could see what everyone was looking at.

It was a lavish buffet table, probably twelve feet long and eight feet wide, laid out with a dazzling assortment of desserts. Cakes, pies, plates of cookies, bowls of chocolate dipping sauce, cupcakes, and fruit – grapes, plums, peaches, nectarines, dishes of frosting …

But it wasn't the food the men were looking at. It was the table's centerpiece that had captured their attention. In the middle of the table, surrounded by the desserts, was a man. Sprawled on his side, looking like some decadent Roman emperor, was a gorgeous young man – seemingly perfect: muscular arms and legs, handsome face, sparkling smile, dark ringlets of curly hair on his head but the rest of him hairless, his big thick beautiful cock erect and sticking out from his crotch at the men watching him.

On the table in front of him was a sign that said 'HELP YOURSELF.' The centerpiece man was smiling serenely, as if there was nothing unusual about this opulent scene.

A few of the guys watching picked up cookies and munched on them, but no one partook of the dessert buffet's 'main course.' I figured a sex party was the last place I should feel inhibited and told myself 'what the hell?'

I picked up a large, ripe strawberry from one of the fruit bowls and held it between my fingers for a few seconds. There were tiny beads of moisture on the berry. When I realized that the man on the table, as well as all the other guys gathered around were now watching me, I put the strawberry up to my mouth and licked it, absorbing the moisture and adding a shiny sheen to the fruit.

Then I took the strawberry and held it up to the centerpiece man's lips. He opened his mouth obediently, and I gently put the berry inside. The guy bit down firmly, his eyes never leaving mine as he chewed and swallowed. I watched the pieces of the berry as they traveled down the man's beautiful neck and disappeared into his flat, perfect stomach. I noticed that some of the other guys had started stroking their hard dicks, and that my own cock was stiffening up again, even so soon after shooting down the cocksucker's throat.

I dipped a finger deep into a dish of chocolate syrup, then lifted it to the centerpiece's mouth and gently pushed it inside, very slowly. I could see some of the young man's composure break down when he realized he was in my power – he wanted my whole finger, all of it! – but I inserted it only a millimeter at a time, until finally my whole finger was inside him. He sucked it, swallowing the chocolate hungrily until it was all gone. I pulled my finger out of his mouth, and he looked disappointed, like he wished I'd leave it in there.

But I wasn't done yet. I picked a few grapes off a bunch overflowing out of a wine glass, and the guy on the table looked hopeful. I knew he thought I was going to feed them to him. He was right, but not exactly how he imagined. I put the grapes in my own mouth, then I leaned over the table, careful not to knock anything over. I put my lips to the centerpiece's and kissed them, then firmly pushed the grapes with my tongue from my mouth into his. He moaned in response, gladly taking what I gave him.

When I broke the kiss, he gave me a big smile and started chewing the grapes I'd given him. I took his hard cock in my hand and jacked it a few times, causing him to groan through his full mouth. I gave his dick a hard squeeze, then let it go.

I winked at the centerpiece and turned to go; I'd seen enough here. He looked like he wanted me to stay, but his attention was diverted when one of the other men watching picked up a can of whipped cream and shook it up. The man squirted whipped cream all over the centerpiece's cock, decorating it like it was a dessert. And it was.

As I left the kitchen, I glanced over my shoulder one more time to see the man sucking the centerpiece's dick, licking and sucking up the whipped cream as he did so. The young man's head was titled back and his eyes were shut in ecstasy. The men watching had started jerking their own cocks at the sight of this.

I walked back out into the entry room, and headed for the hallway that led to the rest of the rooms in Russell's apartment. The corridor was long; it was a big place as I said, with doors on both sides all the way down. At the end of the hallway was the door to Russell's bedroom.

As I took my first few steps down the corridor, I heard smacking sounds coming from the first opened door on my left. I stopped and listening – it was definitely the sound of bare hands on bare flesh. A handwritten sign next to the door read NAUGHTY BOYS REPORT HERE.

I had to see what this was about, and walked through the door. In what was normally Russell's home office, several men were standing or lying in different positions. A sexy man sat in each of the rooms' three chairs, and each of those men had another man slung over his knees, whom he was spanking. My cock, already re-energized by the scene in the kitchen, stood up at what I was seeing. One of the spanking men looked up at me and grinned.

"Come on in," he said, "I'm just teaching this naughty boy a lesson." I obeyed and came in closer. The light was dim, but I could still see the bright pink blush of the naughty boy's ass. Both men were handsome, the one doing the spanking older and more muscular than the slim boy across his knee. The man gave the boy a swat on one butt cheek, flat-handed and hard. I knew it had to hurt, but between the man's legs I could see the boy's cock, and it was stiff as a board.

"You're a bad boy, aren't you, Jeremy?" the man asked in a stern voice.

"Yes, Sir!" the boy said. "I'm a very bad boy!"

"And bad boys get punished, isn't that right?"

He spanked Jeremy hard on the other cheek, and the boy let out a yelp like a puppy dog.

"That's right, Sir!" Jeremy said, his voice breaking.

"And what do you say when I punish you?"

"Thank you, Sir!" the boy said, "Thank you for punishing me, I've been a very bad boy!"

The man started spanking the boy, faster now, hard and solid. Jeremy started moaning quietly, his face blushing with humiliation. Soon his face was as pink as his ass, and my cock was as rock-hard as his. I took my dick in my fist and jerked it a few times. Damn, that felt good! Almost as good as the sight of this baby bad boy getting spanked by an older stud. The man looked up at me again. I must have been drooling, because he laughed.

"Come on," he said, "I know you want to do more than watch."

He was right, of course. I stepped closer, and I could see Jeremy's whole body was tense and quivering, his cock aching for attention. From this new angle, I could see that the man's dick was hard too, as hard as mine and the boy's.

"What should I do?" I asked.

"What do you want to do?" the man asked me back.

"I want to … touch him," I said.

"Then touch him."

I knelt down in front of the man and his boy, so I was on Jeremy's level. Reaching out with both hands, I rested them on the boy, my left palm on his back, and my right on his butt. I felt him breathe, in and out hard, his chest and abdomen filling with air then pushing it back out.

Jeremy's butt was warm from the spanking, and it felt good under my hand. I kneaded the firm flesh of his ass cheek with my fingers, pinching and massaging it, first gently then harder.

"Give him a swat," the stud said. "Go ahead," he added when I hesitated.

I slapped Jeremy's ass with my right hand lightly, then again.

"That's it," the man said. "Now harder,"

I swatted him harder this time, and Jeremy let out one of his little yelps. When he did my cock pulsed. I was getting off on this! I started spanking him in rhythm then, like the man had done, one slap after another. I switched from one cheek to the other, slapping him ass again and again.

The stud with the boy over his knee grinned at me.

"Looks like you got the hang of it," he said. "What's your name?"

"Chris," I said. He grabbed a handful of Jeremy's hair and jerked his head back, and the boy gasped.

"What do you say when Chris punishes you, boy?" he asked him.

"Thank you, Sir!" Jeremy said breathlessly. "Thank you for punishing this bad boy!" As if it were possible, my cock somehow got harder when he said this.

"I'm Rick," the stud said to me, releasing the boy's head, "C'mere."

I did what he said and leaned over Jeremy to bring my face closer to Rick. The man kissed me, his lips hard and strong and wet, and I responded. Rick stuck his tongue into my mouth and moved it around, exploring me from the inside out. Then he broke the kiss and started feeling my face with his lips. He kissed my cheeks, my nose, my eyelids. His unshaven face scraped against mine, and I loved it. Between us, Jeremy shuddered and quivered with passion.

Then Rick looked me in the eyes.

"You're pretty fucking hot, Chris," he said.

"I was going to say the same thing to you …" I answered.

"Then say it."

"You're pretty fucking hot yourself, Rick," I said.

"What do you say we finish this boy off?" he asked.

"Sounds good," I said, "How?"

"How about I spank him and you jerk him off,"

"I'm there." I said, and reached under the boy to find his dick. When I found it, it was hard as a steel rod, and the boy moaned as I gripped it in my fist.

"You like that, Jeremy?" I asked him, as Rick started spanking him again. "You like two hot men taking care of you like this?"

"Yes, Sir!" he answered, "Thank you, Sir!"

I started jacking his cock then, and his breathing got even harder. The sound of Rick smacking his ass was very loud in the small room.

"Yeah," Rick said, "I'm punishing you for being a bad boy, and Chris is rewarding you for taking it so well,"

"Thank you, Sirs!"

This was fun! The boy started groaning loudly as the excitement and intensity increased inside him.

"Shut him up," Rick told me. I took my left hand and covered Jeremy's mouth with it. He didn't stop moaning, but it did muffle the sound.

"You almost ready, bad boy?" Rick asked him. Jeremy nodded so vigorously that Rick and I both laughed. "When we tell you to, you gonna shoot for us?"

"Yes, Sir!" the boy said through my hand. I jerked him faster and Rick really started wailing on his butt, whacking it over and over again.

Rick raised his eyebrows at me, and I nodded.

"Come for us, bad boy!" he yelled at Jeremy. "Shoot your load and make us real happy!" The boy let out a noise that was half-grunt and half-scream.

"That's it!" I said, "Shoot for us, you naughty, naughty, naughty, NAUGHTY BOY!"

Semen spurted out of Jeremy's cock and his whole body convulsed as if he'd had the wind knocked out of him. Rick stopped spanking him, and I let go of the boy's cock as his orgasm rushed through him, rocking him. The other men in the room paused in their scenes to watch the boy's climax. Cum kept squirting out of his cock, splattering down onto the towel. As we watched, Rick and I took hold of our own dicks and jacked ourselves.

"Thank you, Sirs! Thank you, thank you, THANK YOU SIRS!" Jeremy moaned when he could speak again.

"Oh fuckin' yeah, bad boy!" Rick said, and he came himself, shooting his load up onto his hairy chest. His head rolled back on his neck, and his Adam's apple stuck out. I was about ready to come again myself, but stopped jerking because I wanted to save it. I knew there was lots more to experience here, and in between, it was fun to help other guys reach their climaxes.

When Jeremy and Rick had recovered from their orgasms, the man helped the boy get off his knees and Jeremy stood up. I did the same, and when I was up he hugged me tightly.

"Thanks, Chris," he said, "That was unbelievable,"

"You're welcome, bad boy," I said with a grin. Then Jeremy turned to Rick and the bigger man pulled him into a tight embrace. Over Jeremy's shoulder Rick winked at me.

"See you later?" I asked.

"Count on it," he said, and then started passionately kissing Jeremy. I headed out of the spanking office, and walked back into the hallway. The next door on the right-hand side caught my eye. The sign on it read ROCKS OFF ROOM, and I knew I had to see what was up with this.

I opened the door. It was Russell's guest bedroom, not that I could see much of it. There were men everywhere, and a lot of them were fucking. There was a couple screwing on the bed, another on a couch, and more on some mattresses that had been laid on the floor. The other guys were watching the fucking, and I realized that there was a pattern to the layout, that they weren't just standing around.

Each fucking position – the bed, the couch and the mattresses – had a line after it. The men were standing in line to fuck the guy who was lying down, taking turns! How civilized, I thought. Well, I had to get me some of this, so I checked out each of the guys getting fucked. I knew I could screw them all if I wanted to, but I was almost ready to shoot my next load, and I wanted it to be inside somebody. Unfortunately, all the guys getting fucked looked tasty to me, so it was going to be a hard decision. I considered each one:

The guy getting fucked on the bed was slender and black, with the long, toned legs of a dancer. His eyes were shut tight and his jaws were clenched as he took the hard thrusting of the man that was doing him.

The fuck-boy being plowed on the couch was hot, too. He had short brown hair and was kind of small, at least compared to the big muscle-bound gym jock that was boning him like there was no tomorrow.

On the mattress closest to me, two punks with shaved heads were getting it on. The one getting screwed was on his stomach, pushing his ass back against the other one's cock. They had so many piercings between the two of them that there were loud metallic clinking sounds every time the top pushed in.

It was fun and sexy watching all this, but my attention was drawn to the far side of the room, where the unmistakable grunts and moans of a man about to come were emanating. I stepped around the punks to get a look at who was making those groans of mounting passion. On the second mattress, up against the wall, a hunky and horny Latin boy was getting fucked. He wasn't very tall, but he had nice muscles from what I could see of his body. The man fucking him was the one making the noises, and I understood why – I'd moan, too, if I got my cock into that boy. The guy had the boy's legs up on his shoulders and was pile-driving his way to heaven between them.

I stepped closer.

The man didn't notice, but when I did, the Latin boy caught sight of me. He raised his eyebrows and grinned at me, which I took as a good sign.

"You're fucking hot," he mouthed to me, and I pointed back at him to show him I thought the same about him. The man on top of him was about to come.

"Oh yeah oh yeah oh fuckin' YEAH!" he said before letting out an animal groan of bliss. His body went rigid as he climaxed, and I knew he was shooting his load deep into his bottom-boy. But the bottom-boy kept his eyes on me, even when the man pulled out of him. But the guy was flying so high on his orgasm he didn't seem to notice. He peeled the condom off his dick and dumped it in a wastebasket next to the mattress. Then he gave the boy a quick kiss.

"Thanks, man," he said. "That was fuckin' awesome."

The freshly-fucked boy smiled and nodded at him, giving him the thumbs-up sign. The man got up and walked past me to the door.

The Latin boy sat up as I hunkered down in front of him. His body and smile were even hotter close up, not to mention his long, perky cock that was standing straight up.

"You're sexy," I said to him. He nodded and pointed to me. "What's your name?" I asked.

The boy put his finger to his lips and shook his head.

"You can't speak?" I asked. His shook his head no again. "You're deaf?" He nodded, and I realized he'd been reading my lips all this time. I was a little surprised, and unsure what to do.

I started to stand up.

"Maybe this isn't such a good idea ..." I started to say, but the boy put his finger to my lips and shook his head. He reached up and took my cock – which was instantly fully erect again at his touch – in his hand and gently pulled me back down so I was at the foot of the mattress between his legs. Reaching for the small pile of condom packages on the floor near us, the boy took one and unwrapped it. His beautiful face intent in concentration, he unrolled the rubber onto my hard dick and covered it with lube from a bottle next to the mattress. Then he lay back and put his legs in the air.

When I hesitated again, he hit me with his smile one more time and gave me a 'come here' gesture. I couldn't resist him anymore and moved forward onto the mattress. There was no need for foreplay; we were both totally aroused and ready for action. His asshole was open and lubed, and I slid into him easily. I rested his legs on my shoulders and started fucking him. It felt so fucking good, I could hardly describe it.

Something happens sometimes when two guys fuck – when you're totally in sync with each other, when your minds are connected in the way your bodies are connected. It's an incredible feeling, and I was having it with this hot little Latin boy. He kept his eyes open the entire time, looking at me, his eyes locked on mine. My cock loved being inside him as I thrust into him, then pulled out almost the whole way before thrusting in again.

He couldn't speak, but he was communicating in other ways – it was like his mind was sending me messages: his eyes were saying 'I love what you're doing to me,' and his body was definitely communing with mine, with that long rigid cock that was bouncing against my abdomen as I fucked him.

It was ecstatic and wonderful, and when my orgasm started I had no doubt where I wanted my second load of the night to go. But I wanted him to come with me, not just lie there and take it as he had with the guy before me. I wanted him really there, with me. I took his dick in my hand and jerked it, and the boy opened his mouth in a silent moan of pleasure. I grinned at him and kept my eyes open as I came. My load pumped into him, and I must have made him feel equally as good because his whole body tensed, and his cock flexed in my hand as it squirted a load of spunk onto his chest. The boy's head tilted back on his and his legs straightened on my shoulders.

"Oh God …" I groaned as my own orgasm peaked and the last of my jizz shot into him. I collapsed on top of him, and he put his arms around me.

We stayed that way for a few minutes as our hot bliss subsided into fantastic afterglow. Then we caught our breath and disentangled ourselves. I took off the condom and wiped the boy off with some paper towels that were on the floor. Then we lay back down on the mattress together and I held him tight, his back to my chest. I kissed his ear and squeezed him. He nestled against me like we were out camping sharing a sleeping bag. I knew he was done for a while, but didn't want to leave him in the ROCKS OFF room, so I picked him up, cradling him in my arms. He snuggled against me. I carefully carried him out of the room and looked down the hallway.

Luckily for both of us, the next door on the right side of the corridor was labeled REST ROOM – SLEEPING ONLY!!!

I gently nudged the door open with my shoulder and entered what was usually Russell's den. In it there were stuffed chairs, Futon beds, bare mattresses; and sleeping men everywhere. Some were holding each other, others nestled alone hugging their pillows. The combined sound of a stereo playing soft ocean sounds and an air conditioning unit blowing cool air drowned out the noise of the rest of the party. It was a peaceful scene.

There was only one man awake, and he sat in the far corner, watching the others.

"Hey, what's up?" I whispered to him.

"I'm the babysitter," he whispered back, "I'm here to make sure no one fucks with them while they rest."

"Cool." I said. "Any room for this one?" The babysitter gestured to an empty Futon next to him.

"Put him here," he said. I did what he said and gently set the Latin boy down on the Futon. The babysitter handed me a blanket, and I covered with boy with it. He smiled a big happy smile, and I knew he was already asleep.

"Thanks for taking care of them," I said to the babysitter.

"No problem," he whispered. "I get my payment later tonight. I get first pick of them when they wake up."

I saluted him and left the room, closing the door quietly behind me.

I walked back out into Russell's hallway, wondering what other amazing things were happening here tonight. The noise and music continued, as if it would never stop.

The next door on the left was closed. I thought I remembered it was the room Russell kept his exercise equipment in, and that it had a balcony with a view of the hills.

The sign on the door said SMOKING ROOM.

I opened it and was hit with air dense with smoke. It stung my eyes a little as I stared at the scene in the room. Because of the way the room was built, part of it was blocked from my view. Metal squeaking noises were coming from that unseen part of the room. But my eyes were full of what was occupying the area of the room I could see.

The bench press, treadmill and exercise bike had been moved against the wall. The door to the balcony was open, the night visible through it. There were four or five guys standing around or leaning on the walls talking. They were hairy and muscular, smoking cigars – they didn't need to be wearing any clothes for me to know what they were – leathermen. The tallest guy was the hottest – he had short brown hair and a goatee and a very hairy chest. His cock was huge even when soft. He was blowing smoke when he caught my eye and saw me staring.

"Get your ass in here and close the door!" he ordered me, and I obeyed. When I turned around I saw that the other leather guys were watching me, too, with smirks or grins on their faces.

"Come in, boy, we won't hurt you," one of them said.

"Unless you really want us to," another added. I stepped further into the room and saw the area that had been hidden from the doorway. I'd never noticed the four 'O' rings built into the ceiling of this room before, and if I had, I probably would've figured they were for some exercise equipment or something. And on some days, they probably were. But tonight the rings were attached to four lengths of chain from which a leather sling was suspended about four feet off the floor. There was a man in the sling, his arms and legs up in the air, locked to the chains at the wrists and ankles with leather restraints. Another leatherman sat in a chair between the tied-up guy's legs, fisting him. I'd never seen fisting up close, and was fascinated to watch the man's hand disappear into the guy's asshole to the wrist. The tied-up guy was moaning softly, lost in bliss, with his cock standing straight up at the ceiling. The man fisting him was concentrating hard, sweat dripping out onto his forehead from under the leather cap he wore.

I stepped closer and saw that both of the men's cocks were hard. My own cock stirred at the sight of the fisting, despite having already shot twice tonight.

Suddenly there was a hand on my shoulder.

"You like that, boy?" its owner asked in my ear. I recognized the voice – it was the tall hot leatherman. He was behind me, and pressed his crotch against my butt. His big cock smashed up between my ass cheeks – it was so hot it was almost enough to make me swoon. I pushed back on him, trapping his dick between our bodies. Both of the man's arms went around me, holding me close to him. His breathing was loud in my ear, his breath hot on my skin. His right hand moved down my chest and abdomen until it found my hardening cock and gripped it tight.

I watched the guy getting fisted while the leatherman played with my cock with one hand and felt my chest with the other. The fister's hand disappeared into the guy's asshole, and the leatherman's hand found one of my nipples and pinched it hard. I let out a grunt as he rubbed his dick against my ass.

"Yeah, boy," he growled, "that's it …"

"Excuse me," a new voice said suddenly, and I felt the leatherman let go of me.

"What the hell?" I heard him say, as I turned around to see what was happening. A gigantic black bodybuilder-looking guy had the leatherman by the arm. I guessed he'd just pulled him away from me. Now the leatherman was tall, but this new dude was one powerfully-built motherfucker. He towered over the leatherman, his shoulders looking about five feet wide and his cock hanging down between his legs as big as my arm. A spiked leather collar was locked around his neck. He looked like one of those pro wrestlers on TV.

What was going on?

The leatherman jerked his arm out of the bodybuilder's grip and pointed at me.

"That ass was mine!" he said angrily.

"That ass is wanted in the back bedroom," said the bodybuilder.

"Shit!" the leatherman said.

"Sorry," said the bodybuilder, and with very little effort leaned over, picked me up off the floor, tossed me over one broad shoulder and headed out of the room.

"Uh …" I said, stupidly.

From my reverse angle I saw one of the leatherman's buddies hand him a fresh cigar.

"Maybe next time?" he yelled after me.

I nodded as the collared dude lugged me back out into the hallway and down the corridor. I'd never been carried like this before, and it was pretty sexy. Some of the men we passed cheered and gave me the thumbs-up signal when they saw me getting carried away over this guy's shoulder slung like a stuffed laundry bag. I couldn't see where we were going but I knew where I was being taken – the end of the hallway, to Russell Sander's bedroom. When we got there, the bodybuilder stopped, and I hear him knock on the door.

"Yes?" a voice said.

"I've got him, sir," the bodybuilder said,

"Bring him in," was the response.

I heard the door open, and I was brought into the private bedroom of the party's host. The smell of incense was strong. The bodybuilder put me down, and I turned around. As always, Russell's bedroom was an orgy of black. The floor was black, the walls and ceiling had been painted black, the furniture – he'd even found and bought a black computer, for God's sake.

But coolest of all was his bed.

Besides the obvious black blankets and black pillows, Russell had hung black sheets from the ceiling, so they hung down around his bed and framed it, making it look like the bed of a king.

Or a vampire.

There was a naked man lying on the bed, waiting for me.

It was Miguel, the incredibly sexy Latin guy who'd answered the door when I'd first come here tonight. He was sprawled seductively, resting his head on one hand while the other played with his big Latin cock that was already half-hard.

"Thanks for getting him," Miguel said.

"Of course, sir," the bodybuilder answered.

"Wait in the hallway and make sure we're not disturbed."

"Yes, sir," the bodybuilder said, and left the room, closing the door behind him.

"You are so fucking hot." I said, and Miguel laughed.

"You're looking pretty tasty yourself," he said. "Come here." I obeyed and stepped up to the foot of the bed. The sexy Latin boy reached out and took my cock and balls in his hand. We both watched as my dick reached full erection at his touch. Miguel pulled me by my cock and balls up onto Russell's bed until we were lying on our sides facing each other.

He kissed me then, his lips soft and his tongue warm, and it was wonderful. Somehow, despite the workout my libido had been getting all night it rose to the occasion and got me jacked up and ready for more action. I figured I had one more load to blow tonight, and I was going to make it an orgasm to remember. It was incredible to be so intimate with Miguel, so vulnerable.

We touched and caressed each other's chests, squeezing pectorals and teasing nipples. In some way, it felt as if the whole night had been leading up to this – from the moment I saw Miguel I wanted to do this with him. All the while our kiss continued, our eyes closed. I imagined Miguel in my mind, his dark tan skin, his full thick hair, his rich chocolate brown eyes, and especially the supple lips I was massaging and exploring with my own.

He was so choice, so perfect, exactly what I'd hoped for when I first got the invitation to this party. Miguel was mine – or was I his? Did it matter? Not with my throbbing cock still held tightly in the Latin guy's hand as we kissed. He squeezed my ball-sack gently and I gasped like a virgin. Somehow being with Miguel was different from the other guys – it was almost like starting over. I remembered where I was then, in Russell Sander's bed, and realized that all bets were off – in this bed, anything could happen.

Miguel broke contact then, releasing my cock and balls and drawing his mouth back away from mine. I must have given him a pitiful, pleading look because he raised on eyebrow and gave me a devilish grin before diving between my legs. I expected him to suck my cock, but he gave it just a quick kiss before lifting my legs up and showing me what his preferred main course was – my asshole.

With my legs in the air and out of the way, the Latin guy pressed his incredible mouth between them. The sensation of him touching my asshole with his face was fucking incredible. He kissed my butthole, then pressed his lips against it, hard, caressing it, stroking it, loving it – it felt so good, and I was so swooning in the pleasure that I was totally unprepared when he stuck out his tongue and licked me down there in my most sensitive place. I closed my eyes again and let my head loll back on my neck. Waves of ecstasy washed over me, and I swam in them, body-surfing on my own bliss. And as if licking me there wasn't enough, Miguel took that tongue of his and started gently working my hole with it, opening it up, until it was soft and giving and ready for him to push it inside me. When I was ready, he tongue-fucked me, pushing himself into me, tasting me from the inside, then pulling out not all the way but just enough to tease me and make my cock jerk and ooze pre-cum out onto my stomach.

This was so amazing, so delicious, I didn't know how anything could get better.

Until I heard Russell Sander's voice, that is.

"Is he ready?" he asked. Miguel pulled his tongue out of my butt, and I let out a little moan of protest. Both men laughed.

"I don't think he could be more ready than he is right now," Miguel said.

"Perfect," Russell said. "Thanks for preparing him for me."

"No problem," Miguel answered, "it was my pleasure."

"I'll see you when I'm done with him," Russell said.

"Okay, boss," Miguel said, and I heard the bedroom door open and close. Then I heard footsteps getting closer. They stopped at the foot of the bed.

"Now," Russell said, and only then did I open my eyes.

Framed between my legs, standing looking down at me, was the sex god that was named Russell Sander. The man who knew the hottest guys in town, the man whom other men traveled across the country and across continents to worship at his feet, was turning his full attention on me.

He was tall, not as big as the bodybuilder had been but certainly taller than I. Blessed with a naturally muscular physique, he's spent most of his thirty years playing sports, and playing them long and hard. His body was literally to die for. Toned and sculpted, not like a steroid-pumped gym jock, but a man whose body had been shaped by a life of rough sports. The hair on his head was thick and flaming red, and the freckles were dark on his flawless, pale skin. He was breathtakingly handsome, and his smile broke hearts and stiffened cocks for a ten-mile radius. His dick was like him, not too big, not too small, but just right, its uncut foreskin pulled almost all the way back from the bright pink head in the intensity of its straining erection.

Nobody's perfect, but Russell Sander was as close as anyone was ever going to get.

"I'm glad you could make it," he said, and it was my turn to laugh.

"I couldn't miss it," I said, "your parties are legendary, and now I know why."

"I'm going to fuck you now." Russell said, and my cock spurted a fresh round of pre-cum.

"Thank fucking God," I answered, "I've been hoping all night for this."

"Haven't you been having a good time?" he asked, his face concerned.

"Of course I have," I said, "It's just that – I've been fucked by you before, and once you've had the best, the rest just can't measure up."

He smiled at me, and it was a fantastic sight.

"You're one of a kind, aren't you?" he asked.

"I think we both are," was my answer. "Please fuck me, Russell."

"No one's ever had to ask me twice," he said, and crawled panther-like up onto his bed between my legs. The jungle cat comparison didn't stop there – Russell looked down at me hungrily, like a tiger at his prey. And I was happy to be his prey – he could've eaten me alive and I'd have loved it. I hiked my legs back up in the air and grabbed my heels with my hands – I wanted him to have as little resistance as possible. While I did this Russell unrolled a condom onto his cock and slicked it up with lube. I was giving him total access to my asshole, I was his for the taking.

"I'm ready," Russell said.

"Me, too," I answered.

"I'm too horny to be gentle," he warned me.

"I don't care, man," I said, "please just take me, I'm fucking yours!"

Without another word he fucked me, shoving his magnificent cock into me and filling me with his power. The rest of the night, everything that had happened before, had merely been prelude, foreplay, this was the moment I'd been hoping for since I'd gotten the invitation to come tonight. My butt took him willingly, gratefully, as if this big organ pushing into it was not an invader but instead actually necessary. It was as if we were one person, joined in the most intimate and physical way two people can be connected. Russell made love to me, thrusting his cock into me, then withdrawing, then back in again. I moved with him, pushing against him to give him maximum penetration. I wanted to be his best bottom ever, the one he remembered, the highlight of this and all future parties.

He started grunting in animal passion, and I knew he was close. I reached down to jerk my cock off, but Russell pushed my hand away so he could grab it himself, which was of course infinitely better. He jacked me in rhythm with this thrusting, and I realized he was planning for us to come together.

Everything that had happened that night rushed through my head, down my chest and into my cock.

"Are you ready?" he asked me breathlessly.

"Yes, please!" I said.

"Now!" Russell said, and we hit our climaxes at the same time. His muscular body jerked and spasmed on top of me as his orgasm burst through him. His cock unloaded itself inside me, shooting jet after jet of white-hot fire into me. My own climax was like an explosion whose shockwave engulfed my whole body. I convulsed in ecstasy, but Russell wrapped his arms around me and held me tight. The electricity in our bodies was pulsing and powerful, as if our orgasms and ejaculations were happening with such force we had to hold on or we'd be blasted off the bed, through the ceiling and up into the night sky.

I felt the last of my load spurt out of my dick to splatter all over my chest and neck. The man on top of me let out a long groan of passion and release, and it was over. We just held each other for a few minutes, as if afraid to let go. We bathed in our mutual after-glows as the bliss of our orgasms slowly faded into ecstatic euphoria.

Only when Russell let go of me did I realize how tired I was.

He pulled his cock out of me and got up off the bed. I kept my eyes shut as I heard him take off his condom and run water in his adjoining bathroom. Then he walked back over to his bed, and I felt the pleasurable sensation of a warm washcloth wiping me clean of sweat and spunk.

I was covered with a blanket, and I snuggled happily into it. As I drifted out of consciousness, I heard Russell talking to someone, probably Miguel.

"Do you want me to have him moved?" Miguel was asking.

"No, he's good where he is. He'll sleep with me tonight."

"How was he?"

"Just about the best ever."

I smiled, and when the lights were switched off a moment later, I fell asleep instantly.

# X. STREET HUNTER
# Hunters of Men 2

MEET ME OUT BACK FOR HEAD, the scrawled writing on the inside of the restroom stall said. Fuck, Garrett thought, this'll be easy. His victims were now announcing themselves to him, he hardly had to hunt at all. The sorry specimen that had written this message in the childish hand would most likely be his last catch of the day.

Garrett finished pissing into the dirty toilet bowl and shook his sizable cock to free the last drops of urine before tucking the organ back into his camouflage pants. He hit the flush lever with his booted foot and the noise of draining water and groaning pipes seemed very loud in the tiny restroom. Something touched his boot, and he looked down. His lip curled with disgust as he saw a grimy tennis shoe sticking under the wall of the stall. Obviously the guy using the urinal next to the stall wanted to know if Garrett was available for some action.

The hunter pulled his boot away and slammed open the door of the stall. He strode out and glared at the obviously drugged-out young man cowering in front of the urinal.

"Fuck off, scum," Garrett said, "or I'll smash your head through that wall." Without waiting for a response, he headed for the door. Since the restroom was located at the back of the bookstore, he had to walk the entire length of the establishment to get to the front door. As he walked among the racks and shelves, he ignored the attempts at eye contact the other customers tried to establish with him.

Garrett knew he was hot, with his sleeveless T-shirt, bulging bicep muscles and military buzz-cut hair. He exuded unselfconscious sexuality. His physical presence, which made him so attractive to gay men, had also made him arrogant. He felt disdain for the guys who tried to connect with him, considering them wretched souls who weren't even worthy of a few moments of his attention.

They were weak.

But he was strong.

He took what he wanted, when he wanted it. And what Garrett wanted right then was one more catch to finish off the day's hunting. And he had a feeling he'd find it behind this very store.

He walked out of the store's entrance and headed to the rear of the building. Reflections of headlights from cars driving by fell across him as he walked. It was very late, but this part of the city never slept. It was cruising time, Garrett's favorite time of the day or night. As he walked, he pulled a small amber bottle and a grimy hand-towel out of his pocket. When he saw that no one was looking, he dumped some of the contents of the bottle into the towel, then stuffed them both back in his pocket.

Behind the bookstore it was dark, with trees from the public park next door blocking out most of the moonlight. But there was enough to see the overflowing garbage dumpster and the nervous, twitching man who was haunting its shadow.

This is appropriate, Garrett thought. Trash by the trash bin. And trash is free – anyone can take what they want from it, just as I'm going to do right now.

The young man made a little noise of excited surprise when he looked up and saw Garrett standing there. His eyes went wide as he took in the sight of the stud that had accepted the invitation he'd written on the bathroom wall. Garrett cocked his head slightly, evaluating his prey. The guy was slender, almost gaunt, wearing dirty cargo pants and a torn T-shirt. His hair was messy but he had what might have been called a pretty face, before a few years of booze and drugs had taken their toll. He was probably about twenty-five and was wearing new athletic tennis shoes that he'd most likely stolen from his last trick.

He made a 'come here' gesture with his hands, and Garrett obliged, stepping out of the fragile moonlight into the shadows next to the dumpster. The guy started to sink down on his knees, but the hunter stopped him.

"Get your back against the wall, cocksucker," Garrett growled, and the guy obeyed, scooting back on his haunches. Garrett stepped forward, trapping his prey between the rear of the building and his own bulky body. "What's your name?"

"M-Mark," the guy stuttered. Garrett unbuckled his belt and let his camo pants open by themselves from the pressure of the hard cock within. The erect rod jutted out like a prong, and Mark practically licked his lips with anticipation.

"Open your fucking mouth, Mark," the hunter said. Mark did what he was told, and was rewarded as Garrett forced his big cock between the young man's lips. Mark choked on the size of it, but Garrett didn't give a shit, and started pumping his hips, face-fucking his prey until the young man was hacking up bile.

"Yeah, you're a good little cocksucker, a good little cock-whore, aren't you?" Garrett rumbled as Mark did his best to service the huge organ that had been stuffed into his mouth. It never took long for Garrett to get off, even when he was enjoying himself and wanted it to last longer. "Good little cock-whore, that's what you are, Mark …" he said, "and now you're gonna eat my cream."

Garrett's powerful body flexed as his orgasm shuddered through him. He kept a firm grip on Mark's head, so the young man couldn't pull away, and his prey swallowed greedily as the hunter's sperm shot down his throat in three massive spurts. Only when the last drop had been squeezed out did Garrett let go of Mark, and the young man gasped for air.

"Mmmmmm," the hunter said, "that felt good, cocksucker. You made me feel nice. And now we're gonna see how much money you're worth."

Mark looked so surprised by this statement that he didn't notice Garrett pulling something from his pocket.

"What are you talk …" was as far as he got before the hunter smashed his hand against Mark's face, pinning his head to the wall and covering his nose and mouth with the chloroform-soaked towel.

Mark tried to dislodge the towel from his face, but Garrett was much stronger than he and easily kept it in place over his victim's nose and mouth. The young man punched his fists against the hunter's muscular chest and abdomen, but he might as well have been pounding on a brick wall for all the good it did him. Mark tried to call out for help, but the noise was muffled by the towel and went unheard.

Not that anyone would come to his rescue anyway.

Mark's struggles became less insistent and slowly ceased altogether as the chemical fumes did their job. His body sagged against the wall as he lost consciousness.

Without wasting any time, Garrett stuffed the rag back into the pocket of his camo pants and grabbed Mark under his armpits. Lifting the smaller man up off the ground easily, the hunter ducked down and hefted his prey's body over one shoulder. Standing up, Garrett adjusted the weight of his burden on his shoulder and secured him in place with one arm around his legs. Mark dangled over Garrett's back, his arms swinging as the bigger man started walking.

The hunter walked out of the alley, back around to the sidewalk near the front of the store. He carried his prey easily, as if the young man weighed no more than a bag of laundry.

A few late-night cruisers walked by, but Garrett ignored them, twisting his face into a silent snarl. He had his last catch of the day; he was done hunting for tonight. Mark would be out from the chloroform for a while, so he didn't have to worry about him regaining consciousness. Not that he would be able to free himself if he did – Garrett could just get a good solid punch to Mark's face, and he'd be out like a light again.

But he hoped he wouldn't have to do that. Undamaged merchandise was worth more money. If the dealer had to give medical attention to a catch, the hunter's fee was lowered. And Garrett needed money. He had rent and utility bills hanging over him that needed to get paid.

As he carried his catch down the street, the hunter ignored the curious stares of people in passing cars. He guessed it was sort of unusual to see a man carrying another man over his shoulder, at least outside of a wrestling match or a battlefield, but he didn't care. No one had ever called the police on him, and he hoped that would remain the case.

Turning down a side street, Garrett brought his prey to his parked truck. It was an older model, dented in a few places, but with a lot of character. Sort of like Garrett himself. There was a canopy over the bed to enclose whatever cargo he was carrying. Keeping Mark slung over his shoulder, the hunter used his other hand to reach into his pocket and pull out a set of keys. After looking around to make sure he was alone on the dark street, he unlocked the canopy and pulled his truck's tailgate down.

It was dark inside the canopy, but there was enough light from the moon and nearby street lamps to see what was inside. Two big duffel bags, military-style and stuffed to capacity lay on the floor of the pick-up bed. Each bag was big enough to hold a man inside, and that in fact was exactly what they both contained – one man in each. Hunter's prey, to be exact. One of the bags stirred at the noise and squirmed.

"Wh … happening … help …" a muffled voice came from the squirming bag. Without losing his grip on Mark, Garrett reached into the bed and gave the bag a punch in the general area of the stomach.

"Shut the fuck up!" the hunter snarled, and the man inside the bag yelped with pain and stopped moving. The hunter lowered his burden down onto the tailgate of the truck. Mark didn't move. Garrett opened a side panel just inside the canopy and pulled out a few coils of rope and some long strips of black cloth. He sat Mark down on the tailgate, then grabbed his wrists and tied them together with one of the ropes, pulling the knots tight. Then he did the same with the young man's ankles, anchoring them together with rope. One of the black cloths was wound around Mark's head then, covering his eyes and getting tied behind his head. Last but not least, the hunter shoved one of the cloths into Mark's mouth and then secured it in place with the last cloth, tying it around his head to hold the gag in.

Garrett checked over his work and was pleased. It wasn't high-tech or complicated bondage, but it was good enough for him. This guy wasn't going anywhere. After checking again that no one was watching, Garrett reached into the pick-up bed again and grabbed a third duffel bag, this one empty. The hunter maneuvered Mark into the bag head-first, stuffing him in until his entire body was contained inside the canvas sack. Then he closed the bag and pulled the drawstrings tight before tying them securely.

The hunter pushed his bagged prey into the pick-up bed with his other catches and closed the tailgate and canopy door securely.

When he was satisfied, Garrett got back into his truck and started up the engine. He found himself wiping his forehead with a dirty towel from the passenger seat. He was tired. Three catches in one night was a lot of work, he reflected.

He was still horny though, his big cock flopping around inside his camo pants ready for more action. He just might have to make use of one of his catches before he brought them to their new home. But he'd need to get to a more deserted spot for that. Garrett checked his watch and was happy to see that there was still time to get some fucking done before the deal closed for the night.

He drove around until he found another dark alley, this one between two closed office buildings. The hunter parked his truck among the shadows and got out. Going around to the rear of his vehicle, he opened the canopy and climbed in, closing it behind him.

Hmmm. Three catches. Which one should he fuck? He'd already shot a load into Mark, so he figured he'd use one of the others. Which of the other two would be hottest to fuck? Garrett decided on David, the guy he'd caught before Mark.

David had been hustling on the boulevard, giving his skinny 20-year-old body to anyone with a few bucks to share. It'd been easy to bag David – Garrett had simply pulled his truck over to the side of the road and got out, walking over to the young man. The hustler barely had time to introduce himself and ask the big man what he wanted, before he was punched in the face and knocked out cold.

After a quick look around to make sure no one was nearby, the hunter had tossed him over one shoulder and carried him to the back of his truck. He'd tied David's hands and legs together and duct-taped his mouth shut then stuffed him into one of the empty duffel bags in the back.

Now the hunter pulled the bag containing the hustler closer and untied the sack's drawstrings. He opened the bag, grabbed his prey's feet, and yanked his legs out to the waist. Garrett untied David's feet and removed his shoes, the pulled a switchblade out of his pocket. Extending the blade, he cut the young man's pants off and tossed them aside. Where David was going he didn't need pants. Or clothes.

Garrett hiked David's legs up onto his shoulders and undid his own belt. The hunter pulled his camo pants down far enough to allow his hard dick to pop out. Spitting into his hand for lubrication, the big man saw that his second catch of the night (David) was still knocked out from the punch he'd dealt him earlier. He figured he'd cold-cock the guy again if he woke up.

A few strokes with his sticky hand and Garrett's cock was ready for fucking. The hunter pulled the unconscious hustler's body closer and pierced him, leaving his torso, arms and head still in the bag. Burying his cock deep into David, the hunter fucked his catch hard, grunting like an animal. Within a few minutes, he was ready to come again. Gritting his teeth and closing his eyes, the hunter deposited his seed into the young man.

When he was done shooting, Garrett stuffed his cock back into his pants, then retied David's legs together and shoved him the rest of the way into the duffel bag and cinched it shut.

He had to get some sleep before he got up tomorrow. After jumping out of the canopy and locking it closed, Garret got back in the cab of his truck and started it up again. The hunter drove the rest of the way to his destination, an empty-looking office building in the city's grubby downtown.

He pulled the truck up to the loading dock at the back of the building and after making sure no one was watching, turned off the ignition and got out. Garrett opened the canopy and grabbed the duffel bag that contained his first catch of the night. He briefly considered taking two bags at once, then decided against it – didn't want to hurt his back. Leaning over, he hoisted the first duffel up and over his right shoulder. Locking the canopy once again, the hunter carried his catch to an unmarked door next to the loading dock. He knocked, then turned to face the domed camera on the wall to the left of the door.

After the person on the other end of the camera had gotten a look at him, the door was electronically unlocked with a loud click.

Garrett carried his prey into the building and the door closed behind him. He hefted the duffel bag on his shoulder and walked down the short corridor the door had opened onto. At the end of the hallway, another door buzzed open to admit him. The room he walked into was small and dimly lit, with a long counter and black curtains behind it. The man standing behind the counter had once been hot, but now looked gaunt and tired.

"Hey Jarvis," the hunter said as he carried the duffel bag over to the counter.

"Garrett," Jarvis said with a nod, "whatcha got for me?"

"Three catches tonight," Garrett said as he swung the bag down off his shoulder onto the counter.

"Let's take a look," Jarvis said, untying the bag's drawstrings. He opened the top of the sack and revealed the head of the hunter's first catch of the night. Together, Garrett and Jarvis pulled the young man out of the duffel bag and laid him on the counter.

He had short blond hair. His eyes were closed, and his chest expanded and contracted with deep breaths of unconscious sleep. His wrists and ankles were bound in the same way that Mark's were. Jarvis looked down at the captured young man, evaluating. The hunter was impatient; he wanted to know how much his catch was worth, but he knew better than to interrupt Jarvis. The dealer would give his appraisal when he was ready to.

The man behind the counter took the young man's chin in his hand and turned his head from side to side, getting a good look at his face, then checking his teeth. He lifted the catch's T-shirt to examine his flat, hard belly. He unbuttoned his jeans and pulled the young man's cock out, hefting it in his hand, checking it for size and weight. Then he looked up at Garrett.

"Not bad," he said, "you got more?"

"Yeah. Two more."

"Bring 'em in."

After the hunter had carried his other two catches into the room and Jarvis had taken his time evaluating them, the dealer looked up.

"I'll give you $500 each," he said.

"$1,500 for three catches?" said Garrett in disbelief. "I remember when you used to give me $1500 for each catch, and I was giving you a break!"

"Tough shit. $1,500."

"Come on Jarvis," the hunter said. "We go way back. Don't tell me demand is low, man, I follow the industry; demand's never been higher!"

"Take it or leave it."

"You're an asshole. I'll take it," Garrett said.

Jarvis pulled the cash out of a safe under the counter and handed it to the hunter.

"Give me my fucking bags back," Garrett said, and took them out of the dealer's hand. Tossing the empty sacks over his shoulder, the hunter left the building, swearing under his breath. How was a hunter supposed to earn a living if this was all he could make? He wondered. He could try to find another dealer, or he could shoot for more than three catches a night.

He was too tired to think about it now, he decided. The hunter threw the duffel bags in the back of his truck, got into the cab, and headed home, into the night.

# XI. SWEATY REVENGE

I didn't know how heartless I could be until I heard Brent screaming for mercy, and I ignored him. But the fucking bastard had it coming. It's important to understand that from the beginning.

My buddies and are aren't cruel by nature, not at all. But we can be mean motherfuckers when we get pushed too far, and that's exactly what this asshole did.

I don't know why Brent moved into our apartment building in the first place. He had to have known that it was mostly gay guys that lived there. It was pretty obvious, I mean, pretty much all of us had gay freedom flags or pink triangles or leather flags in our windows. You didn't have to be brilliant to figure it out.

Maybe he secretly wanted what ended up happening to him. But I don't know. I'm not one for psychoanalysis. I just do what I think is right.

And Brent had it coming, the little fucker.

He was cute. That almost made it worse – he was always a jerk, but add his good looks and we had one stuck-up bastard on our hands. He started soon enough. As soon as he moved in, he started acting as if he was better than the rest of us. Everyone in the place was familiar with everyone else – it was almost like college or high school all over again – we were a pack of guys that pretty much did everything together.

I mean, we all had our own lives, our own jobs, some of us even had boyfriends, but there was always the group of us at the apartment building to fall back on. You could always rely on the group to be there no matter what shit was going on in your life at the moment. The group would help you through it.

We all hung out together – swimming in the pool, sunbathing to soak up some rays, sometimes smoking cigars after sundown and shooting the shit. I won't bore you with long descriptions but leave it to this: Blond-haired Danny's excellent physique was always on display because he hardly ever wore a T-shirt; Ted was tall and black and looked like a football player; Jeff was dark-haired and skinny; Greg was Hispanic and sexy; auburn-haired Barry had an intensity that was all his own; and me, of course, tanned and burnished by the sun, hotter than sand on a beach.

If I do say so myself. (chuckle)

It started soon after Brent moved in. We wondered why he moved in at all, it wasn't like it was a secret the place was occupied by gays. It was certainly no place for a straight boy with a prejudice. Some straight guys are cool with gay guys, but Brent wasn't. He was pretty cute, like I said. He had reddish-blond hair and a goatee. It's funny how many things the straight fashion world has stolen from the gay fashion world – goatees, earrings, tattoos, piercing – and then forgotten where they came from. The point is Brent had a couple of earrings and a goatee. He sort of looked more gay than some of the guys in the complex. In any case, he was probably about 5'10", weighed 170, not gym-buffed but in shape.

He acted like he was better than the rest of us from the beginning. We'd smile at him and say, "Hey, how're you doing?" and not only would he not respond, he'd actually turn his face away as if we were being rude. After a while, he started swearing at us under his breath. Me and at least one other guy warned Brent about this, telling him it was uncool, that we wouldn't take that from him for very long.

The final straw came a few months later.

My twenty-year-old cousin, Louisa, came to visit me. She flew from Seattle to see me at least once a year and stayed with me a few days. All my friends had met her and liked her, and she them. Brent took an interest in her, too, but I didn't think much of it until it was almost too late. Louisa felt comfortable and at home in our apartment complex, she'd visited so many times. That was probably why she went to the laundry room un-escorted. I was working from home that day and on a tight schedule with a deadline approaching. When Louisa left the apartment figured, she was just going out to the pool.

A few minutes later, I heard her scream.

I jumped up from my desk and saw that the laundry hamper was gone. In that instant, I understood what was happening. She had gone to do the laundry but was now in trouble and needed my help.

I pounded on the wall and yelled to my adjoining neighbor.

“Barry! Call the others and get to the laundry room, NOW!”

I was already out my door when he hollered okay back to me. It didn’t even occur to me that my guys might not have been home – whatever was happening to my cousin, I was going to deal with it, with or without help. Racing around the pool to the stairs, I heard Louisa scream again. Our laundry room was on the basement level, below the first and second floors where the apartments were. I thundered down the stairs and slammed the door open.

Brent had Louisa up against the wall. Clothes were strewn all over the floor – there had been a struggle, and her T-shirt was torn. It looked as if Brent was trying to kiss her, and she was fighting him, but he was obviously stronger.

“What THE FUCK do you think you’re doing?” I hollered at the top of my voice. I ran into the room and pulled him away from her, just as my buddies ran down the stairs and stopped in the doorway, piling up against each other like in a cartoon.

It might’ve been funny if my cousin hadn’t been being assaulted.

“Get her out of here,” I said to Danny.

“Right,” he said and ran over to Louisa. She’d started crying, and Danny put his arm around her as he led her out of the laundry room and back up the stairs as quickly as possible. I looked over at the rest of the guys: Barry, Greg, Ted and Jeff and saw that they were ready; all they needed was a signal. We all knew what we had to do. I was so furious I was literally seeing red. Brent looked at us as if we were rude to interrupt him. He really didn’t see it coming – he must’ve really thought we wouldn’t do anything to him.

“What do you faggots want?” he sneered at us.

“We want you, you son of a bitch.” I said, and Ted and Greg, the two biggest guys, grabbed Brent, each one holding one of his arms.

"What the fuck are you doing?" Brent said as he struggled in the stronger men's grip. Jeff got behind him and clamped his hand over Brent's mouth, so he couldn't scream. Then I walked over and punched the asshole in the stomach, hard. All the air in Brent's lungs was forced out, and he doubled over in pain. I got myself between his legs and grabbed them up, one in each hand, and together with Ted and Greg lifted him completely off the ground.

He started struggling wildly, but when I hissed at him, "Knock it off or you'll get punched again, shithead!" he stopped.

We awkwardly carried Brent up the stairs out into the pool area. We were in luck, since none of our neighbors in the buildings next-door were looking out their windows at that exact moment. Danny and Louisa were out of sight, too, most likely in his apartment.

We bundled our captive into the first door we came to, which happened to be Ted's place. "Get something to gag him with," I said, and Jeff jumped to obey me. With Jeff's hand no longer covering his mouth, the bastard started screaming.

"Let me go you freaks!" he yelled. "You'll pay for this I swear you goddamn faggots!" Jeff came out of Ted's bedroom with a pair of socks. I hoped they were dirty and sweaty from the gym as he stuffed one in Brent's mouth and tied the other one around his head to hold it there.

"Bathroom!" I said and we lugged our prisoner across the living room into Ted's bathroom which was (lucky for us) quite large with its own bathtub. We ripped Brent's clothes off and tied his hands behind his back and his ankles together with towels.

Brent was nice-looking naked, with a dusting of hair on his chest, the same reddish-blond of the rest of his hair. He had light pale skin and an average-sized dick, soft of course while under attack. He struggled to talk, but his makeshift gag prevented anything but grunts to escape his mouth. Danny joined us then.

"Your cousin's in my apartment," he told me. "She's lying down. She doesn't know what we're doing."

"Good," I said, smiling maliciously down at the man in the tub. "This'll be our little secret."

"Are we gonna teach him a lesson, Scott?" Barry asked me with a big grin on his face.

"You know it," I answered. "We're gonna teach him that when a girl says 'No' it's time to take his FUCKING hands off her and keep his FUCKING dick in his pants."

Brent grunted loudly at that, but whether it was out of anger or fear I don't know. He tried to get himself up to his knees, but it was impossible to move with his hands tied behind him and his ankles tied together. He looked a little like a turtle trying to right itself after being flipped over on its back.

But I didn't even want him to have the satisfaction of struggling. I wanted him silent, submissive and immobile.

"Greg ..." I started.

"I'm way ahead of you, man," Greg said and brought his heavy-duty construction-booted foot down between Brent's legs, squashing the man's cock and balls under it. Brent bellowed in pain, loudly even with the gag obscuring most of it.

"You gonna hold still now?" I asked the writhing man in the tub. Brent nodded vigorously and stopped squirming, whining softly.

"I'd say some clothespins are in order, gentlemen," I said. My buddies murmured their approval, a few of them even laughed. I watched Brent's eyes dart around in confusion and desperation, as Ted ran out to get what was needed. He was back a second later with a big plastic bag full of clothespins.

I took one 'pin out and pinched Brent's right nipple with it, leaving it hanging off of him. The pin's greedy little jaws refused to release his tit. Pleased with my handiwork, I continued to attach pins to Brent, creating a line of them that led from his right tit to his left. The asshole stayed still, even though I could sense his growing anxiety and saw him flinch as each clothespin was affixed to him.

I was pleased with the nice horizontal line of pins I'd finished, but I wasn't done yet. Starting in the middle of the line, I created a vertical line that stretched from Brent's chest down to his navel. Now he had a nice T shape on him.

Now it was time for the main event.

"Get down on all fours, man!" I said sharply to Brent. He obeyed, and then I had him get partially out of the tub, so the lower half of him was hanging out, making his butt easily accessible.

"Ted," I said. "You got any condoms around here?"

"Right on, man!" he said, running out of the bathroom.

When Brent heard that and realized what was about to happen, he started screaming again, trying to stand up, to somehow get out of the tub. A few hard slaps to both sides of his face subdued him once again, as Ted returned the works.

We gang-fucked him then, all of us getting at least one turn in the saddle, each of us using a fresh rubber. Brent's asshole was virgin-tight, but a little patience and a whole lot of lube came through in the end. I took the first turn, so I could officially say I'd busted his cherry and been the first to screw our little straight boy neighbor. He tried to fight me, bucking like a bronco, but he knew he had no choice and gave up soon enough.

The whole time the clothespins remained attached to him, hanging off him like some kind of weird jewelry. The flesh around the pinch-points was white by now, blood blocked from entering there. Somehow, they all stayed on despite his thrashing around.

We all fucked him in our own way. Ted hard and fast like a man possessed, Greg taking his own sweet time, Barry raping like a wild man, Jeff gently like a lover, Danny with his strange stop-and-go, stop-and-go action and me, of course, deep and long so every thrust would remind him of the experience as it occurred. As long as he lived, Brent would never forget what happened to him that day.

Never forget what he had brought upon himself.

Hell hath no fury like a group of gay guys that gets pushed too far.

Because of his awkward position, slung face-down over the edge of the tub, it was hard to see Brent's cock. I don't know for sure, but I think I caught a few glimpses of it hard, but I could be wrong. I suppose it might be some kind of weird justice if he got off on what we were doing. But in my state of mind, I didn't want him to experience anything even remotely resembling pleasure, so I slapped his ass hard and tweaked his clothespins to make him as uncomfortable as possible.

When we were all done and had shot our loads, we all pulled our pants and shorts back up and looked down at our prisoner. Brent lay there, breathing heavily, waiting for his ordeal to end.

But it wasn't over yet.

I slapped his butt, saying, "All right, man. Stand up." There was no response. He just lay there without moving.

"Do what he says, you fucking asshole!" Greg said angrily as he kicked Brent. Slowly, Brent obeyed, standing up, so his clothespins were sticking straight out.

"It's time to lose the pins," I said, and we pounced on Brent, yanking the clothespins off of him roughly. Some of the guys slapped them off without even loosening the pin's grip on Brent's skin. Our straight boy started to scream, and I knew it was the pain from the blood rushing back into his pinched areas, suddenly freed from their clenching bondage. Lucky we had him gagged – these screams would've brought neighbors and police if heard beyond that room. We slapped and prodded the areas where the pins had been, irritating the already super-sensitive skin. Brent tried to twist away from us, but he was surrounded – the tub and the wall on one side and six men on the other.

There was nothing he could do, except take it.

When all the clothespins had been removed from him, I ordered him back into the tub, this time lying on his back. He obeyed, whining like an injured animal.

"All right, guys." I said. "Are we ready to show Brent here what we think of him?" My buddies laughed, pulling their soft dicks out, guessing what I had in mind.

We pissed on him. Six streams of urine curved through the air, the stinking liquid splattering down all over Brent. Some of it was dark yellow, some pale yellow, some almost clear, but whatever the color, our piss splashed down onto him and covered him. Some of it drained off to the sides, some was caught by the hair on his chest.

Brent, obviously disgusted, squirmed in the tub, but he knew as well as we did that there was nothing he could do about it.

"You're lucky you're gagged, you little shit," Greg said to Brent. "If you weren't you'd be getting some of this in your mouth. Our offender stopped moving then, his eyes full of resignation and fear. Soon enough we were out of piss, so we shook the last few drops out and pulled our pants up for the last time that day. It was over.

"I'm sick of this," I said, sneering down at the man in the tub. "And I'm sick of you. Get him outta here, dudes."

My friends untied Brent's wrists and ankles and helped him out of the tub. They wrapped him in towels so he wouldn't get piss on Ted's floor. Brent had been broken completely. He made no hostile move against us at all. He just leaned on the guys to help support himself as they walked him back out in the main room.

"Hey Scott!" Jeff said. "Are we gonna give him his clothes back?"

"Of course we are," I said, putting my hand on Brent's shoulder. "And to return the favor, he's never going to talk about this to anyone because if he does, we'll tell them what he tried to do to Louisa."

We gave Brent his clothes and shoved him out of Ted's front door. We watched him through the window hastily yank his shirt and pants back on before anyone could see him naked and dripping with piss. He ran to his apartment and was gone.

Nothing ever came of it. Apparently Brent followed through for us, not telling anyone what we had done. In any case, no cops showed up at our door charging us with assault. For his part, Brent was never rude to us again. He moved out of the complex a few weeks later, and we never saw him again. I guess we'll never know if he provoked us on purpose because he WANTED to get tortured and humiliated. A new guy, who was gay and cool, moved in to Brent's old place after he was gone, so no trouble there.

My buddies and I never spoke of Brent or what happened in Ted's bathroom ever again. But we had an understanding among us. If any more smart-ass straight boy assholes moved into our place, we weren't gonna wait till he tried to rape someone first. We'd teach him a lesson he'd never forget.

# XII. BEAR WORSHIP

I hadn't known what I was missing until the big hairy guy grabbed the back of my head and forced it down into his furry crotch.

Guys like me usually hang out in groups, I guess. I'm hot, blond, swimmer's body, done my share of print work and even some porno now and then. I'd only ever had sex with guys like me. We are all pretty much the same: hot, young, slender, hairless bodies, you know the type. Lots of people think we don't have a thought in our heads, and I'll admit that's true sometimes.

But, not me. I'm pretty damn smart, thank you very much. Smart enough to know that there was something missing from my life. I didn't know what it was, but I knew I never really felt satisfied. When I was on my back getting fucked by one of my buddies, I got hard and shot off and everything, but it just didn't take me anywhere. You know what I mean? I always thought sex was supposed to be incredible, amazing, not just sort of ho-hum-are-you-almost-done? Like it was when we did it.

I guess it was like we were a bunch of boys, just hanging out together, fucking each other 'cause there was no one else to fuck us. It got kinda weird after a while. Sometimes it was almost like getting nailed by my twin, we were all so much alike.

Now some guys might get off on that, and more power to them. But, not me. To me it was like kissing myself in the mirror, you know what I mean? There was nothing there.

I didn't know what to do about it, though. I'd heard talk of older men, but I was never thought that was the answer to my problem.

But, it was.

Because one day I was walking out of the local gay video store, and I saw a sight that made my jaw drop and my dick get stiff. This huge shit-kicking truck was pulling up to the curb. It was a monster rig with a huge open pickup in back. In it were three big dog carriers, two of them with dogs inside. They looked like Huskies or something. The third cage was empty. Out of the truck stepped two of the hottest – no make that the hottest – men I'd ever seen.

The driver was tall, probably 6'4" or so, with a full beard and mustache. His flannel shirt was open and the fur on his chest was sticking out. The sleeves had been cut off so his big beefy arms were visible all the way up to his powerful shoulders. He was strong and muscular, with a little bit of a belly hanging over his belt. Rugged torn jeans covered his legs down his dirty work boots.

His buddy was just like a smaller version of him. He had just a mustache and was very hairy also. They were both wearing baseball hats. I was totally struck by the sight of them. I literally couldn't take my eyes off of them. A word appeared in my mind: BEAR. I'd heard the word before, but never really thought about it.

But, I sure did now. These guys were bears. That's what they were! And man, were they hot! I watched them walk around to the back of the truck, mesmerized by the way they moved, the easy-going way they walked, the unconscious masculinity they projected, the macho confidence they had in spades.

The bears put the truck's tailgate down and unlocked the dogs' cages. Expertly, they attached leashes to the animals' collars and helped them down onto the pavement.

"Come on boys," the big bear said, as they pulled the dogs into position next to them. The two guys started walking then, heading away from the store down to the nearby boulevard. Looks like it was dog walking time. Well, I couldn't let these guys out of my sight. I headed out of the store and trailed behind them, seeing I wasn't the only guy noticing these two. Left and right men were turning to follow their progress.

But the bears had eyes only for each other and their dogs, keeping them under tight control. I followed them for a long time, until I realized they probably knew I was trailing them. After a while, the pedestrian traffic on the street thinned out, until there was hardly anyone left. I knew I was walking way out of my way, but I had to keep following them. The idea of letting the bears out of my sight was unthinkable. I was riveted by the sight of them. They were so hot, so manly, so very different from myself and the other twinky boys I hung around with. Here were some real men, some bears!

Suddenly they turned left into an alley. Not even thinking to listen for their retreating footsteps, I just turned the corner and almost ran smack into them. They were waiting for me, looking at me with their hard stern faces. Their dogs eyed me suspiciously.

“Why are you following us?” the big bear said.

“I ...I ...” I stuttered. “I was just ...”

“He’s nice looking, isn’t he, Robert?” the smaller one said. Robert shrugged his shoulders.

“He’s a twink,” the big man said, as he leaned over to stroke his dog’s head. “You know guys like him, Bill. They’re all the same. Vain, selfish, shallow.”

Used to being praised and adored for my hot looks, I was a little angry. How dare this guy insult me? Who did he think he was? But for some reason my cock had come to attention in their presence.

Robert looked at me again, a sneer on his lips.

“He’s harmless. All twinks need is some bear dick up their butts, then they’d be a lot nicer to be around.”

Bill laughed. I couldn’t believe what I’d heard. My heart was pounding.

“What did you say?” I said.

“You heard him,” Bill said. “All you pretty boys need is some real men’s cocks in you, and your attitude would change.”

“Yes, Sir.” The words came out of my mouth before I could stop them. I don’t know where they came from, but there they were, out in the open, too late to take back.

Robert looked at Bill and grinned.

“Get him,” he said.

Frightened, I tensed to run, but I was too late. Bill tossed his leash to Robert and jumped behind me, blocking my escape.

"Wait a second!" I said.

"You asked for it, twink," Bill said as he grabbed my shoulders and pushed me down on my knees. The dogs jumped to their feet, growling at me. I was amazed that no one had seen us yet, but I realized we were standing in the shadow of a building. Even if there had been anyone around, they wouldn't have seen us.

But maybe they could hear me.

"Help!" I started to yell. The dogs began barking with excitement.

"God, listen to this," Robert said, then turned to the dogs. "Shut up!" he yelled and instantly they stopped. The bear tied their leashes to handle of a nearby garbage dumpster before looking back at me. "Looks like we'll have to fill this one's mouth to get him quiet."

Bill laughed again.

"Looks that way," he said, and suddenly shoved me forward. I yelled in fear and surprise as I tumbled towards Robert. Before I could crash into the ground with my face, the big bear had grabbed me and put his hand on the back of my head.

"Keep a lookout, Bill," he directed his buddy, as he undid his pants with the other hand. I barely had time to see the big hard cock surrounded by its nest of pubic hair before my face was pushed into it.

"Suck it, twink," I heard his voice above me. "Take my big bear cock in your mouth and keep quiet." Without thinking, I obeyed him. The huge organ forced itself into me, pushing against the back of my throat. I started frantically sucking it, slurping it in and out of my mouth like there was no tomorrow. I'd never felt anything like this before, it was fucking incredible. For the first time in my life, I was really having sex. I was being put to good use, taking care of a real man. Sex with my buddies was nothing compared to this. And I knew why. The bears were right. We were twinks. We didn't know what being a real man was all about.

But, these guys did. And I was going to learn from them. There on my knees in the dirty alley I decided this was what I wanted to do with my life. I was going to serve these men so well they wouldn't want to let me go.

"Mmmmmm," the bear murmured above me. "That's good, pretty boy, you're doing just fine ..."

"Robert?" Bill said behind me.

"Yeah?"

"Can I get me some of that? Please? There's no one coming, it's late ..." he pleaded.

"Sure," Robert said. "Why not? But we'll trade places." He pulled his dick out of my mouth and I felt empty without it. "Get those shorts down boy, let's see that butt of yours."

"Yes, Sir!" I said as I shucked my shorts down to my ankles. My bare ass was exposed now. Bill whistled.

"You should see this butt, Robert," he said.

"I'm going to," the big bear said as he gently pushed his friend out of the way. "I'm going to plow this pretty twinky butt. You get his mouth. I don't want him yapping again."

I braced myself, my dick aching now that it was free. Bill unsnapped his pants and forced me down onto his thick pecker with both hands. I started choking immediately, gagging and hacking loudly. The smaller bear's dick was not as long as Robert's, but it was sure thicker. Meanwhile, the big bear had grabbed me by the hips and was lining himself up for penetration. He hocked up some spit and then I guess greased up his cock with it, because a second later I felt his big knob pushing its way at my eager hole.

Nothing like this had ever happened to me before. I was on the ground in an alley, getting stuffed at both ends by the hottest men I'd ever seen. It was unbelievable.

I grabbed my straining dick and started pumping it. Robert reamed me, pushing into me with the bully club between his legs. It felt like I was getting split open as he popped past my sphincter ring and shoved it in as far as it would go. Slobbering all over Bill's fat cock, I pushed my butt back, shoving myself further onto the rear intruder. The big bear started really fucking me, holding my hips for balance and to time his thrusts right. It was incredible to be used that way, by a real man, just used for his pleasure.

I was loving every second of it. This is what I'd been missing, this is what all my friends and I had never realized was out there for us. This is what we were good for.

My climax was getting closer and closer. I moaned around Bill's dick as I felt it welling up inside me.

"That's it, pretty boy," Robert said as he fucked me. "Push back on my big bear cock, you've been needing this for a long time ..." The smaller bear groaned in delight as I started impaling myself on his dick, taking it down my throat further than I thought was possible. Robert's balls were slapping against my ass cheeks as he pushed in and out.

"Robert, I'm gonna unload, man," Bill said.

"Good!" his friend said. "Give this twink a good load."

And then he was shooting, his warm milky cum coating my mouth and sliding down my throat. The feel of it filling me up combined with the big hairy man behind me, plowing my ass, was too much for me. I had to let it out. I started to scream, and Robert clamped his hand over my mouth as I pumped my dick and came. My jizz shot out and landed on the pavement, painting it white. The orgasm shuddered through me, but it wasn't over yet.

"My turn," Robert said as he started porking me faster and faster. "I'm gonna fill up this end of you, twinky boy, yeah, fill you up with some nice hot bear cum ..."

His dick swelled up in my ass and fired off, once, twice, three times, shooting his jizz into me. It was so hot it was like being on the receiving end of a flame-thrower.

When he was done I sank down to me knees.

"Thank you, Sir ..." I said, looking up at both of them. "Thank you, Sir, thank you, Sir ..."

The bears pulled their pants back up and started untying the dogs, who'd been watching anxiously the whole time.

"Let's go, boy," Robert said. "Get those shorts back on. It's late."

Too full of cum and pleasure to think, much less question, I obeyed silently and happily. I followed the bears back the way we had come, trailing behind the dogs. When we got to their parked truck, it was dark and the video store had closed.

Robert and Bill helped their dogs get back up into the truck and into their cages.

"Shuck those clothes off, Twink," Robert said.

"I'm sorry, Sir?" I asked.

"You heard him!" Bill said. "And that's your name now. When we call Twink, we want you. You got that?"

"Yes, Sir," I said, delirious with excitement and disbelief. I took my clothes off and Robert tossed them into a nearby trash can. Then he tapped the tailgate with his fist.

"Up, Twink," he said. "Get up here!"

I obeyed, jumping up and landing on all fours in the back of the truck.

"Looks like that third cage'll come in handy after all," Robert said as he stroked my hair like he had his dog earlier.

"Good boy, Twink," Bill said as he petted my back. I thrilled to the feel of their hands on my naked body. My cock was already hard again. "Good boy."

"Get in your cage, boy," Robert said. Obediently, I trotted over to the empty cage and got inside. It was just big enough for me. I settled down onto the blanket that had been placed on the floor. I was so happy I couldn't think straight. What was happening to me was bizarre, unbelievable, and yet the most totally hot and mind-blowing thing ever.

After closing the tailgate of the truck, the bears got into the cab. Bill slid open the window that connected the back to the cabin.

"Looks like we got ourselves a new bitch, Bill," the big bear said.

“Looks that way,” the smaller bear said.

And as the truck started and pulled out into the street and drove away, as I felt the wind whip through my hair, as I sniffed my new home and panted happily with my new brother dogs, I knew that I had found my real life. I was not destined for a life of modeling, porno and getting fucked by other pretty boys, do you know what I mean?

I was destined for a life of bear worship.

# XIII. BONDAGE SURPRISE

I always loved surprises. My ex, Randy, had hated them. Maybe that was one reason we broke up.

It all started on my first night in my new place. I had just moved into this single apartment in a nice new building. My stuff was all there, but hardly any of it was unpacked. Aside from my TV, VCR and a few other essentials, everything else was still stacked in boxes that I didn't feel like emptying.

I was bored and lonely, I guess. Randy and I had called it quits a few months before, and I hadn't had any decent sex since. There was an itch in my crotch that got hotter every day. Figuring I had nothing better to do, I grabbed an old porn mag out of one of the boxes and plopped down on the floor. I leafed through the pages and the pictures started a major hard-on growing in my boxers.

Splashy drawings of naked men and boys in bondage filled my vision. Their eyes seemed to follow me when I turned my head. When I found my favorite picture, I stopped and looked at it long and hard.

It was a picture of a man tied to a bed. Young and hot, with a tremendous boner sticking up like a periscope in a war movie, the guy had rope wrapped around his wrists and ankles. The ropes had been stretched tight and tied off to the bed-posts. Grimacing in either pain or pleasure, the boy looked ripe and ready for plowing.

I loved the picture because it reminded me so much of what Randy and I used to do. Almost every night I'd tie that hot little boy to our bed and screw his ass till he moaned for mercy. Then, and only then, did I let loose and shoot a nice load of cum into him. The guy in the picture looked a lot like Randy, too. They both have those floppy bangs that so many boys like these days. Thin, pretty face and a body so steely and sculpted it looked like there was no flesh on it at all. They both were blond, even down to their pubes.

Fucking Randy was the best part of our relationship. We never got along too well, as you might have figured since we broke up. But the sex was great. I absolutely loved fucking him, and he got off on it, too, blowing his own cum as soon as he felt my boner spurting inside him.

I used to tie him up lying on his back. None of that bottom-on-his-stomach rear entry shit for me. I liked to see his eyes, liked to see the passion and struggle and ecstasy in them as I took him and made him mine, night after night after night. He never did the same to me. I thought myself too much of a top to take the submissive position like that.

Uncomfortable pressure in my boxers made me squirm around on the floor and re-adjust myself. My own meat was getting bigger and bigger. If I wasn't careful there'd be pre-cum stains on my new floor before long. Who gives a shit, I thought. There's going to be plenty of them before I move out of here, so why bother putting it off?

I suddenly realized how much I wanted to tie somebody up. Somebody hot, like Randy. That feeling of power, of control, of mastery over another man was intoxicating. I wanted it badly. Grabbing a local rag out of another box, I turned to the middle section where the phone sex ads were. There were so many of them, how to choose? There had to be at least one of them with a picture of a guy tied up, yeah, there was.

I knew it was a long shot, calling these lines was always a gamble, but I figured I had to try. My boner was starting to leak, and I knew just jerking it off wouldn't satisfy me, not tonight. I just had to tie up a guy on my bed.

I picked up my portable phone and started dialing. The connection was made, and after wading through the maze of key-pad commands, a voice was in my ear.

"Hello?" it said. Young, I thought, probably early twenties. That's a good start.

"Hello?" I answered back.

"Hello? Are you there?"

"Yeah. What's your name?" I asked.

"Rex," the voice said.

"How old are you, Rex?"

"Twenty-one. What's your name?"

"Jack," I said. I wondered if I might have been lucky and gotten a good one right off. If I played my cards right, I might have this kid bound and gagged within an hour.

"Jack," Rex repeated. "I like that name. How're you doing tonight?"

"Great," I said. "Just to save time, I'll tell you what I look like. I'm about six foot, blond, blue eyes, good bod."

"Yeah?" he said. "I'm 6'2", dark hair and eyes, and I'm real muscular."

Mmmm, he sounded tasty, if a little too tall. I wanted him there with me. But I still had some scoping out to do.

"Rex?" I asked.

"Uh huh ..."

"Have you ever been tied up before?"

There was silence for a minute. Did I blow it? No, he wouldn't have called this line unless he was at least curious.

"A couple times." he said. "It was pretty hot."

"Yeah, it is," I said, relief flowing through me. "You know what I think, Rex?"

"No, what?"

It was time to pull the lever and hope for three cherries.

"I think I'd like to tie you up tonight."

"You do, huh?" No pause this time.

"Yeah," I said, rubbing my crotch through my shorts. "A lot."

"I think I could be up for that," Rex said.

"Cool," I said. "You like surprises?"

"Love 'em ..."

"You ever play games?"

“What kind of games?” he asked.

“Well, there’s this game I used to play with my boyfriend. We called it ‘Surprise’,” I said.

“Oh yeah? How did you play?” Rex asked.

“Well,” I said. “I’d start out by blindfolding myself, getting myself ready to be tied up before he got home from work, then he’d come in to the bedroom like he was going to finish the job.”

“What was the surprise?”

“As soon as I felt him touch me, I pulled off the blindfold and grabbed him. I’d yell ‘Surprise!” and throw him down on the bed, tie him up and fuck him.”

Rex let all his breath out.

“Wow, that sounds really hot. Are you for real?”

“As real as you,” I said. Light from the hallway spilled into the living room, and I could see the shape of my dick tenting my underwear.

“Where do you live?” he asked.

As I gave him my address I could hardly believe I had scored so quickly . But it was crazy to get mixed up with people you met on phone lines and computer bulletin boards, wasn’t it? Usually, yeah, but there was something about this kid that made me want to be with him now, right now.

“So I’ll leave the door unlocked, and sit on my bed blindfolded ...” I started.

“And I’ll come in and we’ll play ‘Surprise’,” he finished.

“Yeah ... I can hardly wait, Rex.”

“Me either, Jack,” he said.

“I’ll be there in a little while. Be ready.”

I hung up the phone, hardly able to believe my luck. Was this too good to be true? Maybe, but the guy had sounded so into it that he had to be real. Besides, I was tough and knew how to take care of myself. If he gave me any trouble, I'd kick his ass out the door, settle for a good jerk-off session and be done with it.

Now I had to get ready.

Quickly I closed all the drapes and blinds and unlocked the front door. I let my boxers fall to the carpet, and my cock flexed outward like the branch of a tree. After a few more preparations, I went to the bedroom. It was still bare and empty looking. I hadn't unpacked much in here either. As I shut the blinds, I glanced outside. It was a gorgeous night, the moon red and bursting like a ball-sack full of cum and the stars shining like a thousand highlights on a gigantic studded harness.

I got a few more things ready then sat myself down on my bed. With my foot I opened the bedside table drawer. When Rex came in he couldn't miss it, it was so overflowing with rope, cuffs and other bondage stuff. I pulled a blindfold out and pulled it over my eyes.

Just in time, too. I heard the front door creaking open. My dick was dripping with anticipation. I hadn't played this game with anyone since Randy left. The potential danger of inviting a total stranger into my apartment just added to my excitement.

Rex closed the door. Any second I expected to hear his steps walking the short distance from the main room to the bedroom. But I didn't. There was nothing to hear. No footsteps. Had he left? Had the sound of the door closing been Rex leaving?

Then I heard a noise. He was still here, all right. But he was in the main room. What was he doing there? Didn't he see my boxers lying on the floor? He didn't have to be a rocket scientist to find his way back here. Didn't he want to start the game?

I could hardly wait to jump him, tie him up and fuck the shit out of him. I wanted to say something, but the tension was so thick you could hang a tit clamp on it. If I said anything it would ruin it, I knew, so I kept my mouth shut.

Finally, the sound of his footsteps started moving toward the bedroom. At last, I thought, now the fun'll begin. Closer and closer he came until he was right at the side of the bed where I was sitting.

I could hear his breathing, hot, heavy and close. He was right next to me. It was almost time. I heard him start to lean forward, toward me. At that second, I reached up and tore the blindfold off, getting ready to shout the word ...

... but a gag was shoved into my mouth before I could make any noise. What the fuck was going on? This wasn't how the game went. I started to stand up, but he was on top of me. In a split second a hundred thoughts raced across my mind.

One of them was that Rex was incredibly hot – dark olive-skinned, probably Italian, long hair, eyes that were so black you couldn't see where the irises ended and the pupils began, and big, 6'2" like he said, and strong, his muscular forearms were practically bursting out of his shirtsleeves. His mouth was big and sensuous, curling into a wicked grin.

Another was that he wasn't acting right: Randy had always been startled when I yanked the blindfold off, jumping back and yelping like a frightened puppy no matter how many times we played the game. Rex hadn't batted an eye, but continued his bee-line right for me.

Another was surprise at my body's reaction: my hard-on had stayed up, maybe even gotten harder – I would've thought it would gone down when something as weird as this happened.

Rex grabbed me by the shoulders and threw me backward onto my bed. I was so stunned my reflexes, were slower than usual. By the time I tried to move and get off the bed, the bigger man had already jumped me, something in his hand. Before I knew what was happening, he had slapped a pair of handcuffs on one of my wrists and was fastening the other end to my bed post. Trying to protest, my yells were cut off my the gag. A second later, Rex had done the same thing to my other wrist, cuffing it to the bed post on the opposite side.

With the agility of a jungle cat, the man jumped off the side of the bed and yanked something up off the floor I couldn't see. Then he was fastening leather ankle cuffs to my feet and locking them down at the bottom of the bed. He smiled at my struggling as if it amused him, easily overpowering me.

Then he was done and crossed his arms while he looked over his handiwork.

I looked down at myself, not believing it.

We had agreed that I was going to jump him and tie him up, and there I was, trussed up just like I used to do to Randy with this hot stud standing at the foot of my bed with a big smile on his face.

"Surprise," Rex said.

"You gotta be fucking kidding," I tried to say, but the gag didn't let anything out of my mouth but muffled grunts.

"You look good this way, Jack," he said.

Fuck you, I angrily thought, wondering why my dick was still hard. Rex walked back around and sat down next to me.

"I like you like this. Maybe I'll just leave you this way and go."

I frantically shook my head, my eyes pleading. If he left me like this, I'd never get loose. But wasn't it kind of hot, being in this guy's power? No, he could turn out to be a psychopath or something. I liked how he smelled, it wasn't a cologne scent, it was just a musky natural body odor; it made my dick harder.

But wait a minute, I was angry. This son of a bitch had gone back on our agreement – we had made a deal and he had broken it. I was going to kick his ass when I got out of this.

If I got out of this, I realized. Maybe I'd better cooperate with him.

"I'm going to take the gag out, Jack ..." Rex said. "But only if you promise not to yell for help. If you do, it'll go right back in. I'm about twice as strong as you, if you haven't figured that out yet. Do you promise?"

I nodded. Anything to get that thing out.

He lifted my head and unfastened the gag. As soon as he pulled it out, I started talking.

"Now listen, asshole," I said. "What the hell do you think you're doing? If you don't let me loose in ten seconds ..."

With an unimpressed look on his face, Rex shoved the gag back into my mouth and my tirade was cut short. I tried to force it out with my tongue, but it was too late, he'd already re-fastened it. I struggled against the bonds, but I knew I wasn't nearly strong enough to break them.

"What am I doing, Jack?" he said. "I was going to ask you the same question."

I stopped struggling for a second to look at him with questioning eyes. He grinned again.

"What are you doing, Jack? You told me you loved surprises ... well, I bet your boyfriend never did this with you, did he?"

I shook my head, wondering where he was going with this.

"I'd say I've given you a pretty damn good surprise, haven't I?"

I just stared at him, suddenly confused. Rex put his hands on my chest and started massaging my pecs, kneading them in his big firm palms. It felt good. But I didn't want to feel good. I wanted to get out of this. Or did I? Maybe that was why I was confused.

The probing hands moved to my nipples and began gently tweaking them. It was hot, I couldn't deny it. My dick was raging. Rex followed my eyes and smiled again. God, he was even more handsome when he smiled like that. Two rows of even white teeth that lit up his face.

He put his hand to his mouth and licked his palm, then wrapped his fist around my boner. Oh, man! It felt so fucking hot. I was totally in this man's power, bound and gagged, with my cock in his hand. I felt a little trickle of pre-cum slide down my cockhead onto Rex's gripping hand. He saw it too and his smile widened. His hand gave my dick a few little strokes that made me gasp through the gag before he let go.

"And all the thanks I get for giving you a new surprise is name-calling and angry words, Jack? I'm disappointed in you."

His smugness was driving me crazy, but his touch and the feel of him was making me crazy in a different way.

"You need to be punished," he said.

Oh shit I thought. What the fuck is he going to do?

“First,” Rex said, the grin never leaving his face. “I don’t like that mouth of yours, so it’s going to stay filled. No more talking for you tonight.”

I must have let out a little moan or whine or something because he laughed at me.

“You can make all the noise you want, Jack, no one’s going to hear you. No talking.”

He stood up and went to the end of the bed near my trussed-up ankles where he had gotten the foot cuffs. He leaned down, and when he came back toward me something long and shiny was dangling from his hand.

“Second,” he said as he sat down next to me again. “I think you’ll need a little pain to remind you to be more respectful of me, a little more grateful, if I ever let you talk again.”

Too late I realized what he had picked up. Not that it would have made a difference anyway. They were tit clamps. The tiny toothy mouths seemed to grin at me as Rex slowly lowered them down to my chest. Then he attached them to me, and they were biting into my nipples. I whimpered through the gag as the sharp little fuckers sank into my tender flesh. Those were going to kill when they came off. I remembered how Randy had screamed when I pulled off clamps that had been on him a while. It always made me hot and horny.

I wondered if it did the same for Rex.

For some reason, I found myself hoping that it did.

Ouch! I was brought back to reality by ragged little slivers of pain from my tits. Rex was flicking the clamps with his fingers, making them bob up and down like oil wells. I closed my eyes. It was strange pain, unlike anything I’d felt before. Somehow it seemed to be a mixture of pleasure and pain, one second hurting and the next glowing.

Rex’s voice came to me as if in a dream.

“You know what, Jack?” he said. I moaned in answer. “I think there’s something here you’re not telling me ... and maybe it’s something you haven’t even told yourself.”

I didn't know what the hell he was talking about. But, it didn't matter because he had started running his hands up and down my chest. Every time his hands got close to my hard cock, I shivered. I desperately wanted him to touch it again, to take it in his hand and stroke it. Then it happened. One of his hands closed over my engorged organ and the other took my balls in its palm. Aahh, it felt so good! He stroked me a few times, and I pulled against my bondage. I was tied up good and tight. Again, I had the strange feeling like that was good, that I was glad I was in the place I was in.

His hands moved off my chest and I was left panting, my chest heaving up and down. If he stroked me a couple more times, I was going to come, I just knew it.

Then I felt him unfastening the gag again. I wondered why, he had told me no more talking, that my mouth was going to be filled up. Just then he leaped onto me, straddling my face, and yanking open his jeans shoved his own boner between my lips as soon as the gag was out of the way.

It was so fucking hot. His big hard meat was in my mouth, and I was just couldn't help sucking like a baby with a bottle. It tasted so good. I loved the feel of that firm hard pole inside me. I could hear Rex murmuring in approval above me. I glanced up and saw him looking down at me, that grin on his face again as he starting fucking my mouth.

No more sucking now. All I could do was give his dick the best ride it had been on in months. Carefully keeping my teeth out of the way, I formed my mouth into a soft warm tunnel of pleasure for him to ream and plow as much as he wanted.

"That's it, Jack," I heard his voice from high above me. "Take it all, serve my hot dick with your mouth ... don't hold back, give me everything you've got ..."

Every nerve in my body was on fire. The feel of his weight on top of me, holding me down, as if I wasn't already tied to the bed, almost made me shoot off like his stroking me nearly did. I was super-sensitive, as if all my senses were on the alert. I was so entranced by the pleasure of his cock in me that it seemed like my tongue was memorizing the welcome intruder, committing every vein and contour of it to memory.

I slobbered up spit and bathed his meat with it, slicking my tongue all around with as much energy as I could. He started slamming me harder, really screwing my mouth. His dick was hitting the back of my throat every few seconds as he plunged in and out, in and out. There was no doubt about it. I liked his cock filling my mouth more than the gag. Little tremors shot through his dick like electricity in my mouth. It felt as if he was going to shoot off. That must have been why he pulled out, leaving a trail of spit down my chest. My mouth felt empty and lonely without him, but that was fixed soon enough. True to his word, Rex gagged me again.

I didn't know when my anger had changed to passion, but somewhere along the line it had. Instead of being upset with him, I found myself grateful for the experience he was giving me. Everything was new and exciting, and I couldn't wait to see and feel what came next.

The answer was fast on its way.

"I'm going to untie your legs, Jack," he said. "But only if you promise not to try to kick me or escape in any way. Do you promise?"

I nodded my head vigorously, my nostrils flaring in anticipation. A second later, I heard the sound of the ankle cuffs clattering to the floor, and Rex's strong hands wrapping around my legs and lifting them up in the air.

Now I knew what was coming all right, and I couldn't wait. It had been years since I'd been fucked, and I guess I didn't think about it much. But now, it was all I could think about. I wanted that hot cock that had just been in my mouth to be up my ass, reaming and plowing me like I used to do to Randy.

Rex reached down to the floor to get one more thing, than leaped astride me again, this time further down between my legs. Making sure I could see him doing it, he tore open the small square package and unrolled the condom down his long erect dick. I wanted that thing in me so bad. I rubbed my legs up and down his sides as if I could pull him inside me. He got into a comfortable position and leaned into me. I felt the hungry cock feeling around my asshole, sniffing it like a dog would sniff out a rabbit. Licking his hand again, Rex slimed up his dick with it. He hadn't used lube once, just his own spit. For some reason that totally turned me on. It was so manly, as if he didn't need anything to fuck me but himself, just him, nothing else.

He started pushing inside me, and it hurt like hell. I yelled through the gag. He worked his cockhead around the entrance, tenderizing me, trying to get me ready. But I was still too tight. He couldn't even get his fingers in there when he tried.

Then he got that grin again, and I didn't know if I should be excited or scared.

Without any warning Rex yanked the tit clamps off me. The screams came even before the blood rushed back into my nipples. With my eyes clenched shut, I yelled and screamed into the gag, it was the worst pain I'd ever felt before, worse than appendicitis, worse than breaking my arm in fourth grade.

I opened my eyes, hoping to plead with Rex to make it stop, please, I'd do anything, and I saw him moving towards me and away, towards me and away, grinning all the while.

It almost looked like ...

... he was fucking me. Oohh, shit! The pain dissolved away into ecstatic pleasure. I was realizing he had used the tit clamps to distract me while he forced his tool into my butt. God, it felt so fucking good I couldn't believe it.

I was like an electric light grid that was getting a tremendously strong power source plugged into me. Every part of my body was glowing, pulsing, flashing in the same rhythm Rex was fucking me, in and out, in and out, in and out. It was so euphoric. I may have almost passed out more than once, his grin filling my vision until it was all I could see and the rest of him seemed to disappear as if the Cheshire Cat had turned himself into a *Playgirl* centerfold.

Straining against my bondage, I had never felt so good. The few times I had gotten fucked before had been boring, nothing special, so dull I didn't know what all the fuss was about. But now it was a whole different story. Bound and gagged in my own house by this hot stud, totally naked while he kept all his clothes on, just his cock sticking out of his jeans and into my asshole.

The combination of feelings was pushing me to the point of coming. Rex's cock fucking my butt, the feeling of being tied down and unable to move, a prisoner in my own apartment with this vision of a man above me, taking his pleasure out of me however he wanted it. It was almost too much.

Then he spoke again.

"I know what you're not telling me, Jack," he said. "I'm going to say it, so we'll both hear it out loud ..." I was hardly listening, so enthralled by his dick reaming my butt, but I kept my ears open.

"You always wished Randy would do this to you ..."

Oh my God, he knew.

"You know in your heart and soul you're a cocksucking bondage boy that needs to get tied up and fucked by a man more than you need food and water..."

He was speeding up his strokes, matching the growing intensity of his words and my feelings.

"... but you could never admit it to yourself or anyone else. But now you can because it's okay to be what you truly are ..."

I could feel my body tensing up, shoving me toward the point of no return.

"... the other thing you didn't tell me was the last rule of the game: that whoever gives the other guy the bigger surprise wins ..."

He thrust his dick into me as far as it would.

"Surprise!" he yelled as he grabbed my dick and stroked it fast.

The truth and clarity of his words hit me with the force of a hurricane, and the confusion vanished. With that I fell over the edge and came, shooting huge loads all over myself, him, my bed, even the walls. The white-hot orgasm shook my body to the core. A sunrise of ecstasy was happening inside me, the rays of light hitting every inch of me and lighting me up like the aurora borealis. I screamed into the gag, even louder than I had when he'd pulled the clamps.

"Oh yeah!" Rex yelled, and I could feel his cock flex inside me, jetting burst after burst of spunk into the condom. In that second it was like we were a single being, fused together by passion and two hot dicks. Without a doubt it was the hottest fuck I'd ever had.

He slowly pulled out his cock out of me and carefully removed the condom, tying it off at the end. He fell forward onto me, wrapped his arms around me, and hugged me tight. I wanted to squeeze him back, but could not bend my arms to embrace him. We lay there, enjoying the afterglow and the feel of our bodies next to each other.

After a few minutes, Rex put the blindfold back on me. I didn't want it on, but he'd just given me so much pleasure I wasn't going to give him any trouble. He untied me, releasing my aching arms from the bed-posts. The gag was pulled out of my mouth.

"Jack," he said. "You did real good. Now leave the blindfold on until after you hear me leave."

I wanted to protest, ask him to stay, at least get his phone number, but I couldn't. I felt an obligation to play by his rules after all the hot action. So I just lay there, panting, still trying to catch my breath after my mega-orgasm. I listened to him pack up his stuff, then walk out into the main room. He walked to the door, paused for a minute, then I heard the door open and close.

Rex was gone.

Pulling the blindfold off, I sat up slowly. What an incredible experience. I looked around my room, hoping to find some trace of him left. Nope, nothing, not a thing besides my cum splatters on my body, the bed and the walls. He'd even taken the tied-off condom full of his jizz that I'd hoped to keep as a souvenir.

Damn him.

Rubbing my eyes, I went out to the main room. Nothing disturbed, nothing out of place. Looks like he didn't notice the closet door was open a crack. He had given me a serious surprise, yet I wondered, as I walked over to the closet, if he might not be even more surprised when he saw what was inside.

I opened the closet to reveal, on an old tripod, one of my two videocassette cameras. Obsessed with recording my sex with people, I had bought them several years ago and had taped all the sex I had at home since. It was too weird for most people, which is why I stopped telling guys about it. It was another reason Randy wanted out of the relationship. He was freaked out that there were hundreds of hours of him getting tied up and fucked on videotape.

I stopped the camera and rewound the tape before pulling it out. Back in the bedroom, I opened the closet doors where my other camera had been taping from. Taking that tape out, too, I plopped down on my bed to watch what had just happened.

As I did, I found myself grinning like Rex had. He thought he was the one with the big surprise, but I was the one who had given him the biggest one. I popped the bedroom tape into the VCR first, since that's where the action happened. Sometimes I wondered why I bothered taping both rooms, but I knew why: I got off on watching people so much, especially people that don't know they're being taped, that I couldn't resist getting as much recorded as I could.

The action was hot. The big stud came into my room with an army-issue duffel bag slung over his shoulder, which he put gently on the floor near the foot of my bed. So that was what he kept getting all his gear from, I realized. The rest of the stuff was pretty much how I imagined and remembered it. He was so damn good-looking.

Watching Rex overpower me and tie me to the bed fascinated me. I knew I would watch that tape many more times. After it was all over, I figured I'd watch the other tape, just to see if anything interesting was on it. Now that I thought about it, I could find out what he'd been doing all that time before he came into the bedroom. It seemed like he had been hanging around in the main room for a long time before getting down to business.

The image came on, a good view of the whole main room. Rex came in, his duffel bag over his shoulder, closing the door behind him. Then he looked the room over, checking out the place. He even glanced in some of the unpacked boxes, picking up photos and letters. I felt like my privacy had been invaded for a minute, until I realized how ridiculous that was when I was sitting watching a tape of someone who didn't know about the camera.

He seemed to be scanning the room, taking in what little information there was. I remembered how well he had seemed to know me, especially the way he dug my long-repressed bondage fantasies out of me. He must have been a therapist or something; he read me so well and figured out my story just from the stuff he looked at in the room.

He looked over the room so carefully I was surprised he didn't find the camera. He got so near the closet a few times I didn't see how he couldn't have not seen it through the door. But his face never showed any reaction, so I guessed he never saw it.

After he finally came into the bedroom, there was just a long time of empty room while he was in there with me. I fast forwarded through it, figuring I was done for the night and better hit the sack.

I'd won the game.

I'd given Rex the biggest surprise, even though he didn't know it and probably never would.

But I like doing things all the way through, so I stopped the fast forwarding at the point when Rex came back out to leave and let the tape play from there.

I couldn't believe what I saw.

Without even slowing down, he went right to the front door mat and reached under it, pulling something out. My mouth dropped open, but it was nothing compared to the shock what I saw next made me feel.

Rex walked up right up to the closet where the camera was, opened the doors, got real close to the lens and held up what he had taken from under the mat.

It was my spare front door key.

He grinned hugely, and his mouth silently formed the words: "Surprise. I win."

Then he put the key in his pocket and returned the doors to their nearly-closed position. Grinning all the while, Rex slung his duffel bag over his shoulder and went out the front door, closing it behind him.

After a few minutes of staring at the screen, I started to laugh. I rolled back onto my bed, giggling like a maniac. No one had ever beaten me in the Surprise Game.

That had sure changed, and that was the best surprise of all.

Now it's the next morning, and I'm lying in bed with the sun hitting me in the face. I realize a few things.

One, I'll have to move the bed.

Two, a man that I know next to nothing about is out there with a key to my apartment.

Three, I'll have to get the lock on my front door changed.

My rational mind knows that for sure.

But my cock has a surprise for my rational mind.

# XIV. IMMORTAL ALONE

The boy's head tilts back, and his bared throat exposes itself to me. There is no sweeter torture than this, I realize, nothing so enthrallingly tempting as a victim giving himself to me, even if he is unaware he is doing so. The boy stretches his chin back even farther and takes a deep breath. His neck enlarges just slightly as he sucks in air, and for an instant the blue veins within bulge slightly. I imagine I can actually see his blood as it is pumped through the vessels, but push the thought away.

Must concentrate, I order myself, must not descend into bloodrage. That temporary frenzy would lead only to a crimson mess that would take days to clean up, which was bad, and would signal a loss of control, which was infinitely worse. Control must be maintained. That is the core of all dominant/submissive interaction, I reminded myself. As the top, I must control this situation in every way – physically, mentally, emotionally and spiritually.

I will give this boy the sexual domination he wants, and I will take what I need from him. Control of him, and myself, must be absolute. I cannot lose my grip on this experience even when faced with such tempting gifts as a ripe throat exposed in submission. He doesn't know what he's doing, I say to myself, he thinks he's just here for a rough fuck with a hot top he met at a leather bar. That's true, but the rest of the story is that I am a vampire, and after I fuck him, I will drain his veins of blood and his body of life.

He doesn't know this.

Or does he?

A flicker of doubt flashes across my mind, almost too fast to catch.

"Please take me, Sir," the boy says, "please make me yours."

Submission is so delicious. My cock hardens from mere stiff flesh to what might as well be a spike of steel. I wonder suddenly which of us is the sadist and which the masochist. This human boy lies naked beneath me, arms and legs outstretched, his wrists bound with rope to the bed frame and his ankles tied together – I lie on top of him, a vampire, not only larger but infinitely stronger and more powerful than him in every way, and I find myself needing to slow down and take stock and remember that I am the dominant one.

But how can I resist him?

He is perfectly my taste: slender, white-skinned, muscles toned, a shock of sandy brown hair adorning his fair head, his body having drawn breath for twenty years yet housing a mind uncluttered with the resentments and regrets of even that young age.

I believe myself to own him, able to do with him as I please, yet he does exactly what excites me, exactly what I want a victim to do, and in so doing ensnares me with his own submission. Is he controlling me rather than the reverse? Again, I push the thought away.

Such doubts are unbecoming of a vampire of my age and experience. Yet, I wonder if my brothers have ever had thoughts of this nature, and what they would think if they knew I was having them.

Enough!

This is my bed, my home, my domain.

He is my victim, mine to control and dominate and after I've used him sexually, I will kill him and drink his blood until I am bloated with it.

"You are mine, boy," I say, answering his plea. "All mine."

"Please fuck me, Sir!" the boy begs. "I need you to fuck me! I need to be your fuck-hole!"

As I prepare to fuck him, I remember what has come before and led us to this moment, the time and place earlier tonight where I'd caught him.

It had been around midnight, I suppose, for the time, and the place was as usual, a leather bar. As you might expect, leather bars are about as close to an ideal hunting ground as vampires are likely to get in this day and age. The needs and hungers that compel men to go to leather bars are very similar to those that drive vampires there as well – a desire for privacy and anonymity, an urge to seek experience that is beyond normal and acceptable by regular people, the drive to push oneself into realms other might consider depraved or sick. Men leave with each other to consummate their needs and attractions in cars, public parks, private homes. They frequently leave the bars with men they know nothing about, except that they may be able to quench their desire, fill the need that yawns within them like a gaping mouth.

And sometimes they never return.

The leather bar I found my current victim in was an hour or so from the house I call home. There were hunting grounds closer, to be sure, in a big city like Los Angeles, but too many disappearances within a small radius of city blocks would undoubtedly be noticed and investigated. I have long avoided contact with local law enforcement, and have no plans to initiate any now.

The bar was in a grungy section of the valley, with deserted streets, dark and ominous buildings and the only businesses open were porn shops. I found a spot on a nearby street to park my car and got out, being sure to arm the alarm. Never know what kind of thieves or vandals were lurking in dark corners around here, I thought. Can't be too careful.

I figured I looked reasonably threatening enough myself to avoid getting harassed or mugged on the short walk to the bar – I was 6'2", 220 pounds, short brown hair under a motorcycle cap, mustache and goatee, white T-shirt, leather jacket, blue jeans and black boots. I'd been a 35-year-old gay man when I'd *Ascended*, so I was suspended at the age in appearance, and I still preferred to hunt men. I can drink from females, of course, and their blood will sustain me, but male blood just tastes better. It feels better going down, too, saltier maybe than girl-blood, richer and fuller-bodied.

No one bothered me.

I turned a corner, and there was the bar on the edge of the street. DRINKIN' HOLE, the old sign on the side of the building said. The irony of the name was obvious, but it still made me smile. I walked around to the back where the entrance was. ENTER FROM BEHIND, it said in smaller letters. Just like a lot of guys there tonight, I thought, they are hoping to be taken home with someone and entered from behind before the sun rose again.

There were a few men hanging around the entrance, but they weren't what I was looking for. I walked up the short flight of steps and into the open door. I paid the burly attendant the cover charge and strode into the main bar. It was dark and loud, full of pungent smoke and pounding music. There was a decent crowd, not as packed as the place got on Friday and Saturday nights but pretty full for a week-night.

The scent of the men excited me, and I flared my nostrils to inhale more of it. My cock stirred in my jeans, aroused by the prey possibilities here. When I was human I had been an aggressive and dominant top, so hunting other men came easily to me. A few guys noticed me, their gazes lingering. I acknowledged their attention, but not in an inviting way. Going up to the bar itself, I bought a bottle of water and admired the young bartender and his bar back. They looked tasty, but were out of the question – too easily traced. If either one of them disappeared, everyone that saw us leave would know my description.

No.

I needed someone who wouldn't be missed and couldn't be tracked. A big muscleman with a shaved head and pierced nipples joined me as I walked through the crowd to stand against the wall. He took one look at the bulge between my legs and met my eyes hungrily.

"Hello, Sir," he said, revealing himself as a bottom. Who would've thought this hulking behemoth wanted to get tied up and fucked just like the other desperate men there that night? If I ever meet God, one of the questions I'll ask Him is, "Why did you create so many bodies that were perfect for dominating and making other men submit yet endow them with submissive spirits?" Bottoms trapped in tops' bodies. Did it have a purpose in the Grand Plan, or was it just another phenomenon to amuse Him, as were so many other things?

"I could serve you well, Sir," the behemoth said.

"Not tonight," I said, not unkindly. "I'm looking for something very specific." His disappointment was palpable, but hope sprung eternal in his eyes.

"Another time, Sir?" he asked, not realizing that by denying him a hot fuck I'd granted him a longer life.

"Maybe," I said, in a tone that meant we're done, go away. He did so, and I began to scope the crowd for what I really wanted. I leaned against the wall and looked at the men around me. With my heightened vampire senses, I could feel each of them: their smells, their tastes, the beating of their hearts and the songs their blood sang as it was pumped through their veins. Each was a unique individual, with his own configuration of blood and flesh and bone.

But which of them did I want?

Which would be mine?

I was hungry, but I could wait. There were still many hours before the dreaded sunrise. It was more important to find just the right boy then it was to find a victim quickly. I wanted someone special, not just a warm body. I'd drunk from enough anonymous men, tonight I needed something unusual.

A special victim.

I was confident I'd find him. I just had to be patient.

I myself was not going unnoticed, but I ignored the eyes that roamed and lingered over me.

Where was he?

I glanced toward the door just as a new guy walked in. He was young, probably mid-twenties, dressed in denim cut-off shorts, hiking boots and a white tank-top undershirt that made his already-tanned skin even darker in contrast.

He looked delicious.

The new boy stopped and looked around, scoping the scene as I had been doing. I looked around myself, watching the other man notice him. He was hot – I could see the bottoms envying him and the tops coveting him. I knew if I wanted him for myself I had to move fast. The other tops were moving toward him, circling like sharks around a bleeding fish. I watched the hot boy look around, see the other guys scoping him, and knew that whatever I was going to do I had to do it now.

I pushed off from the wall and headed toward him, hoping I looked forbidding enough to drive the vultures away. But the hot boy didn't even give the others a second look. He caught my eye and gestured toward the bar with his head, asking without speaking. I nodded and we both headed that way.

We met at the bar, ignoring the other men who tried to get our attention.

"Hey," I said to him.

"Buy you a beer?" he asked me.

"Water," I said, "lots of lemons."

He got the bartender's attention and ordered my water and a beer for himself. He drank his beer suggestively, sucking on its phallic neck while watching me without blinking. He didn't seem surprised when I fished a lemon shard out of my water and ate it, peel and all.

"You're pretty sure of yourself," I said to him.

"Thank you, Sir," he said, "and I bet your mouth tastes fresh and sour."

"You like sour?" I asked.

"I love sour," he said.

"Good, maybe you'll get a chance to taste my mouth tonight."

"I hope so, Sir," he said. "I'd hate to have driven all this way for nothing." The possibility of distance aroused me as much as his flirting. An isolated victim far from home was easy to trap. I kept my voice level, not wanting to seem too excited.

"You live far away from here?" I asked.

"In Costa-fucking-Mesa, Sir," the hot boy said, then took another pull on his beer. "It's a fucking hour-and-a-half drive."

"Does anyone know you're here?" I asked. "Family? Friends?"

"No family," he said, "and my 'friends' care more about crystal meth than they do about me … or themselves."

I moved closer to him, purposely invading his space.

"Why did you come here tonight?" I asked, curious in spite of myself. It didn't matter why for my purposes, but I found him so interesting I wanted to know more about him.

"I need something special tonight," he said, "I need something new, something … extraordinary."

I smiled, realizing that he thought he was talking about a night of hot dominant/submissive sex, maybe some bondage and SM; when what I had planned for him was going to be a thousand times more lasting.

Maybe even extraordinary.

I leaned in close and saw that his cock was hard in his shorts.

"I'm going to take you home with me tonight," I whispered into his ear.

"I was hoping you'd say that, Sir," he whispered back.

"You want to be mine, boy?" I asked him, taking the beer from his hand and setting it on the bar.

"More than anything, Sir."

"Good," I said, leaning down. I lifted him up off the floor and hoisted him over my shoulder. He submitted willingly, hanging limp. I adjusted him on my shoulder, so his weight was distributed evenly, then secured his legs in place with one arm. The men around us noticed and stepped back to give me some room, with looks ranging from curious to interested to surprised and jealous. I could tell there were plenty of guys there who wished they were in our places, some as top, some as bottom.

I was grandstanding, I knew, and showing off was never a good idea. After the boy disappeared tonight, any of these men could describe me if asked by police who the victim had left the bar with.

But I couldn't help it.

Even though I was a vampire, an undead creature, and really not comparable to anyone else at the bar, I still wanted to show them that I was the hottest top there, that I could get any boy I wanted. The boy hung limp and loose over my shoulder, exactly like the piece of meat he was. As I carried him out of the bar, I thought about what I was doing. I was enacting a ritual as old as humanity – carrying home food for the night. I could have been a Neanderthal man carrying a kill to his tribe, or a hunter in colonial America bringing a deer home to his family for dinner. This boy I had slung was my food for the night, my sustenance. In some strange way, I sort of loved him for that, as much as I could love a person I was going to kill and drink blood from.

I carried the boy out the exit and down the stairs. The men hanging around outside watched silently, their eyes locked on me and my prey. As I carried the boy out onto the street, I found myself clutching him tighter, as if worried someone would try to take him from me. There was something different about this boy, something not really definable yet. Somehow, it just felt right that he should be mine tonight.

I don't often use the word perfect, but it most closely described what was happening. This boy had looked and acted just how I'd always hoped and dreamed a victim would. Having him slung over my shoulder just felt fantastic, like it was supposed to be that way.

We got to my car, and I put him down gently into the passenger seat. When I got in on the driver's side I looked at him. He was lying back against the seat, eyes closed, breathing slowly and deeply.

"You okay, boy?" I asked.

"Yes, Sir," he said, "I'm just trying to prepare myself for what's going to happen soon." I put on my seat belt and turned the key in the ignition.

"I don't think much of anything's going to get you ready for what I'm going to do to you tonight," I said. The boy just smiled and didn't say anything. I wondered what he was thinking, but his face was passive, blank, unreadable.

The drive to my place was uneventful, yet full of unspoken tension. I was getting more and more excited as killing-time got closer, and the boy seemed to be in an almost meditative trance, silent and unreachable. When we got to my house, I parked in the driveway and unlocked the car doors. I got out and waited for him to do the same. When he didn't, I walked around to his side and opened his door.

He just sat there.

"Boy?" I asked, and he murmured something inaudible. I leaned closer.

"What did you say?"

"Please carry me again, Sir," he said softly.

"You liked that?" I asked.

"Yes, Sir. It felt so fucking great – like I was ... yours."

"You are mine, boy," I said, and without saying anything more I took hold of his wrists and pulled him out of the car. Leaning down, I hoisted him back up and over my shoulder. I closed the car door with one hand and held my human burden in place with the other. After arming the car alarm, I carried him up to the door of my house. I took him inside and locked the door behind us.

When we reached my bedroom, I laid him down on my bed. His white tank-top and tanned skin stood out very starkly against the bedspread and walls, all of which were black. I kept my eyes on him as I pulled off my boots and loosened my belt. My jeans fell to the floor and I stepped out of them before peeling off my socks.

The boy gasped when he saw my cock, long and thick, erect and dripping, jutting from between my legs, pointing at him like a divining rod that's found water. I took off my jacket, vest and T-shirt, revealing my large chest with it dusting of hair and large nipples, never taking my eyes of the boy. I took my cap off last.

Now fully naked, I walked toward him.

I reached forward and took his tank-top in my hands and tore it off of him. There was no cry of surprise, no whimper of fear. The boy just sat there at the foot of my bed, looking at me with fuck me eyes. I removed his shorts, underwear and boots, leaving him naked and ready.

But instead of climbing up onto him, I walked around the side of the bed – I lifted up my pillow and picked up the coil of rope I always keep underneath it. Looping it through my steel headboard I brought the rope to the foot of the bed where the boy was waiting for me. Pulling his arms gently behind him, I coiled the rope around his wrists and tied them together. Neither of us spoke as I tied his arms to the headboard. The boy just sat there, waiting, maddening in his beauty and submission.

I wanted to take him quickly, but I knew I had to control myself.

If I wasn't careful, bloodrage would take me, and I would go into a feeding frenzy that would be orgasmic for its duration, but would leave me bloated, the boy mutilated and his blood and entrails all over the bed, walls and ceiling.

No, I had to stay calm, and savor this as it deserved to be savored.

I stepped around until I was facing my victim.

He looked at me without expression, just waiting. It was almost like he knew – no, that was impossible. He couldn't know what I was or what I was going to do; there was no way he could. I crawled up onto the bed, spreading his legs and sliding between them. It's as if I can hear his heart beating, every second pumping blood in and out, to all his extremities filling them with life-sustaining elixir.

Waiting for the perfect moment to take him is such sweet agony – how I long to end this yet the anticipation is so exquisite. He's doing everything so perfectly, it's as if he knows just what excites me. A willing victim, as I've always wanted, he seems to know what's happening yet is not afraid!

Soon, I cannot deny my cock any longer and plunge forward into his willing asshole. Impaling him is penultimate pleasure – it feels magnificent yet I know even greater bliss awaits when I impale his neck with my teeth and drain him of his life.

I force myself into him.

"Thank you, Sir," he says through his scream, "thank you for taking me."

My response is to slide my arms around his torso and crush him tight to me as far as his restraints will allow. I squeeze him so hard the air rushes out of his mouth as his lungs are compacted. Like a rod of iron my penis cleaved into my victim, seemingly so strong it could split him in two. But no complaint escapes his lips, no protest sullies his mouth. He wants what I'm giving; he needs what I'm doing! After decades of feasting on fear and terror I am finding that willingness is an even more potent aphrodisiac!

Well, I tell myself feverishly, he won't be expecting how this is going to end! But his willingness, his utter submission, is so delicious! I fuck him brutally, pumping my cock in his hole harder than I've ever done to anyone before.

I suddenly realize I don't want this to end.

Normally, I would be salivating for his blood by now, just dying until the moment he reached orgasm, and I could finally pierce his neck and feast. Blood is at its most oxygenated and potent when the victim is experiencing sexual climax, so it is the best time to feed. But I am enjoying fucking him, enjoying the closeness, the connection we seem to have …

Enough of this, I think, time to pull myself together and put an end to this!

I grab the boy's raging cock in one hand and pull his head toward me with the other. Kissing him roughly, I swallow his gasp of ecstasy as I jerk his cock to orgasm. Behind my lips my canine teeth begin to extend, their tips sharpening in anticipation of the kill.

"Permission to come, Sir?" the boy asks desperately.

"Yes," I say, "now, boy."

And as his semen shoots from his cock, splattering onto his chest and neck, he howls a cry of pleasure as wild and passionate as any creature of the night. My mouth closes on his neck and my teeth pierce his tender skin.

But what is this?

His blood is sweet – not salty and heavy with iron like blood usually is – but rich and succulent, more delicious than anything I've ever tasted! I drink from him, and as I do my body releases its own pressure, shooting my come out of me into the boy.

I drink from him, too quickly, in a vulgar manner I haven't taken since I was newly *Ascended.* My instincts have taken over, my rational mind banished.

His blood tastes so good, more, more, I must have more! The boy moans beneath me, straining against his bonds. This sweet ambrosia is unlike any blood I've heard of in tale or song. I slurp and suck from him, heedless of the blood that drips down onto our naked bodies and stains my bed beneath us.

Suddenly reason crashes through my lust – this boy is special, I mustn't drain him completely – I need to keep him alive and make him my companion. I could make him immortal and drink his exquisite blood for eternity! This is the boy, the one I've always wanted, the boy that knows what I need and acts just like I want him to! This creature is a priceless treasure to be savored for all time – he must truly be mine. I must disengage, must stop drinking so his life will be preserved.

What's happening?

I can't pull away! It's as if my fangs are stuck in his neck, unable to remove themselves. I sense something I've never experienced before, a strange power nearly equal to my own – the boy! He's holding me in place! He's preventing me from disengaging – making me drain him beyond redemption!

What power enables him to do this? Nothing I've ever experienced…

Must stop drinking!

Must stop!

Must save this boy, keep him as mine, mine to suck, mine to fuck, mine forever!

NO!

It's too late. It can't be, but it is. He releases his hold on me, and I stumble back off of the bed, falling on my ass to the floor. I've drained him too deep; he's too far through death's gate to come back.

But why? Why? How could he make me do this to him?

I glare up aT him as despair fills my heart. He stretches his arms out as far as he can, like a crucified martyr, like Jesus. I hated him in that moment, rage replacing sorrow.

How could he do this?

Why would he do this?

He gave me everything I ever wanted, than took it away almost as soon as the gift was received.

Why?

How?

*I am a telepath*, his voice spoke directly into my mind; *I'm also telekinetic.*

"What?" I said out loud.

*I can hear your thoughts*, his voice in my head said, *and I can project mine into your mind.*

*I don't understand*, I thought at him.

*I read your thoughts in the bar tonight*, he projected to me, *in that moment I knew what you were, and that you could give me the death I wanted.*

*The death you wanted?* I repeated.

*I have a unique blood type*, he thought, *no one else has it; it's mine alone.*

*That's why it tastes so different, so good?*

*Yes*, he projected, *but because it's so rare, no one can act as a donor for me. I have a non-contagious but incurable disease. Without a transfusion from a healthy donor I'm going to die a slow painful death.*

*But there aren't any donors if you're the only one who has your blood type!* I think back at him.

*That's what I wanted to choose my death. Without a donor I'm going to die anyway, so I wanted to decide when and where I would die.*

*Why did you choose me?*

*Because I've always had such a boring, ordinary life*, he projects to me, *I wanted a glorious, spectacular death, and I knew you could give me that, and if you refused, I had my mild telekinetic ability to make you do what I wanted.*

"You used me!" I say out loud.

"You use people all the time," he says weakly, "and even kill them sometimes. How does it feel?"

"Fuck you!"

"You did," he says, "was it worth it?"

"Best victim I ever had," I say, rising to my knees at the foot of the blood-stained bed. The boy sagged backwards.

*Don't go!* I beg him with my mind.

*Too late* he projects, *thank you – I love you.*

And he dies.

I throw my head back and roar a scream so powerful all the windows in my house shatter, and the shards of glass fall around me like the tears I'd cry if I still had a soul.

# XV. ROPED BY A WRANGLER

He stood above me, the moonlight making long shadows around him as I knelt before him. He'd bound my hands behind my back with rope, and my clothes were torn and dirty.

My head was bowed before him, and I could feel his gaze on me.

I could feel his eyes move over the back of my head, my neck bent in submission, onto my back. I half-expected my shirt to ignite under his scrutiny, burning to ash and falling away. Between my legs, my cock throbbed. The blood within pulsed with each beat of my heart. My tool strained against my jeans, desperate for release. But I knew my pleasure was unimportant.

All that mattered was the cowboy, and what I could do for him.

I kept my eyes down, transfixed at the sight before them.

"You like my boots, punk?" he asked.

"Yes, sir," I said as I felt my tongue involuntarily slip from my mouth to lick my lips. His boots were well-worn, dusty, dirty from a hard day's work. They had a lot of character, just like their owner. This man had something scores of would-be cowboys and wanna-be wranglers could never have – the dirt of authenticity.

His jeans were threadbare, pale and bleached by the sun, his legs long and lanky. His fat, full cock was clearly outlined under the denim, tucked to the left side. A wide black leather belt with a big silver buckle held his pants in place, and a patterned flannel shirt concealed his thick torso. The shirt's sleeves were long but I could see bicep muscles bulging beneath the fabric. I'd hardly seen his face, most of which was shadowed by his traditional broad-brimmed hat. What skin I could see was darkly tanned by the sun. His lower lip stuck out a little, undoubtedly from a dip of tobacco tucked inside. A day's growth of beard covered his cheeks and chin. I couldn't see his eyes, but I could feel them burning into me.

"Reckon I'd like to plug that mouth of yours with my cock," he said.

"Please, sir," I said. "I'd like that, too."

"I don't give a rat's ass what you'd like, punk!" he said sharply. "Now get up here and open wide."

My knees groaned as I leaned up on them, my kneecaps protesting against the hard wooden floor of the shack the cowboy had brought me to. He unbuttoned the fly of his jeans in one smooth motion – no underwear – and his rod flopped out, already stiffening at the thought of an expedition down my throat. I raised my head, mouth gaping, drool flowing down my chin at the sight of the cowboy's dick. He fisted his tool a few times, coaxing it into full hardness. He leaned forward, bringing it tantalizingly close to my lips.

But instead of sticking his cock in my mouth, he pulled it tight against his abdomen and let it go. The thick tube of muscle popped out and down, smacking against my chin. I yelped in pain and surprise.

"Listen to you," the cowboy growled above me. "whining like a fucking pansy. You want this dick, punk, huh? You want it? You gotta earn it, you hear me?" He punctuated his questions by cock-smacking me, letting his tool pummel my mouth and chin. Tears sprang to my eyes, but I willed them not to fall. It hurt, but I wasn't a pansy, and I'd prove it. I closed my eyes and made no noise as he continued to dick-whip my face – not just my mouth and chin but my cheeks, eyes, nose and forehead.

"A thief is what you are," he said, "nothin' but a low-down, no-good, mother-fucking thief!"

A few seconds passed with no cock-smacking, so I risked opening my eyes. He was glaring down at me, his lip curled in a sneer as he lined up his tool with my mouth again.

"You hungry, thief? Eat this!" He rammed his dick between my lips. I gagged and choked as the intruding organ slammed against the back of my throat. Bile and saliva flowed, trying to lubricate his cock, but it wasn't enough. I coughed, hoping he'd show mercy on me.

He did, sort of.

He started fucking my face, ramming his cock in and out of my mouth as if he was drilling for oil. I was able to breathe again, not for long, but it was better than nothing. My arms were aching from being stretched behind my back, and my wrists were raw where they were bound by the rough rope. But servicing the wrangler was the most important thing right then. I was embarrassed, humiliated and fucking turned on at the same time. My cock burned between my legs, protesting being trapped untouched inside my jeans.

The cowboy started cursing gutturally, keeping a running commentary to his face-fucking me.

"Fuckin' thief is what you are," he muttered, "low-down cocksucking thief, stealing from Mr. Franz, well now you got somethin' in your mouth, don't you? Are you still hungry, punk?"

I was, but it didn't make any difference. Soon enough I was going to get a meal unlike the one I'd imagined earlier that day.

"Uuunnnggghh," the cowboy groaned, "gonna come down your throat, thief, give you the only food you're fit to eat … uuunnnnngghhh!"

Jets of hot spunk spurted out of his cock and down my gullet, and I swallowed hungrily. When he was done he extracted his tool and left me there with cum and drool dripping from my mouth. The cowboy looked down at me contemptuously, and I met his gaze with my own.

"Please, sir …" I whispered. Instead of answering me he grabbed me by the arms and yanked me to my feet. Roughly flipping me around so I was facing away from him, he started untying my hands. When they were free, I turned back to face him.

"Thank you, sir," I said, "my wrists were really hurting." He didn't say anything, just looked at me, so I kept talking, like an idiot. "And thanks for not giving me to the police."

His brow furrowed for a second like he didn't understand what I was saying.

"What, you think I'm done with you?" he asked.

# # # # #

It had all started several hours before.

I was on my cross-country move, driving from Los Angeles to Sparkling Springs, Florida. I was in bad shape. I'd made mistakes in my planning, and now was critically short of money. It had come down to this: I could eat, or I could fill my gas tank. One or the other.

While I was crossing through one of the Southern states, I came upon what I thought was an abandoned ranch. There weren't any people visible, and no lights burned in the windows of the buildings I could see. I drove around until I found a gate that wasn't locked and parked my car. I slipped through the gate and walked quietly to the closest building. The sign above the door said Stores & Supplies. I said a short prayer of hope that there would be something inside I could use.

I found the door unlocked, and I opened it slowly. It was dark inside, and I couldn't risk turning on the lights, so I opened the door wide enough for some stray beams of moonlight to get in. Creeping into the storeroom, I found more than I could've hoped for. The place was full of food – boxes of beef jerky, rows and rows of peaches in jars, jugs of water and lots more – I almost cried in relief. I opened one of the boxes of jerky and helped myself. It was dry and salty and so fucking good. Uncapping one of the jugs of water, I drank out of the top like a dog. Eating peaches out of a jar without a fork was a sloppy messy business, but I was so happy I didn't care.

Suddenly the room was bathed in bright light. Almost blinded by it, I looked behind me.

Two figures stood in the open doorway. One of them had a double-barrel shotgun aimed at my head. I clenched the muscles in my abdomen to prevent my bladder from emptying itself.

"Put your hands where I can see them, you son of a bitch," a gruff voice said. I obeyed and stretched my arms out, so they could see I didn't have a weapon.

"Stand up, slowly."

I did what he said, turning around as I did.

I could see a little better now – the one with the shotgun was a tall brute of a man, decked out like a real-life cowboy with a menacing look in his eye and a coil of rope attached to his belt. The other guy was shorter and much older, probably in his sixties or higher. He was wearing a robe and had glasses.

"What have we here?" the older man said. "What do you think you're …"

"I'm sorry!" I said, jumping in. "I was driving by and I've got no money and I'm so hungry …"

The cowboy shoved the shotgun in my face.

"Shut the fuck up you little cocksucker!" he snarled at me. "Don't interrupt Mr. Franz when he's speaking!"

I obeyed, lowering my head in shame.

"It's all right, Dalton," Mr. Franz said.

"What should we do with him?" the cowboy asked. Mr. Franz stepped closer to me, looking over what I'd done to his food supplies.

"It doesn't look like he's eaten much," he said. "I don't think we need to involve the authorities." I said a silent prayer of thanks. "Just teach him a lesson about stealing from this ranch."

My gratitude turned to terror.

"Will you hold my gun for me while I tie him up, sir?" Dalton asked. Despite my fear, I was smart enough not to resist when the cowboy handed his shotgun to Mr. Franz and stepped toward me. He grabbed me by the arm and pulled me roughly to my feet. He forced my hands behind my back and with the coil of rope from his belt he tied them together at the wrists. Then the cowboy turned me around to face him, leaned down in front of me and picked up me, tossing me easily over one shoulder. I hung down his back, too scared to move, although my cock started to harden against Dalton's shoulder. If he noticed he gave no sign.

"I'll teach him a lesson, all right," he said.

"Will you be wanting your gun back?" Mr. Franz asked. The cowboy snorted.

"I reckon I can handle this punk," he said.

"All right," the older man said. "do whatever you want with him, but I want him gone by morning."

I wondered with something like panic what the word gone meant in this case.

"Yes, sir," the cowboy said.

"Good night, Dalton."

"Good night, sir."

The two men walked out of the storeroom, turning out the lights and locking the door behind them. Then they walked away in opposite directions. From my vantage point upside-down over the cowboy's back, I saw Mr. Franz walked toward a large building that probably held the living quarters. Dalton carried me deeper into the darkness of the ranch grounds, obviously knowing the way so well he didn't need a light or a path. Even though the older man had the cowboy's gun, I was no less afraid of this man who'd thrown me over his shoulder like I was nothing more than a sack of grain.

But I had to do something.

"Uh, hello?" I tried. "Sir?"

"You'll keep your mouth shut if you know what's good for you," Dalton growled at me. I obeyed him. So much for resistance.

He took me to a small shack, about half the size of the storeroom. The cowboy snapped on the single light bulb that hung from the ceiling. Dalton carried me in, and I saw what looked like an old tool shed that hadn't been used in years. He closed the door behind us. He swung me down off his shoulder and stood me up, so I was facing him.

I looked up into his contemptuous eyes.

"Get on your fucking knees, cocksucker."

# # # # #

"But I thought …" I started to say.

"That was your first mistake," the cowboy said, grabbing me by the arms and tying them up again at the wrist, this time in front of me instead of behind my back. “I just wanted to get your hands out of the way. Now you’ll see what happens to thieves on this ranch.”

Dalton spun me around, so I was facing away from him, then kicked my feet from under me and shoved me forward. But instead of crashing to the concrete floor my fall was broken by an old sawhorse. I yelped in pain and surprise as I was jackknifed over it, my ass in the air and my arms and legs hanging down uselessly on either side.

The cowboy wasted no time.

He came up behind me and grabbed the waistband of my jeans and yanked them down, exposing my naked ass to the air.

“No!” I said, “please!”

“Shut the fuck up, punk!” he said, slapping my butt hard. “You did this to yourself.” I heard him spit into his hand and slick up his tool again before I felt his monster between my cheeks. Dalton nosed around my hole for a minute, then shoved his meat into me up to his pubes. I cried out, but just like before my own cock responded to his dominance and stiffened uncomfortably against the wooden sawhorse. Then the cowboy fucked me, shoving himself in and out of me like I was his last fuck on earth. I began whimpering in pain and excitement. My waist and abdomen hurt where they were smashed over the sawhorse, my hands hurt where they were tied together and most of all my ass hurt where he was fucking me.

Luckily it wasn’t long before Dalton started grunting as he had when he came last time. He punctuated his last few thrusts with words snarled at me through his teeth.

“This – is what you get – when you steal – from this ranch – you stupid – fucking – cocksucking – punk – thief!”

Then his grunts turned to moans as he came, shooting his seed deep into my ass. It felt like gallons of the stuff. When he was done, he yanked himself out of me and put his pants back together. I was exhausted. There wasn’t much more I could take tonight. He pulled me off the sawhorse and turned me to face him. Dalton was grinning at me in a predatory way.

“Please, sir,” I begged, “please let me go …”

"Oh shut up!" he said and cold-cocked me with one fist. I saw stars and felt my knees give out. The last thing I felt before I blacked out was the cowboy catching me as I fell and throwing me once again over his shoulder.

# # # # #

When I woke up the sun was coming up. I was in my car, with the doors locked. I felt in my pocket for my keys. I found them, along with $100 in twenty dollar bills. My hands were sore and my ass was sore, but I smiled, even though no one was watching me. Then I started my car and drove until I found an open fast food joint and bought myself a big breakfast with the money the cowboy had stuffed in my pants.

Then I took a deep breath and got back on the road, resuming my drive to Sparkling Springs, Florida.

# XVI. COMMANDER ZANN

“Lieutenant!” the Commander barked.

“Yes, sir?”

“Do we have any recent acquisitions?”

“Yes, sir, one. A colonist from planet Gaeta Prime. He was captured yesterday. No orientation yet.”

“Have him brought to my quarters.”

“Yes, Commander Zann.”

Zann stood up from his command chair. The viewscreen at the head of the bridge showed the stars streaking past as the Commander’s spacecraft hurtled across the solar system faster than the speed of light. He smiled as his underlings huddled over their control consoles, hoping not to be noticed or singled out for punishment by him.

The Commander strode across the bridge as if he owned the place, which he did. The spacecraft, and every man on it, belonged to him as his sovereign property. Rightfully won in battle or dishonestly stolen from others, it was all his.

His knee-high leather boots were polished black as space, his latex and rubber bodysuit captured every curve of his exquisite physique, his cock and balls clearly visible between his legs, and his muscular arms were bare, their bicep muscles round as setting suns.

He reached the door in the corner of the bridge that led to his private quarters. Sensing his presence, the door slid open. Before he entered, the Commander turned back to the man sitting directly in front of his command chair.

“Lieutenant,” he said.

“Yes, sir?” the man answered.

"Do not interrupt me unless we are under attack, or someone more powerful than me contacts us."

"Understood, Commander."

With a nod, he turned back to the door and entered his quarters.

He gave a sigh as the door slid shut behind him. Here, with the hum of his ship's engines a dull roar in the background, he could relax. Of course, to an outside observer, his method of relaxation might seem strange. But the Commander was under no such scrutiny and would proceed, as he always had, as he saw fit.

He sat down in his favorite chair and waited.

Seconds later, his door chime sounded.

"Enter," he said.

The door opened to reveal a burly guard, almost as muscular as Zann himself, holding a naked man slung over one broad shoulder. The guard's uniform, as were the uniforms all the crew wore, were modified versions of the Commander's own, with the arms bare to expose the wearer's biceps.

"The Gaetan colonist, sir," the guard said.

"Excellent. Bring him in."

The guard carried the unconscious man into his superior's quarters.

"Set him down there," the Commander said, gesturing to a spot several feet away from where he was sitting. The guard obeyed by gently lowering the man off his shoulder and onto the floor.

"His remote?"

The guard pulled a small electronic device from his belt and handed it to the man in the chair.

"Dismissed," the Commander said. The guard nodded and left the room, the door closing behind him. Zann looked at the motionless form of the captured colonist lying in front of him. The man was only a few years younger than himself, probably in his late twenties. The angle wasn't ideal for viewing his face, but he looked handsome enough not to offend the Commander's eyes. His body was not bulky like Zann's own, but rather lean. Gaeta Prime was not a tamed world; its colonists undoubtedly had to labor hard in their struggle to make it habitable.

Fools, Zann thought. Why they would waste their lives working to make a new home for the millions of people who'd been forced off planet Earth by the over-population crisis was beyond him. To work for a better future for humanity was ridiculous as far as he was concerned. Humanity had no future. It would continue to be dispersed and diluted until it eventually degenerated into barbarism.

That is, Commander Zann thought, if it hasn't already.

He returned his gaze to the man on the floor in front of him. The colonist's hands were behind his back, held in place by a metallic binding device made of metal as strong as the hull of the ship. A similar device encircled the man's neck like a collar. Most interestingly of all, a third ring-shaped unit surrounded the man's cock and balls, snug and inescapable. Each unit was adorned with small lights, which at the moment were burning green.

The binding devices were standard issue for captured acquisitions, but they never ceased to amaze and amuse Commander Zann. If he ever met the man who designed them, he'd shake his hand.

He took a deep breath, settled back in his chair, gripped the remote in one hand, put the other between his legs, and prepared for a relaxing session.

The first button on the remote he pushed was labeled REVIVE.

As soon as he did the colonist shook his head, as if awakening from a daydream. He opened his eyes and tried to move his arms but they were held firmly in place by the binders. Zann was delighted by the man's handsome face and the nice display of straining muscles as he tried to break his hands free.

"What …?" the colonist said.

He lifted his head and looked around wildly.

"Where …?"

He became aware of his collar and shook his head back and forth, as if he might dislodge it with the strength of his neck alone. Zann laughed at this, unable to help himself.

Awkwardly, the colonist rose to his feet and staggered clumsily in a circle, trying to decipher where he was and what had happened.

"I don't … understand," he said. His accent was pure Gaetan, and it made Commander Zann's cock stir to life and lengthen between his legs. Zann loved the sound of accents, almost as much as he loved to see a muscular young man struggle against bondage.

Both at the same time was, well, let us say, among his most cherished experiences.

"You don't have to understand," Commander Zann said, "and you don't have to worry. Not anymore. No more being frightened there won't be enough food. No more being scared of man-eating animals hunting at night. No more cold winters, no more burning summers. No, you have nothing more to worry about, my young acquisition."

The colonist, who had been listening intently with an ever-increasing glare of anger on his face, spat his next words.

"You!" he said. "You did this to me! I'll kill you!"

The young man charged forward, teeth gritted, his fury bent on his captor sitting before him. Commander Zann calmly raised the remote control device and pressed a button marked SHIELD.

Suddenly a shimmering cylinder of energy surrounded the colonist, and he smashed against it before he could reach his target. He screamed in pain as the energy shield repelled him and he stumbled backwards. He charged again, trying to reach his captor, but again the shimmering wall shocked him and he gave up. The lights on his binding units had changed to a deep yellow color.

Commander Zann leaned forward in his chair, his eyes burning into those of the colonist. As he spoke his fingers played up and down the length of his hardened cock that clearly showed through his bodysuit.

"There will be no killing today, my young acquisition," he said, "and if there were, it would be done by me. To make things easier for both of us, you must begin to learn what you are."

"And what am I?" the young man snarled.

"Mine, of course," Commander Zann said.

"Where the hell are my clothes?" the captured colonist asked.

"They've been destroyed," Commander Zann said. "You won't need them any more."

The young man angrily punched his fist into the energy shield surrounding him and swore at the pain that resulted.

"What is this … barrier between us?" the colonist said, "what's preventing me from walking over to you and smashing your face into the deck?"

Commander Zann raised an eyebrow at the young man's daring, but knew better than to be provoked by an acquisition.

"It's a precaution to ensure you don't do anything foolish, like attacking me, that might result in your execution," Zann said. "It's generated by the devices that bind you. You cannot escape it."

"I'll escape it when it's deactivated," the colonist said.

Commander Zann raised the hand that was holding the remote control. "Only this can deactivate your shield," he said, "and you will never touch it."

The young man glared at his captor.

"What kind of man are you?" he asked. "Why do you need these machines to protect you? Can't you defend yourself? Can't you back up anything you say with your fists?"

Zann smiled at him with a gleam in his eye. "I have something far more effective than my fists to back up what I say and do," he said, and turned a dial on the remote labeled RESTRICT. The colonist shrieked in pain and crumbled to the deck. He struggled to free his hands, but they were firmly bound behind his back. Writhing on the floor, the colonist curled into a fetal position. His lights had changed to red.

"What …? Stop … please!" he gasped.

The Commander turned the dial back to its off position.

"What you just experienced was another application of the technology that's confining you. By twisting this dial, I can make the metal ring around your cock and balls emit an electrical charge. It will not damage you, but the effect, as you noticed, is quite painful."

The colonist lay on the deck, breathing heavily.

"So as you've seen and experienced, I now control your world," Zann said. "I can make it a painful hell, I can make it a tolerable existence, or I can make it a pleasurable paradise."

The young man raised his head from the floor at these words. He looked at his cock and balls, which were swollen red from the irritation of the shocking ring.

"Are you going to … do that to me again?" he asked weakly.

"Would you like me to?"

"No!"

Zann looked at him silently.

"I mean, no … please."

"That's better," the Commander said. "See how fast you learn? I'm proud of you, my young acquisition."

The colonist struggled up onto his knees.

"Why do you keep calling me that?" he asked. "I'm 28, you can't be older than 35 …"

"It amuses me to call my slaves that," Zann said.

"I will never accept life as a slave, you pig!" the young man snarled.

Commander Zann regarded him coolly, gently stroking himself through the material of his pants.

"This life has been chosen for you. It makes no difference if you accept it or not," he said.

"I will not submit!"

Zann turned the RESTRICT dial again, and the colonist screamed in pain and dropped to his knees. The Commander reset the control and the electrical current was cut off.

"I don't think you have a choice," he said.

The acquisition stayed on the floor this time, lying on his side and breathing deeply.

"Or what?" he asked, less angrily, more resigned. "You'll keep stinging me until I die from shock or pain?"

"You're worth much less to me dead than alive," Zann said, leaning forward to make sure his words were heard. The Commander did not raise his voice unless absolutely necessary. "I have no taste for blood. But if you don't respond to training, I'll be forced to do something I don't want to do."

There was a pause until the man on the floor finally asked "What?"

"Sell you as feed."

"Feed?"

"Food. For livestock."

The colonist looked up at his captor.

"You bastard …" the young man hissed, "you're a coward. You're nothing without your machines!" Commander Zann smiled at him as he stroked his dick through his pants.

"You're missing the point," he said. "None of what you've said changes the fact that you're bound naked at my feet, and I'm sitting above you with the power to reward or punish you." His thumb moved toward the RESTRICT dial.

"Please don't …" the colonist said quietly. "No more pain."

"Get up."

The young man obeyed, and stood before Zann with his head bowed.

"You will address me as 'Sir' or 'Commander', is that clear?"

"Yes, Sir."

"Now raise your head and look at me."

The colonist did as he was told.

"What is your name?" the Commander asked.

"Lode, Sir."

"Lode …" Zann considered. "Yes, that'll work. You can keep that name."

"Thank you, Commander."

"You learn fast, don't you, Lode?"

"I try, Sir."

"Good. Now. Do you have any experience sucking a man's cock?"

"Some, Commander."

"Good. I'm going to de-activate your shield. When I do you will walk over to me on your knees and suck my cock. Is that understood?"

"Yes, Commander," Lode said, his head bowed. Zann pushed the button to drop the shield, and the young man awkwardly stumbled on his knees the short distance to where his captor sat. The Commander loved watching his acquisition's muscular arms strain as they were held in place by the binders.

When Lode was kneeling in front of him, Zann leaned forward again.

"Look at me," he said, and the young man obeyed. Zann showed him the remote control unit in his hand. "There is a button on this device I haven't used yet." With the hand not holding the remote he pointed at a control knob in the lower-right corner.

The button was labeled KILL.

The colonist's face went white.

"I don't want to use that button, Lode," the Commander said. "But I will if I feel your teeth on my cock or if you attack me in any way. Do you understand?"

"Yes, Commander."

Zann removed his cock from his pants and let it jut upwards into the captured colonist's face. Lode swallowed and leaned forward, very conscious of his captor's hand on the remote. He engulfed the Commander's engorged member between his lips and went down as far as he could.

He felt the Commander's gaze burning into him like twin suns. For Lode, the universe narrowed down to two things – him, and the cock of the man he was serving. He forgot everything, the fact that he had been captured and taken far from home, the space cruiser he was on that was screaming through space, nothing else mattered, just the Commander and his cock.

Lode sucked Zann's cock as best he could, and prayed it would be adequate. The Commander enjoyed his prisoner's out-of-practice blowjob, although he was careful not to let the captured colonist see any evidence of that fact. The young man's mouth was exquisite on his dick, soft yet insistent. Fear of death always added something to sex, something indefinable, something desperate that he had come to cherish.

The desperation he was experiencing with his latest acquisition was too intense to endure for long, and soon Commander Zann felt a first orgasm thundering through him. With an animal roar he grabbed Lode's head and held him tight to his body, so he couldn't pull away, and blew a huge quantity of sperm down the young man's throat. Lode almost choked on it, but Zann held him tight until he swallowed all of it. Only then did the Commander allow the colonist to fall back on his haunches and gasp for breath.

The Commander savored his orgasm as he watched the young man stagger back from his ordeal. When the last waves of pleasure had completed their radiation through his body, he started to play with his balls to start them churning again.

"Lode," Zann said.

"Yes, sir?" the young man said breathlessly.

"Turn around so your back is to me. I'm going to release one of your binders in a moment. When I do, you will bring both hands from behind your back in front of you. Then I will re-secure your binders, and you will bend over at the waist and support your weight with your hands. Are your instructions clear?"

"Yes, Commander."

Zann pushed a button on his remote labeled LEFT WRIST RELEASE and there was a loud clicking sound as the binder on Lode's left hand was released. The Commander watched his captive without blinking, his finger poised on the KILL button, waiting for any sign of resistance or attack. But Lode made no such attempt, and obediently followed the instructions he'd been given.

When his hands were once again locked in front of him, the young man leaned over, baring his ass to Commander Zann. A few strokes on his cock, and Lode's captor was fully hard again and ready to fuck. The sight of the handsome prisoner bending over in utter submission was ecstatically exciting to Zann, but he had been in this position many times and knew how to control himself.

Lode's remaining saliva on his cock made it wet enough for penetration, and he stood up from his chair. Zann positioned his dick so it was between Lode's cheeks at the entrance to his asshole. The muscular commander put one hand on each buttock and pulled them apart, revealing the tight asshole within.

There was no more speaking, by Zann or Lode. The time for words was over. The act that was about to happen required no prelude or validation – it was as old as the Earth their ancestors had come from. One man was about to penetrate another, and nothing could be prevent it. Both men knew it, and both men accepted it.

Zann fucked Lode, shoving his cock into the younger man with a powerful thrust. The captive gasped and groaned in shock and pain, but he did not complain or resist. He seemed to be resigned to his fate.

The Commander savored his dick in the other man's ass as he would enjoy choice wine or a fine cigar. He grabbed Lode's hips and held him in place as he fucked him. Zann never screwed long, but he screwed hard. The colonist grunted in pain as the powerful man behind him pounded his ass with his cock. Each thrust seemed more intense than the last, and Lode found himself having to anchor his weight firmly on his outstretched hands to prevent being thrown to the floor by Zann's violent assault.

Within moments the second orgasm crashed through Zann's body, and with a roar he emptied another load of his sperm into the young man. The commander held Lode by his hips until his cock had exhausted itself, and only then released him. The colonist stumbled forward onto his knees, then onto his belly, groaning.

He screamed in shock a second later as the bigger man flung himself down on Lode's back. Zann grabbed the colonist by the torso with both hands and flipped him over so Lode could look up at him with terrified eyes.

"Lode," Zann said.

"S-sir?"

"You've performed adequately today."

"Thank – thank you, Commander …"

"As of now, your orientation is over. During your orientation, you've used several words to describe me, among them 'pig', 'coward' and 'bastard'."

The young man stared up at his captor with wide eyes as Zann continued.

"I let you use those words because this was your first day as an acquisition. But that time is over now."

He paused for effect.

"If you ever use those or any similar words to describe me, I'll chop off your cock and balls and feed them to you, then kill you. Is that understood?"

"Yes, Commander! I understand!" Lode said desperately. "But …"

"What is it, acquisition?"

"I thought you had no taste for blood, Sir …"

Zann grinned down at his slave.

“I don’t,” he said, “but sometimes it has a taste for me.”

Before Lode could say anything, the Commander picked up the remote and hit a button labeled SEDATE. The young man’s eyes rolled back and he slumped into unconsciousness on the floor.

“Guard!” Zann said, and seconds later another burly attendant was at the door. “Return him to his holding cell,” the Commander said to the guard as he stood up and smoothed his uniform.

In one smooth movement the guard leaned over, grabbed the unconscious young man and hoisted him up and over one shoulder.

“Yes, Commander,” the guard said, and headed for the door. Zann followed him back out to the bridge of his starship. The bridge crew huddled over their stations, hoping not to be noticed.

Commander Zann sat down in his command chair and smiled.

Today, life was good.

# XVII. MIDNIGHT BURGLAR

I figured my apartment would probably get robbed sometime in my life, but I never thought it would be me that got stolen.

Work had been hard that day. I was really tired when I got home. Dropping my stuff, I took off my clothes and collapsed on my bed. I was asleep in seconds, unconscious to the world.

I don't know how long I slept, but when I woke up, it was dark. Lying there staring at the ceiling, I tried to figure out what had woken me up. Usually, I was a heavy sleeper; it was very strange for me to wake up in the middle of the night like this. What could have caused it? I didn't remember any nightmares then I heard it.

The noise came from my living room, not twenty feet away from me through my open bedroom door. The blood froze in my veins.

There was someone in my apartment.

I didn't know whether to be scared or furious. Knowing it was important to stay calm, I slowly turned my head, so I could look out my door into the other room. I opened my eyes enough to make out the large shape that was moving in my living room.

It was a man. He was dressed totally in black: black boots, black jeans, black jacket and shirt, black gloves on his hands and a black ski mask covering his face. He was holding a big black bag open with one hand while he put my stuff into it with the other.

A burglar! A thief in my home! I fought down the desire to jump out of bed and tackle the asshole, knowing that was a good way to get myself killed. Who knew if the guy had a knife or a gun? I couldn't take any chances.

But I had to do something! I couldn't just sit there and let this happen! I glanced at the phone on my desk across the room. If I was real fast, I might be able to grab the phone and call 911 before he saw me. But then what? I didn't know. All I could think about was calling the police, letting someone know what was going on here. I started moving very slowly, inching myself to the edge of my bed, trying to work up the courage I would need to jump across the room and grab the phone. The burglar was walking back and forth in front of the door, taking my stuff and putting it in his sack. Maybe if I timed it just right, I could get over to my desk without him seeing me.

My feet were now hanging off the edge of the mattress. I knew it was now or never, I had to do this or I'd lose my nerve and never get it back. Glancing into the other room, I saw the man walk across the doorway into the kitchen. This was it!

Flinging the covers off, I jumped to my feet and headed for my desk. My eyes were on the phone, so I didn't know if the burglar had seen me or not. I grabbed it and dialed just as a gloved hand went over my mouth.

I screamed and dropped the phone. Trying to twist myself around to face the attacker, all I could do was struggle in place. He had grabbed my arm and wrenched it painfully behind my back. I tried to yell again, but his hand clamped down on my mouth even tighter.

I felt the tip of a knife in my back.

"Shut your fucking mouth or I'll kill you, I swear to God," the burglar said. His voice was low and masculine. I couldn't believe it, but my dick started to get hard at the sound of it.

"Do you understand me?" he said, pushing my arm even further up my back. I winced in pain, and nodded quickly.

"Good boy," he said. I felt him put my wrists together and wrap something around them. It got tighter and tighter, and suddenly I realized what he was doing. The burglar was tying me up! Before I could struggle, he had pulled the knots tight and my hands were securely bound behind my back.

Suddenly, we both became aware of a noise below us. It was a voice, faint but insistent.

"Hello? Are you there? This is the 911 operator. Are you in trouble?"

The connection must have been made before I dropped the phone. I wanted to yell out, but I knew this guy could cut my throat if he wanted to. There was no sense in being stupid. I had to stay calm.

Silently, my attacker leaned over, picked up the phone and very gently set it back in its cradle.

"Shit," he said quietly.

I knew we were both thinking exactly the same thing. The 911 operator was tracing the call right now to this location. Policemen would be on their way soon.

"We gotta get out of here," he said. My blood froze again. We? What did he mean we?

He spun me around to face him. He was a big guy, and strong, too, by the look of those arms through his jacket. I could see his eyes through the holes in the ski mask.

Suddenly the burglar hauled off and punched me in the stomach. It felt like an explosion inside my body. Moaning in pain, I stumbled onto my bed.

"Now you won't give me any trouble."

He knelt down next to me, and starting tying my ankles together. If I had been in less pain, I might have thought to kick the bastard in the face and run to a neighbor's apartment, but the pain in my stomach was so intense I couldn't do anything but lie there groaning. Seconds later my legs and feet were bound together. Then I heard him opening my dresser drawers. What was he looking for? A second later he came back into view, a jockstrap and a couple of my bandannas in his hand.

"This'll keep you quiet."

He stuffed the jockstrap in my mouth and tied it in place with one of the bandannas. The other one he used to blindfold me. Now I was really getting scared, although my dick was still hard from being dominated by this guy. Being tied up by him made me even hotter.

But I had to keep my cool. This guy was a criminal, probably a pro. What was he going to do with me? I heard him walk back into the other room. The pain had lessened a little bit, and I tried to move, but it was too late.

I was bound and gagged – the more I struggled, the tighter the ropes got. Loud noises suddenly came from the other room. What the hell was he doing now? It sounded as if he was emptying his sack out on the floor. Why would he do that?

"Let's go, man, time to hit the road. You're coming with me," he said.

I felt his hands on me, trying to lift me up off the bed. Twisting violently, I forced myself away from his hands. Maybe if I could stall him long enough, the cops would get here before.

"You're just determined to be a pain in the ass, aren't you?" he said, and started beating on me. My back, my stomach, my face, everywhere on me was fair game. He punched me in the gut, slapped my face, beat on my back. The blows rained down on me as I tried to get out of his way. But I was tied up, gagged and blindfolded. I didn't have a chance, and we both knew it.

I stopped fighting and tried to catch my breath.

That was the chance he'd been waiting for. He grabbed me by the shoulders and hoisted me to my feet. Too tired and hurting to resist, I just let him do it.

"You're the most valuable thing in this apartment, man," he said as he picked me up and slung me over his shoulder. "I ain't leaving here without you." God, he was strong. Even after our little fight, he lifted me up as if I weighed less than a hundred pounds. What was he going to do?

Then I felt it. He let me slide down off his shoulder into something. I realized he was putting me in his sack. He meant what he said, I thought. He's stealing me! My dick was now rock hard. Once I was all the way in, he pulled the sack up over my head and pulled the drawstrings closed. The light disappeared, and the darkness closed over me as I slid into the big black bag. Now, I was totally helpless. Bound and gagged and inside of a sack. I felt motion above me, and guessed he was tying off the drawstrings, so I couldn't struggle my way out.

What was I going to do now? Nothing, I thought. There's nothing you can do. Just relax and don't panic. But what happened next surprised the hell out of me and made my cock start dripping.

The burglar hoisted his bag, with me in it, over his shoulder as easily as if it was a laundry sack. Either he's spinning on speed or coke, I thought, or this guy lives at the gym when he's not breaking into apartments.

"Now we're ready," I heard him say. "And don't fight me, man, or I'll drop you off on the side of some back road somewhere. Or put you in a garbage dumpster. I don't want to do that, but I will. Don't give me any trouble, you got that?" he shook the sack, and I spoke through the gag.

"Yes, sir, yes, sir!" I said, my voice muffled.

"Good boy," he said. "Now shut the fuck up and keep still."

We were moving. He was carrying me through my apartment. I was getting stolen as if I was an expensive piece of merchandise. My kidnapper weaved back and forth as he walked. I figured he was avoiding the piles of my stuff he had dumped out.

Then we were out in the open air. I heard him very gently close my front door behind him. How had he broken in? I wondered. I'll have to get better security. I almost laughed out loud at myself then, for thinking I would get a chance to come back here. For all I knew, this guy was going to kill me. Maybe I was going to get sold to a maker of snuff movies, one of those psychos who film real people getting really killed, so they can sell the movies black market.

I had to stop thinking that way, or I would really freak out. It was quiet outside; I knew if I made a loud noise my neighbors would hear it. But would they be able to come out here and take the asshole before he could do something to me? I knew the pool was less than five feet away, he could toss me in there, and I'd drown in seconds. Come to think of it, he could just drop me where I stood, and my head would crack open on the cement of the courtyard. No, I had to do what he said. I had to obey him. I had to keep quiet and not give him trouble. The more I cooperated, the longer I'd live.

We were moving again, traveling swiftly across the courtyard towards the back entrance where the cars were parked. My head was spinning. It was very disorienting to be carried backwards and upside-down. If I wasn't careful I'd throw up. That'd be pretty. Puking while gagged was a good recipe for choking to death, I figured.

The burglar carried me down the stairs to the parking area. His boots made loud scuffing sounds on the concrete. Then he stopped. A key was being turned in a lock, and a door was being opened. Carefully, he leaned over and pulled me off his shoulder down onto some hard surface. Where was I? This didn't feel like the back seat of a car. Then the door closed over me and I realized where I was. The fucker had put me in the trunk. My one chance to get rescued was gone. I hadn't tried to alert my neighbors. If the 911 operator had traced the call, the cops hadn't gotten here in time. That's it, I thought. I'm not paying any more city taxes if the cops can't even rescue me when I'm getting stolen out of my apartment! I laughed out loud this time, the noise sounding muffled and strangled through the gag. I was really thinking bizarre things now, I realized. Maybe I'm crazy.

The thief got into the car and started it up, the noise deafeningly loud to me. He quickly backed up and turned around, heading out to the street.

I have to be crazy, I thought. This guy kidnapped me and might kill me, but my dick is hard as a rock and begging for attention. I knew I couldn't reach it with my hands tied up like they were, but maybe I could rub it. Distracting me from my fear, my crotch started moving, as if by itself, back and forth against the surfaces it was pressed up against it. Mmmm, that felt good. It was rubbing against my boxers, which rubbed against my sweat pants, which rubbed against the canvas of the sack, which rubbed against the hard metal of the trunk's floor. Got some good friction going.

At least the night isn't a total loss, I thought as I rubbed and rubbed, loving the feeling on my dick. That's it, I am crazy.

The car got out onto the street and picked up speed. I struggled against my bondage, not really thinking I could get out of it, more to just feel the nylon of the rope rubbing against my wrists and ankles. Somehow that made the burning in my dick flame higher.

Now the thief was driving faster and faster. We must have been on a freeway. Where was I? Where was he taking me? My apartment building was next to a big freeway junction, so he could have gotten onto any highway heading any direction.

We could be going north, south, east or west. I had no sense of direction at all, so much so that my friends told me to my face that I was geographically impaired. Behind my back, I heard, they said I couldn't drive my way out of a paper bag.

Yeah, I thought, or get myself out of burglar's bag.

I almost laughed again through the gag. What was happening to me? My dick felt so good as I rubbed it up and down, up and down. How could I be getting off on getting kidnapped? How could I enjoy getting tied up, put into a sack, carried away and taken who knows where? What the fuck was going on with me?

I didn't know. All I did know was that I was more excited and scared than I'd ever been in my life. This was a real adventure. I felt really, truly, fully alive like I hadn't in months or maybe years. It was so intense, and I may not live through it, but what the hell, I was going to enjoy it!

The car drove on for a long time. I may have drifted in and out of sleep because all of a sudden we were slowing down. I wondered what was going on, had we reached our destination?

The burglar stopped the car a minute later and got out. I heard a zipper get released and a loud trickling sound. He was pissing, right next to the car. I don't know why, but I started thinking about what it would be like to kneel in front of him and open my mouth wide, to be on the ground in front of this stud who had taken me out of my apartment as of I was just another stereo to steal, to feel the flow of his piss as he re-directed it into my open mouth, to swallow down mouthful after mouthful of his juice, and then when he was done taking his whole thick organ into my mouth, caressing it with my tongue and slurping on it like it was a popsicle, hoping I could please him enough to get a load of his come, hoping he would let me serve him a few minutes more before he stuffed me back in the sack and tossed me into the trunk.

What the hell was I thinking! I had to calm down. I racked my brain, trying to figure out what his pissing so close to the car could mean.

He wouldn't have whipped out his meat like that if there were a lot of people around, so we must have been somewhere isolated. Maybe a rest stop, or an empty parking lot. But I'd heard his boots crunching on gravel.

Suddenly, the sound stopped and we was zipping up his pants. He was walking over to the car, and a second later the key was turning in the hole and the lid was being raised. I could hardly believe my luck.

"You okay, man?" he said.

"Let me loose!" I shouted through the jockstrap shoved in my mouth. He laughed.

"Sorry, can't understand you."

"You can, too, understand me!" I yelled louder. "Let me loose you fucking asshole!"

Oh, that was smart, I thought, just before his fist connected with my gut again. My breath flew out of me as I wondered how he could tell where my stomach was through the material of the bag.

"You're not getting away, so stop hoping," he said. I doubled over in pain, trying to shield myself from more assaults. Damn, I thought. This fucker knows how to punch. He had me, I was helpless, did he have to keep reminding me?

"Answer me by moving your head," he said. "I'm sick of hearing your voice."

I nodded my head vigorously, hoping he could see the motion.

"You got to take a piss?" he asked. The thought hadn't occurred to me with my dick being so hard and everything, but now I realized: I hadn't pissed since before I went to bed, hours and hours ago. I nodded again.

"Okay, let's get you out here," he said. "I don't want you pissing in there and stinking up my car."

Then his strong arms were around me, lifting the bag up and out of the trunk. He set me on the ground, and I stumbled a little. I was still inside the sack, and had no way to judge my surroundings I was so disoriented. Now that I was standing up, I realized that my bladder was full and I had to go really badly.

"Don't try anything, man," the thief said. "Or I'll kill you I swear to God."

I shook my head to show I understood, and that I wouldn't. The noise of him untying the drawstrings was loud in my ears, then I felt the chill of the night air as he slid the canvas down over me, revealing me to the world. I felt like a banana getting peeled. There must not be anyone around because the strangeness of this sight would definitely have attracted the curious. The weirdness of what was happening to me, plus my bursting bladder, combined to make my erection disappear.

Waiting to be totally released from the sack, I was surprised when my kidnapper just let it pile up around my feet. Then his hands were grabbing my shorts, yanking them down. He did the same to my boxers, and then my dick felt the kiss of the air.

I felt his gloved hand roughly grab my flaccid meat and point it away from us.

"Let it go, man, I ain't gonna wait all night."

Willing my muscles to relax, I felt the first drops come and then it went all at once. It spurted out of me like a dam had been released. For what seemed like an hour, we stood there together, a bizarre pair, while I relieved myself. I resisted the temptation to turn my body and give the burglar a golden shower. He probably wouldn't have appreciated it. The last few spurts came out and he started putting my equipment back inside. But with the piss gone, my cock was awakened by the incredible hotness of this man holding it. Oh no, I thought. Not now.

But it was too late. My dick was hardening in the thief's hand, as if it had a will of its own. What was I going to do, what if the guy was a gay-hating fag-basher? He was likely to castrate me right then and there! I hoped fear would soften my organ, but it just made it hotter and more erect. My last chance would be for him to not notice, to just put it back in and be done with it.

But he didn't. He paused, my meat still in his gloved hand.

"What's this?" I heard him whisper to himself, and I froze in place, wanting so badly to wish myself out of there, to just be back in my bed.

The burglar laughed softly.

"Looks as of I got myself a horny little gay boy, didn't I?" he asked. Too mortified to answer, I made no noise.

"Answer me!" he said angrily as he slapped the side of my head. I nodded quickly, hoping this was the end of it.

But it wasn't.

"Yeah, just what I thought," he said as he started rubbing my chest with the other hand. He kept my dick in his other hand, caressing it in his palm.

My back arched. I wanted to get away from him, but if I tried who knew what he would do. Not wanting to get punched again, I just stood there. It felt so fucking good! I knew I had to keep my cool, to stay rational, but the feeling was so intense.

"Mmmm," I heard him whisper. "You got me going, man ..." His hands were all over my chest, stroking it up and down, pinching my nipples, slapping my abs.

"I'm gonna put you to good use, horny boy," the thief said suddenly, pushing my shoulders down and forcing me to my knees. "Go on," he said, shoving me forward. I crawled blindly on my hands and knees, the hard gavel biting into my palms and knees. Out of the sack now, I found myself on softer ground. It was grass, thank God.

"Stop," the voice said, and I did so immediately. I heard my kidnapper kneel down next to me.

"Get down."

I dropped down to my stomach. Frightened by what I knew was coming, I started shivering. It would only get worse if I fought him, so I just lay there and waited for it.

Soon enough, I heard that zipper being pulled down again, and this time the sound of him pushing his denim jeans down to his knees. It was so quiet around us, as if there were no animals or people anywhere nearby.

He lay down on top of me then, his chest pressing against my back. He hadn't even taken off his shirt. With one hand he pushed my head down, forcing my face into the grass. I could feel his hard cock pressing up between my naked butt-cheeks. Not knowing why I did it, I pushed up against it, arching my back so my ass rose to meet the dick that wanted inside me.

My kidnapper murmured in approval. I heard him work up some spit and lick his hand, then grease up his meat with it. Now it felt smooth and slippery against my cheeks, and my own penis was raging with desire.

"Please ..." I whispered.

"Please what, man?"

"Please ..." I said. He plunged his cock into me then, and I forced my ass back and up, trying to take as much of him inside me as I could. This man had taken me against my will, he'd abducted me out of my apartment, put me in a sack, drove me away in his car, and now was using me for his pleasure in what must have been a deserted field in the middle of the night. As frightened as I was, it was also totally hot.

He moaned as he started pumping me, pulling his dick out and then pushing it in. It was the best fuck I'd ever had, just getting my ass raped by this stranger who'd taken me as if I was a piece of merchandise that could be begged, borrowed and stolen. Here he was, screwing me, just plowing my ass like there was no tomorrow. I must have let out a little groan because suddenly he clapped his hand over my mouth.

"Shut up!" he whispered fiercely. "Shut the fuck up. Just keep quiet. There's nothing you can do, so just take it like a man."

His hand over my mouth made me even hotter. It flashed me back to earlier when he had cornered me in my room, and I realized something that was more shocking and strange than anything that had happened yet. The burglar scared me to death, yet I really wanted him to fuck me. I had wanted him to take me from the first moment I had seen him loading my stuff into his big black sack. And now it was happening, as incredible as it was. My dick ground itself into the grass, fertilizing it with globs of dripping pre-cum.

"Yeah, that's it," he said into my ear as he started pumping me faster. "Take it, man, take it all, my horny boy, my horny little gay boy ... I bet you like taking it up the butt, don't you, faggot? Bet you like being fucked by a real man, bet it's been too long since you got fucked nice and hard ..."

Then I felt his cock flex and shoot inside me, spurts of his cum splattering, filling me up.

"Yeah ..." he groaned. "Oh yeah ..."

He pulled out of me and grabbed me around the chest, lifting me up to my knees. I figured he was going to take me back to the car, but I was wrong. I heard him hock some more spit into his palm, and then he grabbed hold of my dick and started working it! It was so fucking unbelievable I felt myself lifting up off my knees, as if the feeling could help me shatter the law of gravity.

"Come on, gay boy," my kidnapper said. "I figure this'll help keep you quiet, but I'm not waiting forever. If you're gonna do it, you better do it now!"

At the sound of his command, I felt the orgasm rocket through me like an explosion, tearing me apart from the inside out. I bucked and jerked in his arms, and he held me tight to prevent me from falling. I knew bursts of cum were shooting out of me, firing across the grass like rocks skipping on water. Moaning and panting, I tried to lie back down on the grass.

"Oh no you don't," I heard him say as he jerked me up to my feet. "We're getting out of here." He left me for a second, and even though I was still bound, gagged and blindfolded, I could've tried to get away or call for help.

But I didn't.

Instead I waited for him to come back and then cooperatively helped him get me back into his sack. He tied the drawstrings off again and hefted me up over his shoulder.

"That did it," he whispered to me. "You're going to be a good boy, now, aren't you?"

I didn't need to answer, we both knew I would.

He got me back in the trunk of his car and we drove off. I didn't care anymore where we were going, or what he was going to do with me. I was so high on my orgasm that I just accepted that fate had dealt me a strange hand and there was nothing I could do except wait and see what happened. In some strange way, I felt happy and content because before I knew it I was asleep, the droning sound of the highway passing beneath me as sweet as a lullaby.

The car stopped. I don't know how much later it was, but I sensed that it was still dark through my blindfold. It couldn't have been long. The trunk opened and the thief picked me up again, lifting me out of his car and up over his shoulder again. This time he didn't speak to me, he just carried me a few feet, then up some stairs and into a building of some kind. Beside some faint noise in the background, it was quiet. The burglar carried me down hallways, up stairs, deep into the depths of the building. The noises were so indistinct, I couldn't tell what they were. It could have been a factory, an office building, a warehouse – anything.

Then he finally stopped, and I heard a door close behind us.

"What the hell's this?" a voice said, and I started in the thief's arms. It had been so long since I'd heard anyone but him, it was startling to think there was someone else there, seeing me like this, the helpless victim of another man.

"This fucker called the police on me when I was doing his place," the burglar said. "So I took him instead of his stuff. What do you think he's worth?"

"Gotta see him first," the other voice said, and I found myself being lowered down off my kidnapper's shoulder. The sack was set down on a hard surface, probably a table or a countertop. Someone pulled the drawstrings open, and I squirmed out from inside the sack like an animal being born. Through the blindfold bright light seeped in.

"Hmmm, he's a good one."

I felt hands on me, all over me, caressing and massaging my naked chest. It was probably the other man, assessing the value of me, the stolen property. He pinched my nipples and slapped my face lightly. My sweats were yanked down and my crotch exposed. The hand gripped my hard dick, bouncing it back and forth against my chest.

"You think I could get a good price for him?"

"He's nice all right, but I'd have to be able to tell the buyer about his performance value."

The thief laughed.

"I know all about his performance value! I did him in a field on the way here. He fucking loved it! This little faggot was born to be a slave!"

"Now you know how this works. I can't just take your word for it. I need proof."

"Do you want to use him yourself?" the burglar asked.

"I'd rather see you do him again, that way I can be an unbiased observer. Then I can tell how much we can get for him."

"Fine by me."

My arms were grabbed and I was pulled roughly into a different position, with my head hanging upside down off the edge of the table. I heard the burglar's zipper again, but this time there was more. Lots of sounds, of jeans being pulled down, of a shirt being pulled off; he was completely undressing! Then my gag was removed and my mouth was free. But before I could even yell for help, a big dick, had been shoved between my lips.

"Take it, boy," the thief said. "Take it just like you did in the field ..."

I started sucking his dick, caressing and working it with my lips and tongue. It felt so hot in my mouth, so full. I was totally being used by this man, used like a piece of property in front of someone else, someone that was watching to see how much I was worth.

Suddenly I heard a loud noise.

"Freeze!" the other voice yelled.

"Oh shit!" my kidnapper said, and I could feel his dick get limp in my mouth. "You're a cop? A fucking cop?"

"You got it, man, now just back up nice and easy ..."

"I don't fucking believe this!" the thief said as he backed up out of my mouth. I was left alone, with no one touching me.

"We've been after you for a long time, scumbag," the cop said. "Now I've bagged you once and for all."

I heard the cocking of a gun. Then the sound of lots of voices. A bunch of men ran into the room – it must have been the cop's backup. Many voices assaulted my ears.

"We got him, boys!"

"It's about time."

"Hands behind your back, man!"

Clicking – they were handcuffing him.

"Get his clothes back on him."

Then there were hands on me, helping me to sit up, and yanking the blindfold off of me. The light blinded me, and I couldn't see anything for a minute.

I opened them and saw my rescuer.

He was good-looking, blond, and great blue eyes. His hands were on my shoulders, and he was looking me straight in the eye.

"Are you all right, guy?" he asked.

"I – I think so," I said.

"Did that bastard hurt you?"

"No," I said. "I'm okay," And I glanced across the room, where a bunch of uniformed officers were swarming around a man that had to be the burglar.

He was hot.

About my age, late twenties, dark hair and eyes, clean-shaven. The police had gotten his pants back on him, but his big broad chest was still bare, and his muscled arms were cuffed behind his back. He saw me looking at me, and there was an electric look that passed between us.

For a split second, it was as if we were alone.

He was the thief, and I was his catch.

And, somehow, that was the way it would always be.

Then, a second later, we were back in reality, and the cops were jostling him out of the room. Just before he was pulled out of my sight, the burglar cocked his head and gave me a sly lopsided smile.

Then he was gone.

I went down to the station with the officers and filled out a report like a good citizen. But I refused to testify. I just didn't want to.

Every night after that, I found myself thinking about what had happened. In a strange way it was as if I had never been rescued, as if I was still bound and gagged inside that sack, a prisoner.

His prisoner.

And I jerked my hard cock off to the memory of our split second, the memory of his eyes and his lopsided smile and what it felt like to be slung over his shoulder.

But then it's as if I wake up and the dream is over.

I don't know what happened to my thief. He may have been let off; he may have gotten a jail sentence.

But either way, sooner or later, he's going to be back on the prowl again.

Maybe that's why I never did get better security at my apartment. And why I leave the door unlocked when I go to sleep at night. Someday, I hope, the midnight burglar will come for me again.

And this time, I won't fight him.

# ABOUT THE AUTHOR

Christopher Pierce is the author of the novel *Rogue: Slave* and its sequel *Rogue: Hunted* (STARbooks Press). He co-edited the *Fetish Chest Trilogy* of anthologies (Alyson Publications) with Rachel Kramer Bussel. For STARbooks Press, he has edited the collections *Men on the Edge: Dangerous Erotica*, *Taken by Force: Erotic Stories of Abduction and Captivity*, and *SexTime: Erotic Stories of Time Travel*. His short fiction has been published in more than thirty anthologies, including *Surfer Boys*, *Leathermen* (Cleis Press) and *Ultimate Gay Erotica 2005*, *2006*, *2007* and *2008* (Alyson.) Write to him at chris@christopherpierceerotica.com and visit his world at www.christopherpierceerotica.com.

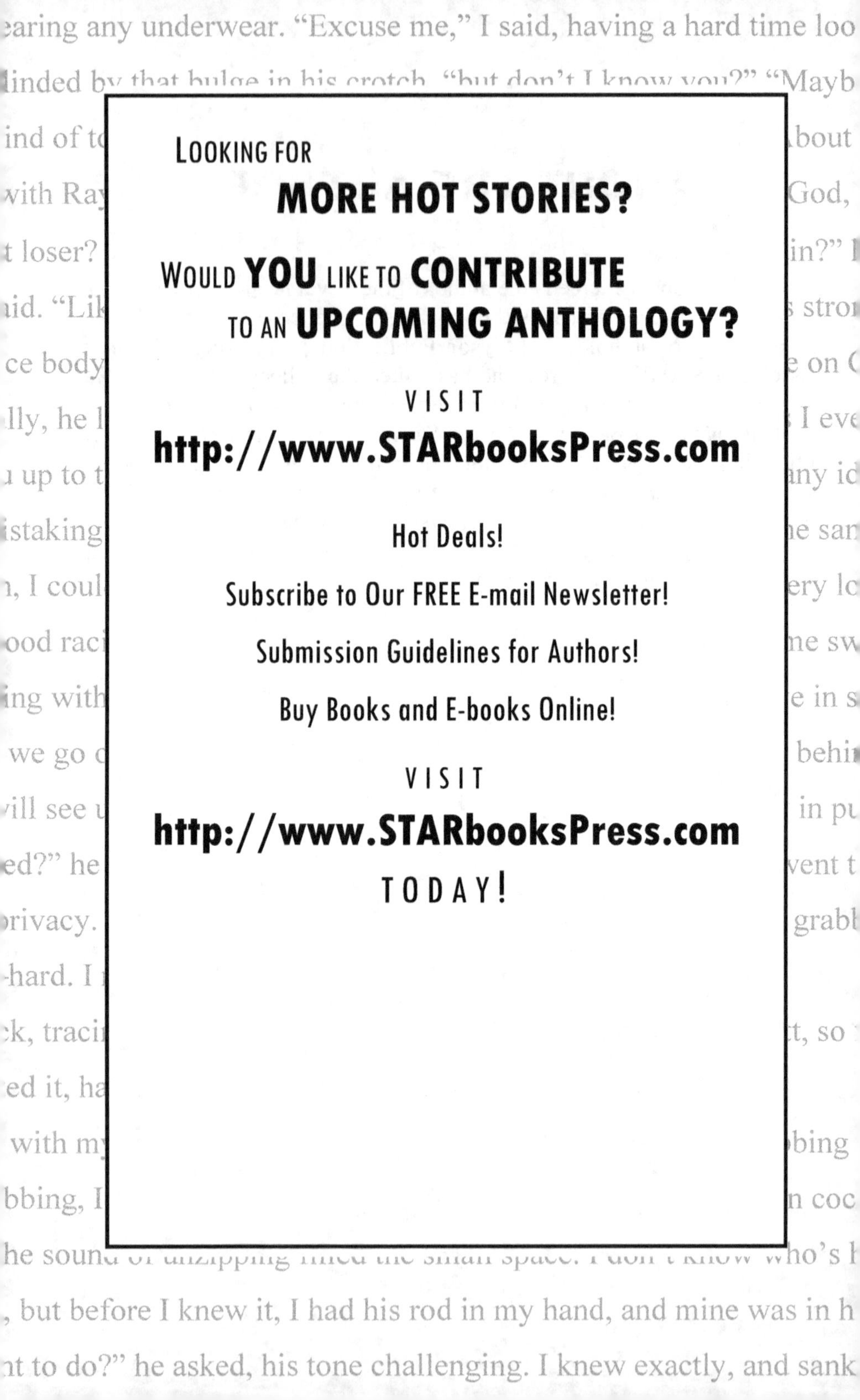
LOOKING FOR
MORE HOT STORIES?
WOULD YOU LIKE TO CONTRIBUTE
TO AN UPCOMING ANTHOLOGY?
VISIT
http://www.STARbooksPress.com
Hot Deals!
Subscribe to Our FREE E-mail Newsletter!
Submission Guidelines for Authors!
Buy Books and E-books Online!
VISIT
http://www.STARbooksPress.com
TODAY!

www.ingramcontent.com/pod-product-compliance
Lightning Source LLC
Chambersburg PA
CBHW051646260626
47170CB00004B/1371

* 9 7 8 1 9 3 4 1 8 7 6 5 4 *

# The Black Path

ALSO BY ÅSA LARSSON
FROM CLIPPER LARGE PRINT

The Savage Altar
The Blood Spilt